Also by Monica Tesler

Bounders, Book 1: *Earth Force Rising*

Bounders, Book 2: *The Tundra Trials*

Bounders, Book 3: *The Forgotten Shrine*

HEROES THE
RETURN

BOUNDERS
BOOK 4

HEROES RETURN
THE

MONICA TESLER

ALADDIN

New York   London   Toronto   Sydney   New Delhi

ALADDIN

An imprint of Simon & Schuster Children's Publishing Division
1230 Avenue of the Americas, New York, New York 10020
First Aladdin hardcover edition December 2018
Text copyright © 2018 by Monica Tesler
Jacket illustration copyright © 2018 by Owen Richardson

For information about special discounts for bulk purchases, please contact
Simon & Schuster Special Sales at 1-866-506-1949 or business@simonandschuster.com.
The Simon & Schuster Speakers Bureau can bring authors to your live event.
For more information or to book an event, contact the Simon & Schuster Speakers Bureau
at 1-866-248-3049 or visit our website at www.simonspeakers.com.
Jacket designed by Karin Paprocki
Interior designed by Mike Rosamilia
The text of this book was set in Adobe Garamond Pro.
Manufactured in the United States of America 1118 FFG
2 4 6 8 10 9 7 5 3 1
Library of Congress Cataloging-in-Publication Data
Names: Tesler, Monica, author.
Title: The heroes return / by Monica Tesler.
Description: First Aladdin hardcover edition. | New York : Aladdin, 2018. |
Series: Bounders ; book 4 | Summary: "Jasper and Mira must escape the rift and deliver a message from
the Youli to Earth Force before the war destroys their planet"— Provided by publisher.
Identifiers: LCCN 2018024629 (print) | LCCN 2018031491 (eBook) |
ISBN 9781534402492 (eBook) | ISBN 9781534402478 (hardcover)
Subjects: | CYAC: Adventure and adventurers—Fiction. | Human-alien encounters—Fiction. |
Ambassadors—Fiction. | Virtual reality—Fiction. | Science fiction. |
BISAC: JUVENILE FICTION / Action & Adventure / General. |
JUVENILE FICTION / Science & Technology. | JUVENILE FICTION / Science Fiction.
Classification: LCC PZ7.1.T447 (eBook) | LCC PZ7.1.T447 Her 2018 (print) | DDC [Fic]—dc23
LC record available at https://lccn.loc.gov/2018024629

For Mom & Dad

I

WHAT ARE THE ODDS? I'VE SPENT MY whole life hearing about the Incident at Bounding Base 51 and the famous aeronauts who were lost that day. Now here I am standing right next to them.

In the rift.

Even though Gedney theorized there may be a place in the galaxy where time moved differently—almost like a rip in space itself—no one knew for sure. I guess the lost aeronauts, Mira, and I are living proof of his hypothesis.

We're living for now, at least. The longer we stay here, the more time we lose back on Earth. The aeronauts say they've been stuck in the rift for two days, but more than fourteen years have passed. Mira and I were here for at least an hour before we even found the lost aeronauts. That's got to be a couple of months back on Earth.

It's not like we can just wave our gloves and go back. For starters, my gloves were lost on Alkalinia. I managed to bring the shield down, giving Earth Force at least a fighting chance against the Alks and Youli, but then Mira bounded us out of the action. I can't believe I abandoned my friends—I abandoned my sister, Addy—on that sinister snake world, not that I would have been much help trapped at the bottom of the toxic sea. The only reason I was trapped at all was that my gloves were stuck. When we bounded, my gloves got left behind.

I doubt my gloves would make much difference here in the rift, though. Mira's gloves don't seem to work. In other words, it's not so easy to get out of here. Proof: the human bones we found a few minutes ago.

The aeronauts won't stop running their mouths. "There's no way we've been here for that long!" "Where are we anyway?" "Why on earth did the Force send *you* to rescue us?"

Even though the glum grayness of the rift swallows their voices into near nothingness, their chatter is still loud enough to obliterate any chance of me thinking things through. I get that this is a stressful situation, but competitive talking won't get us out of here.

Mira squeezes my hand. *Ignore them.*

I wish it were that easy.

"Shut up!" I finally shout.

Everyone stops talking at the same time. Their words fall slowly in the thick air, like feathers on a breeze, until they're absorbed into the spongy ground beneath our feet.

"Seriously," I continue, "if we're going to figure out how to get out of here, you need to stop freaking out! Be quiet and let me think!"

"Listen, hotshot," starts the tall aeronaut with short dark hair. I know from watching web specials that it's Bai Liu. "I don't know who you are or how you got here, but I'm not about to let a kid tell me what to do, especially one who wears the Earth Force insignia. I outrank you. Stand and salute."

"Take it down a notch, Bai," the aeronaut next to her says. "The kid's got a point. If we're all talking at once, we'll never come up with a plan." He steps in front of her and crosses his arms.

Despite how strange and unexpected all this is, I recognized Captain Denver Reddy the second I saw him. He's one of those icons who everyone knows. Tall, brown skin, lots of swagger. Mom says she and her friends used to swoon over Denver.

Bai throws up her hands but doesn't talk back. She was Denver's co-captain on the failed bound and is almost as famous as he is, but it's clear who's in charge.

If I'm being honest, I'm kind of starstruck. It's not every day that you run into the famous lost aeronauts from the Incident at Bounding Base 51.

I shake my head to clear my thoughts and take a deep breath of the stagnant, musty air. "Give me some time to think."

Time we don't have. If they've been here for fourteen years, and it only feels like two days to them, that means we're losing time at the rate of almost two days per minute. A shudder rips through me. Losing more time? It's like a sick joke after being trapped on Alkalinia. The Alks drugged us by loading us up with delicious fake food. Then they poked and prodded us with needles while we slept for days. I can't believe we managed to bound away only to get stuck here, where we're losing more time. A *lot* more time.

We go round and round with ideas but get nowhere. Meanwhile, the clock keeps ticking. Just like that, another hour slips by.

There's got to be something we can do. "Mira, can you bound? Or are you still blocked?"

"Bound?" the older aeronaut who first found us asks. "Do you see a ship around here?"

"We don't need—" I start.

Mira kicks my foot. *Quiet!* She takes my hand and pulls me from the group. The aeronauts start to fade as we retreat into the fog.

"Wait!" one of the aeronaut calls as we disappear into the gloom. "Where did you go? Don't leave us! We need—"

Let's go! Mira's fingers curl tight against the back of my hand. *We need space to think.* We walk farther from the group, our feet sinking, the aeronauts' voices fading, with each step.

The darkness swallows us up, so there's no trace of the lost aeronauts, even though they can't be more than a dozen meters away.

My mind races. How long have we been here already? How long have we been gone? I wish the answers to those questions were the same, but I know they're not. As every minute ticks by in the rift, more days pass on Earth. We've got to get out of here!

The battle on Alkalinia is long over by now. Sure, I got the shield down, but was it enough? Were the Earth Force troops able to thwart the plans of the Youli and Alkalinians? What happened to my other pod mates?

Did Addy survive?

I sink my knees to the ground. "What are we going to do?"

Mira kneels beside me. *Brain-talk.*

She's right. We don't need the lost aeronauts hearing anything that would require us to waste time educating them about stolen alien biotechnology.

I bow my head to my knees and try to clear my mind. For a second, I'm grateful for the utter desolation of this place. It swallows up sound and color and movement so completely that it feels like quicksand for the senses. I can easily forget that a crowd of lost aeronauts stands only meters away, and they're all probably expecting me to come back with an answer for how to get out of this mess, an answer that is not coming.

It's no use, I say to Mira. *We're trapped.*

She presses her palm to the back of my neck, where my Youli brain patch is implanted. A wave of feeling washes over me. Optimism. I know it's Mira's way of telling me that not all is lost.

She's obviously delusional. I close my eyes and try to push back the growing wave of panic.

A bright light shines behind my eyelids.

I bolt upright. All I can see is the brilliant glow. I jump to my feet and spin around. There's nothing but the brilliance and the sucking gray of the rift. Mira is gone.

"Mira! Where are you? Mira!"

The light shifts and solidifies. The ground shakes beside me, like something was dropped from the sky.

I turn. Mira is on her hands and knees. She tries to lift her head. Her arms collapse beneath her.

"What's wrong, Mira? What happened?" I know she wasn't here a second ago. There's no way I would have missed her.

Mira's brain alights with electricity. Something about it is different, more textured, more complex.

"Mira, are you okay? Did you bound?"

She presses her palms against the gray, squishy ground and slowly pushes herself up. I repeat my questions brain to brain, but all I sense from her is static.

The light before us fades, and I realize we're not alone. Three Youli stand directly in front of us.

My senses slam into focus, and I reach for my missing gloves. Then I jump in front of Mira to shield her from the Youli. She's still trying to stand. Her mind is sparking, but it's like she's not fully conscious.

Whatever happened to Mira must have something to do with the Youli. "Stay away from her!"

The Youli don't respond. They tip their huge heads to the side and stare at me with their bottomless black eyes, like they're carefully considering what I said. Their skin is the color of smashed peas. Their bodies pulse with the glowing beat of their alien hearts.

A razor-sharp pain drills at my temples. The loudest, shrillest noise sounds in my brain. I collapse to my knees and press my hands against my skull. How can I protect Mira when my head's about to explode? When I fear I'll lose consciousness, the pain starts to subside and a word rings in my mind, in my body, in the air. Everywhere.

Peace.

I force my gaze to the Youli standing before us. It's clear the word *peace* is coming from them. The same word they uttered on the Paleo Planet, the same word I heard on the Youli ship.

Pushing aside the last of the pain, I keep my voice low and level. "What did you do to Mira?"

Peace.

I surge to my feet and burst forward. Right into a solid wall of nothingness. I bounce backward and land on my butt. The Youli's powers obviously work here in the rift.

Next to me, Mira still struggles to stand. When she finally makes it to her feet, she braces herself against the Youli's invisible wall.

Mira! Get back!

Her brown eyes find mine and I'm flooded with emotion. I can't decipher what any of it means, but my throat turns thick. Mira's eyes fill with tears. She holds my stare, gazing at me like we've been apart for a long time.

What's wrong, Mira? What's happening?

Mira closes her eyes. She reins back her despair and shuts it inside a closed door in her mind. When she looks at me again, her mind is empty, but only for a moment. Her brain touches mine and opens wide. I hear voices, and they're not just Mira's.

Thoughts race around my head, too many thoughts to concentrate. What is going on? Why are the Youli here? What happened to Mira? Did the Youli take her? Were those Youli voices in her brain?

8

Even as my panic rises, waves of calm begin to swish in my skull. They must be coming from the Youli—or maybe even Mira—because there's nothing about me that feels calm. Although now . . . I'm kind of . . . maybe . . . relaxing? It's like I've just sat through an hour of Mom's meditation music, but here the effect is instantaneous.

Which means it's not real. If my time on Alkalinia taught me anything, it's that there are lots of things that aren't real.

Mira's hand is pressed against the invisible wall. Her face has that radiant, open quality I remember from way back in the cell block at the space station. As I stare at her face, searching for answers, her hand drops, and she stumbles.

The wall must be gone. I surge forward. This time, there's no wall, but one of the Youli lifts his palm and grabs my atoms, freezing me in place.

"Let go of me!" At least my mouth and vocal cords aren't frozen. One of the Youli approaches Mira, stepping right through the space in the rift that used to hold the invisible wall.

"Don't take one step closer to her!"

Brain-talk. I hear in my mind from a voice that's unmistakably Mira's. *They'll understand.*

If that's how it is, fine. I focus all my mental energy at the Youli. *Get away from her!*

They turn their large green heads toward me and gaze

upon me with their deep black eyes. Again, one word radiates from them: *Peace.*

Do they think I'm a fool? The Youli on Alkalinia weren't looking for peace. They planned to kidnap me and Mira and kill the other Bounders—they were going to murder *Addy.* I saw them shooting at Earth Force across the Alkalinian sea. I was nearly caught in the cross fire!

"Peace? You weren't saying *peace* back on Alkalinia!" I shout before remembering what Mira said about brain-talk.

I try to clear a space in my mind to form words, but my anger fills up my whole head.

Still that word rings all around: *Peace, peace, peace.*

I want to clench my fists. I want to punch the Youli in the face. But I'm frozen. All I can do is press my lips together and glare at the Youli. *There was no peace for my friends. Not on Gulaga. Not on Alkalinia. How can you bring us here and call it peace? We're trapped!*

Mira steps beside me and places her hand on my arm. Even though I can't move, I can feel her long, cold fingers through my Earth Force uniform.

I brought us here by mistake, she says. *The Youli can get us out.*

MONICA TESLER

"WHAT DO YOU MEAN, *THE YOULI CAN GET
us out?" I demand through gritted teeth.

Brain-talk, Mira reminds me.

"No! The Youli are not calling the shots here! I'll talk with my voice if I want to. What happened to you? Did they take you?"

Mira grabs my frozen hand. *I'm here. I've been right here with you.*

That can't be true. I swear Mira vanished for a moment right when the Youli arrived. When she reappeared, she was overwhelmed with sadness and barely conscious. Now she seems to be pro-Youli. When did that happen? Does she completely forget what went down on Alkalinia a few hours ago (at least for us)?

"But I saw—"

Mira squeezes my palm and sends me an image of the lost aeronauts, who right this moment are probably just a few meters away, swallowed by the endless gloom of this place. *Quiet! They'll hear!*

Fine! I don't know what Denver, Bai, and the other aeronauts would make of this encounter with the Youli, but I doubt it would speed up our exit from the rift. No matter what's going on with Mira, it doesn't change the fact that we need to get out of the rift, and fast.

I force myself to look at the three green aliens standing in front of me. *What do you want with us?*

Peace.

As soon as the Youli thinks the word, the invisible tether that holds my body releases. I'm free to move. It must be the Youli's attempt to demonstrate trust.

I clench my fists, barely holding back from charging the Youli. *Peace, huh? What is it with you and that word? You obviously have no idea what it means!*

Mira squeezes my palm again. *Jasper! Listen to us! Please!*

Us? I shake my hand free. Seriously? She's taking their side? *They took you, didn't they? They're controlling you somehow.*

She turns away as the Youli fill my mind with their message: *Peace.*

No! I silently scream. *I don't want to hear the word peace again! Not until I know what you did to Mira! And not until I have assurances that my sister is safe . . . that all the Bounders are safe!*

A wave of sadness and frustration fills my mind. Is that coming from Mira? Or the Youli? Or both?

As I try to process the feelings and unanswered questions, the Youli in the middle steps forward. Its voice is deep and spoken in such a melodic way it's almost like singing. *We do not speak in the same manner as you, Jasper Adams, but we have studied your kind, including your linguistics, and we will try. We cannot give you the assurances you seek, for we do not know your sister's fate. There were many casualties at the Battle of the Alkalinian Seat—Youli, Alk, and Earthling. The Youli acted without one mind, and the consequences were grave. Those who initiated the attack have been addressed, but division remains deep.*

What does he mean they "acted without one mind"? *Are you saying not all the Youli wanted to fight?*

Before sending me words, the Youli fills my mind with pictures, like Mira does sometimes. It's me and my pod mates on the Youli vessel right before the attack on the Gulagan space elevator. We're planting the degradation patch on the Youli systems. These images must be from the perspective of the Youli we tackled on the ship.

Your technological attack was devastating, the Youli says. *It threatens to undermine generations of peace and principled living among our people and the greater galaxy. Reunification is possible, but it comes at a price. People of both of our planets have perished. If events continue on their current course, we fear the galaxy may pay the ultimate price.*

Is he saying we were responsible for the Youli's attack on Alkalinia? That we provoked and disabled them with the degradation patch, and they were simply fighting back? No way.

Plus, nothing justifies the Youli's plans to exterminate the Bounders—*kids*—on Alkalinia.

As soon as those thoughts cross my mind, Mira turns to me and takes my other hand. She steps close, so our foreheads are almost touching. A door slams closed, a mental door, so that for a moment it's just Mira and me communicating. *The Youli didn't want to kill the Bounders,* she says. *That was the Alks' plan.*

What is going on? Mira is definitely hiding something from me. *How on earth would you know that?*

She squeezes my hands. *Trust me.*

I'm the furthest I've ever been from trusting Mira. I'm about to tell her that, but then she kicks open the confidential door, and the Youli are back in my brain.

MONICA TESLER

The Youli on the left steps forward and speaks with a voice that sounds like wind chimes in my mind. *It is time we put our conflicts to rest and move our joint history into the next phase. We have a message for your people.*

I take a step back, away from the Youli, away from Mira. I turn my back to them and stare out at the gray nothingness. Mira said the Youli could get us out of here. Does that mean they know how to navigate the rift? They must. After all, they got here without a problem. It seems they were looking for us and knew exactly how and where *and when* to find us.

As much as I want to spend the next several hours yelling at these Youli about all the horrible things they've done to me and my friends, every second I waste is more time lost outside the rift. We need to escape. Accepting the Youli's help isn't just our best option, it's our only option.

I turn and face the wind chime Youli. *If I deliver your message, you'll get us out of here?*

Yes, Jasper Adams.

I take a deep breath. *What's the message?*

Peace.

Of course it is. I clasp my hands above my head and close my eyes. Peace? Really? They actually want to end the war?

We sincerely hope you choose to carry our message, the deep-voiced Youli says. *It is the most important thing you can do for both of our peoples. It is the greatest way to honor your sister and friends.*

Does that mean Addy's dead? I thought they said they didn't know. I clench my fists. *Don't bring my sister into this!*

Tell your people we wish to meet and discuss the requirements for your planet's entry into the Intragalactic Council, the Youli continues. *This is our gesture of peace.* The Youli extends his hand toward me. It's large and green and pulsing.

"He actually wants me to shake his hand?" I ask Mira.

He knows it's our custom, she tells me.

The other times I've touched a Youli have been extremely intense, like opening a floodgate of sensations. Still, I'm curious.

I grip the Youli's hand with my own. As soon as we touch, my body is overloaded with a million feelings and thoughts.

We both pull our hands free. The Youli stumbles back like he was pushed. They must not be too big on touching, or at least touching Earthlings.

So, we have a deal, I say. *What's next?*

Wait, Mira says. *The others.* She sends me an image of the lost aeronauts.

Oh, right. Them. They're probably only a few meters away, completely clueless to the fact that their mortal enemies have arrived.

The Youli will take them, too, she says.

"Hold on a minute," I say to her. "Why didn't they tell me

that themselves? What else have they said to you? Why are you keeping secrets from me? What happened to you?"

We're wasting time.

Something about Mira is all wrong, but what she's saying is right. The one thing we don't have is time to waste. Still, I have to know I'm not putting us and the lost aeronauts in jeopardy.

You disappeared, Mira. Where did you go?

She digs her shoe into the gray ground. *It was the only way.*

You need to tell me what happened. Now.

We went with them, she says, gazing off into the fog. *The Youli needed to understand us and—*

What do you mean "we"? I didn't go anywhere with the Youli.

Mira takes a deep breath. *I mean we need to go with them now. They'll take us to the Ezone.*

I drop her hands. *You told them about the Ezone? Doesn't that violate like a hundred Earth Force laws?*

I'm most sure of the coordinates. It was the easiest to relay.

I can't believe this. *You gave them the coordinates?*

Mira's mind swells with frustration. *How else do you think we'll get there? Or would you rather they bound us to their planet? Stop asking questions! We need to move!*

Mira never talks to me this way. There's definitely something she's not telling me. As soon as we get out of the rift, she'll have to explain what's really going on.

"Fine. Let's find the others." I start trekking through the

gray muck in the direction I think we came from. "Denver! Bai! Where are you guys?"

Soon someone returns my call. I head that way and practically collide with Bai.

She shoves me back. "Watch where you're going, plebe!"

"Sorry. Listen, I think we may have a way out of this place."

The aeronaut who found us falls to his knees. "Oh, thank God."

"What's the plan?" Denver asks.

"See, that's just it. . . . It's sort of unusual. . . . Umm . . ."

"Get back!" Bai says, throwing her arms to the side to protect the other aeronauts. Her eyes bug wide, like she's seen a ghost. "Can't you hear? Get behind me!"

I turn around. Mira and the Youli have cut through the gray haze. Since neither Mira nor our green rescue team can communicate with the aeronauts, I guess explanations are up to me.

"It's cool." I lift my palms to the side. "These guys are going to help us."

Denver steps next to Bai. "Get out of the way, kid. You don't know who you're dealing with. These aliens are our enemies."

"Yeah, I won't argue with you there. But the Youli are also our ticket out of here."

"Den, this is obviously a trap," Bai says. "These Youli scum are the reason we're here in the first place. Bounding Base 51 was under attack."

If there was ever any doubt about whether Earth Force covered up the existence of the Youli since before I was born, it was just erased.

"Listen up!" I say. "I'm no fan of the Youli, but we need to act now. While we're in here fighting, we're losing months of Earth time."

Bai angles away from me and speaks to her pod. "How do we know he's telling the truth? Why should we believe him that it's been all these years? Maybe we've only been here two days. They could be working with the Youli! They're strange kids, right? I mean, the girl doesn't even talk!"

That strikes a nerve. "Her name is Mira!" I shout, although the rift swallows most of the sound. "Here's the deal. The Youli don't care whether they include you in this rescue. The more we stand here arguing, the less I care. We're leaving the rift in one minute. You're either with us or not. Your choice."

The aeronauts huddle up and all talk at the same time. They're clearly divided about what to do. With every breath, I feel the moments pass back at home.

"What's it going to be?" I ask.

Denver places his hand on Bai's shoulder. "What choice do we have, Bai? We need to go with the kid."

"You mean with the Youli," she says.

"I mean with the kid. He's wearing the insignia. I trust him."

Denver Reddy scans the faces of his pod mates. One by one, they nod. He turns to face me. "We're in. What's the plan?"

Tell them we'll all join hands, Mira says. *I'll link with the Youli, and they'll bound us out.*

Once I relay the message to the aeronauts, Mira pulls me to the side. She weaves her fingers with mine, and looks up at me with her brown eyes. My mind fills with sadness, and this time I'm certain the sadness is hers.

"What is it?" I whisper.

She reaches her fingers to my face and gently cups my chin in her hand. Her eyes study mine. She's looking at me like she needs to memorize every detail of this moment.

"Mira?"

She bites her lip, and her face sets with a steely resolve.

You're the glue, Jasper. It has to be you. It's always been you.

What are you talking about?

I'm not going back, Jasper.

What do you mean?

I'm . . . Her mind shifts and sorts, like she's looking for the right words. *I'm leaving with the Youli.*

Wait . . . you're kidding, right? Why would you do that?

I have to.

MONICA TESLER

My heart leaps in my chest. What is she saying? Why is she doing this? I can't let this happen. *No, Mira! You can't! That's not part of the deal!*

It's my choice.

No! They're making you do this!

I have to do this, Jasper. It's the only way.

That makes no sense! You need to come with me. We'll figure this out together.

Mira turns away. *I can't go with you.*

You can't or you won't?

She turns back to me, but she won't meet my gaze. *I don't want to.*

Her words punch me in the gut. She doesn't want to go with me? That can't be true. This is all wrong. Everything's happening too fast.

A hand clamps my shoulder. "Come on, kid," Denver says. "Time's a-tickin'." He breaks apart my left hand's grasp on Mira's right. Bai swoops in and clasps Mira's free palm.

Mira, no! Please!

Mira's eyes lift and linger on me for a moment. Then she turns her gaze to the center of the circle. A mental door slams closed between us. She's shut me out.

A strange sensation seizes my body, like I'm a marionette and someone is pulling the strings. Then the strangeness is replaced by the familiar discomfort of a bound.

Bam!

Slam!

My butt hits the ground. Denver still has my hand in his, but where Mira's palm was moments before, my hand hangs free.

"WHERE ON EARTH ARE WE?" ONE OF THE
aeronauts asks.

Denver pushes himself up. "Are we on Earth?"

"How'd we get here?" Bai asks. "It felt like we were just
ripped through space."

Pretty much.

Curling my fingers against my palm, I can almost feel
Mira's skin still pressed against mine. What did you do,
Mira?

"Hey, kid!" Denver says. "Where's the girl? And the Youli?"

I ignore him and look around. The room we're in is dark
and disorienting. A light wind stirs the hair on my arms.

Memories tug at the corners of my mind. This is where I learned to bound.

Just like Mira said, the Youli brought us to the Ezone.

A loud noise sounds in the distance. An alarm.

Denver kicks me in the shoe. "Kid! Snap out of it and tell us what's happening!"

I push myself up to standing. "We're at the space station. This is a training room. I guess we should just head to the—"

The door bursts open, letting in a radius of light along with the wail of the alarm. Six officers rush in, weapons raised.

"What the . . . ?" the one in front shouts.

"Are you . . . ?" another says, staring at Denver and his pod.

"Jasper Adams!" A familiar face topped with bright red hair catapults at me, wrapping me up in a hug.

"Hi, Ryan!" I step back into my personal space. "How's it going?"

"How's it going?" he parrots back. "You're supposed to be dead, and you ask *me* how's it going? How are *you?* Where have you been all this time? How did you get here?"

"Ryan, what happened on Alkalinia? Did my sister make it? How long have—"

"Attention!" Denver Reddy claps his hands. "I am Captain Denver Reddy. Salute your senior officer!"

Ryan and all the Earth Force officers who arrived with him snap to attention. Denver turns to me. "That means you, too, kid. We're not in . . . whatever that awful place was . . . anymore."

Welcome back to Earth Force, I suppose. I resist the urge to glare at Denver and slowly lift my hand to my forehead.

Once everyone in the room other than Denver's pod is silent and standing rod straight, Denver crosses his arms against his chest. "Good. Now, no more questions. Take us to see whoever's in charge. Immediately."

The next few minutes are a total blur. The officers rush me and the lost aeronauts out of the Ezone and through the halls of the space station. As we walk, one of the officers speaks quietly into her com link. When we arrive at the chute, a dozen officers are there to greet us with starstruck looks on their faces. They salute the lost aeronauts. Some of them even bow to Denver.

Geez. The guy's not *that* awesome.

I get that it's a pretty big deal. Most of the officers at the space station were around my age when Denver and his pod disappeared. They probably watched the Incident live on the webs. Seeing Denver Reddy is like seeing someone return from the dead.

"Still using the chutes, eh?" Denver asks the young officer holding open the door to the cube.

The officer opens his mouth, but no words come out. As red rises to his cheeks, he manages to cough out, "Yes, sir, Captain Reddy, sir."

Another officer gestures for the lost aeronauts to enter the cube. She follows them in and activates the system. Denver steps up to the grate and gets sucked in. The other aeronauts follow, then the rest of the officers, until just Ryan and I are left. Now I'll finally get some answers.

"They should have let you go in the front," Ryan says. "You've been missing, too, after all." Ryan is taller, and he's not as round in the middle as he used to be. It's like someone hung him up and let gravity stretch him.

"That's okay," I say. "Ryan, how long have I been gone?"

"You don't know?" When I shake my head, Ryan's eyes go wide. "What happened?"

"Just . . . how long, Ryan?"

He scrunches up his face in thought. "The Battle of the Alkalinian Seat was close to a year ago."

A year? I suck in a breath. No wonder Ryan looks different. How much happened while I was away?

I grab Ryan's forearm. "My sister, is she okay?"

A strange look passes across his face and he flicks his eyes to the floor.

Oh God. She didn't make it. Pain pierces my chest like a twisting knife. How could I let that happen? I couldn't even protect my own sister!

"She was killed in the battle? Was it when the venom tube broke apart?"

"Oh . . . No!" Ryan shakes his head. "She survived the battle!"

Thank goodness. It feels like every muscle in my body exhales.

"It's just . . . ," Ryan continues.

Tensing up again, I tighten my grip on Ryan's arm. "Just what? Is she okay or not, Ryan?"

"She's okay—at least, I think so. The thing is, she's not here. In fact, I'm not sure where she is, although I bet she's with your pod mate Marco Romero."

Huh? What's he not telling me about Addy and Marco? And what else happened while I was away? I can't believe I was gone a whole year!

Ryan's com link buzzes, and we both jump. "Officer Walsh, please escort Officer Adams to the admiral's briefing room immediately."

He rolls his eyes and nods at the chute cube. "We've got to go. You remember how to work this thing?"

"Wait, Ryan, I don't understand. Where's my sister?"

Ryan looks both ways down the hall. "I probably shouldn't have said anything. Most of what I know is rumors. Ask the admiral. Or your buddy Cole. He has top-level clearance now. We really need to go."

As I stand on the crate waiting to be sucked into the chute, my mind spins. Mira left with the Youli, and I don't know why. Addy is gone, and I don't know where. I lost a year of my life in that horrible rift, and now it seems I may have lost even more.

Ryan stands aside to let me enter the briefing room. My heart pounds so hard, I can hardly catch my breath. And I'm exhausted. Even though adrenaline is still coursing through every centimeter of my body, I feel like I can barely stand. I was up all night, first deactivating the shield in Alkalinia, and then trying to find our way out of the rift. Now I'm back and having to wrap my head around all the time I've lost and how much has changed.

At least this room is familiar. It's the same briefing room where Admiral Eames told us that our pod would be the advance team to Alkalinia. For me, that was only a few weeks ago. For everyone else in this room, other than the lost aeronauts, a year has passed since that meeting. My mind spins. How much have I missed?

Trying to focus on one thing is a lost cause. Is Addy okay? Where is she? Why is she with Marco? Cole has top-level clearance? How did that happen? How's Lucy? What about everyone else? Did they survive the Battle of the Alkalinian Seat?

Where is Mira? Is she safe? Why did she leave with the Youli? Why did she leave *me*?

The room is almost full, and no one seemed to notice when I walked in and stood in the corner. Everyone is focused on the lost aeronauts who are in various stages of freaking out. It must be starting to set in that they've been gone for more than fourteen years—make that *fifteen* years now. A year seems like an eternity for me; I can't even imagine how they must feel. A huge chunk of life has passed them by.

Bai paces the length of the room, brushing off anyone who tries to engage her. One of the younger aeronauts begs the officers to let her contact Earth. Of course, that's not happening. Earth Force would never let this media gem get out without proper spin.

Denver is the only one who appears relatively calm. He shakes everyone's hands and smiles in a way that reminds me of Maximilian Sheek but without that weird tipped chin. After all, Denver was the face of Earth Force while Sheek was still in grade school.

"Hey, Jasper," a voice near me says. "That's your name, right?"

It's the aeronaut who first spotted us in the rift. He's leaning against the wall next to me.

I nod.

"What's happening? What are we waiting for?"

I have no idea why he's asking me when there are over a dozen high-level officers in the room. Maybe it's because

I'm the only person he knows other than his pod mates. The other officers in the room were kids when he disappeared.

I shrug. "I'm guessing the admiral is on her way. We'll know more then."

He shakes his head. "We've really been gone fifteen years, huh? This is going to be a very different homecoming than what I envisioned."

I'm not exactly sure what to say. "At least it's a homecoming, right? Everyone thought you were dead. I guess they thought I was dead, too."

"Is that why they're looking at us like we're ghosts?"

The door swings open and in walks Captain James Ridders and Cole. Everyone snaps to attention.

Cole surveys the room. His gaze passes over the lost aeronauts but doesn't stop until he spots me. When he does, his whole body seems to exhale. He dips his chin in a tiny nod.

Thank goodness! I'm finally going to get some answers. I head over to greet my friend but stop when the door opens again. Admiral Eames enters.

"What a momentous day!" she declares as she walks to the head of the table. "Welcome back!" Her voice sounds high and shaky.

Just like Cole, the admiral searches the room with her eyes, but before she finds who she's looking for, Denver Reddy plows through the crowd to reach her. "Cora!"

He swoops her up in his arms. Her feet dangle half a meter above the floor.

For a moment—so quick I'm not even sure it happened—the admiral melts into Denver's embrace. Then she stiffens and whispers something in Denver's ear. He sets her down.

"You'll address me as *Admiral*," she says, straightening her uniform. Her cheeks are pink as she takes her seat. "At ease." She instructs her ranking officers to give up their seats for the lost aeronauts and—somewhat shockingly—me. As soon as we're seated she turns to Denver. "Captain Reddy, please tell us what happened."

"Excuse me, Admiral," Cole interjects, "but I must insist that everyone without a Code One security clearance exit the room, excluding the returning aeronauts and Officer Adams, of course."

The admiral nods.

Half a dozen officers reluctantly leave. Without them, the room is a lot less crowded. I tap my feet under the table. Let's get this started. I have a million questions that I can't wait to ask as soon as someone tells me what happened to my sister.

Denver leans forward and folds his arms on the table. He waits until the door closes and everyone still in the room is paying full attention. It's clear this guy knows how to engage a crowd.

"I'm sure you know the basics," he says. "What started out as a normal bound with live web coverage quickly went south.

As we performed the routine systems check, word came over my headset that incoming enemy was spotted within range. My first thought was to abort, but knowing that the bound was live, with cameras inside the cockpit, I continued as planned, waiting for an abort order to come from up the chain of command. Then the auto countdown initiated."

"Go on," Captain Ridders says. He stands at the admiral's side with his arms crossed.

Denver leans back. "Just before the bound, my systems went down and the cockpit was swallowed in darkness. I assumed it was engineering manually overriding and aborting the bound. Now, my best guess is our signals were scrambled by the alien vessel. The bound proceeded."

So that's the real story of the Incident at Bounding Base 51. The words that just came out of Denver Reddy's mouth explain the greatest tragedy and fascination in Earth's recent history.

"Things felt off from the moment the bound initiated," Denver continues, "like my body was being ripped in a million pieces. But thankfully we remained intact. I believe some or all of my crew was unconscious for a period of time. When we came to, we were . . . somewhere else."

"Where?" Ridders asks.

"I don't know."

"What do you mean, you don't know?" the admiral asks.

"Where have you been all this time? You've been gone for the last fifteen years, Captain Reddy."

"See, that's not exactly true."

As confused looks pass across the faces in the room, Denver turns to me. "Kid, you're the one with the answers. You explain it."

Everyone looks at me, including the admiral.

I press my fingers together beneath the table and sit up straight. "We were in the rift."

Sharp intakes of breath sound around the table. For a moment, no one speaks.

"You mean . . . a rift in space as Gedney has theorized?" Cole asks.

"Right," I say. "I mean, yes, sir." It's clear that's the correct way to address Cole in this debrief, but it feels incredibly weird to call my best friend *sir*. "And like Gedney says," I continue, "time moves differently there."

Cole, who stands on the other side of the admiral, and who doesn't react at all to my formality, braces his hands on the table and leans forward with a familiar look of curiosity. "How so?"

How do I explain? "Well, take me, for example. Ryan . . . or, umm . . . Lieutenant Walsh says I've been gone almost a year. But in my experience, I only got to the rift a few hours ago. In fact, for me, the Battle of the Alkalinian Seat was last night. I don't even know what happened. Did I get the shield down in time? Did all the Bounders survive?"

No one answers my questions, but the room erupts in chatter as everyone tries to make sense of what I said. It's hard to believe the rift exists, let alone that time moves differently there. Cole talks excitedly with Ridders. The admiral takes advantage of the distractions to lean close to Denver.

"You look so young," she says quietly. "How long were you gone?"

His face softens. "About two days."

She closes her eyes, and a pained expression paints her face. "I've aged."

He leans even closer, and I think he grabs her hand beneath the table. "You're as beautiful as ever."

She shakes her head and jerks her hands free. Placing her stacked palms on the table, she straightens in her seat. "Officer Adams, please continue," she says loudly and with enough authority to quiet the entire room. "Describe the rift, and explain how you turned up in the Ezone."

Mira . . . what on earth do I say? I can't just tell Admiral Eames that she chose to go with the Youli. I'm not even sure that's the whole truth. I'll have to be careful how I explain things.

"I'll tell you what happened," Bai interjects. "We spent two days exploring the gray no-man's-land only to have these two kids show up and—"

MONICA TESLER

"*Two* kids?" Ridders interrupts.

"Yes, two, and yes, one of them is missing," she says. "In fact, I'm wondering whether the kids were in on it."

Wait, what? How could she think we were in on it?

"In on what exactly?" Admiral Eames asks.

"An enemy operation," Bai says. "Sure, we're alive and well, and that's something to celebrate, but let's not lose sight of the fact that this could be part of a massive military attack. The last time they showed up, we all know what happened."

"The last time who showed up?" Cole asks.

"The little green men!" Bai says. "Although now that I've seen them up close, they're not so little."

"Someone explain this to me," the admiral says. "Jasper, what happened?"

So much for spinning things my way. I'd better stick to the basic facts. "The only reason we're out of the rift, Admiral, is because the Youli showed up. They got us out of there."

Another round of gasps fill the room, and this time they're laced with fear.

"Sound the alarm and raise the alert level to red," the admiral says. "All weapons personnel to their posts. Scan the surrounding vectors for any sign of quantum activity."

Half of the officers in the briefing room rush out.

As Ridders and Cole drill the lost aeronauts with questions, Admiral Eames signals me. "Jasper, Officer Matheson is the only other cadet who was unaccounted for in the Battle of the Alkalinian Seat. She was with you in the rift, wasn't she?"

In the seconds that follow, I make a decision. The admiral can't know that leaving with the Youli might have been Mira's choice, not if Mira ever wants to come back.

"Yes, she was with me in the rift."

"Where is Mira now, Jasper?"

I cross my fingers beneath the table and force myself to look the admiral in the eye. "The Youli took her."

AFTER ADMIRAL EAMES QUESTIONS US about the Youli's involvement in our rescue, she breaks up the meeting. Apparently, it's the middle of the night at the space station, and the admiral needs to check in with her defensive weapons and quantum detection teams. She asks her staff to escort the lost aeronauts to temporary quarters. Surprisingly, she lumps me in on that request. I'd assumed I'd be headed to the Bounder bunks, not private captain quarters.

As her officers usher the lost aeronauts out the door, I shoot a glance at Cole. I need to talk to him. Alone. Fortunately he seems to understand my signal, or at least he asks the admiral if he can walk me to my room, which means we'll have some time to talk.

Admiral Eames seems perplexed at Cole's request. Then she nods. "That's right, Captain Thompson, you were pod mates with Officer Adams during your Academy days. Of course you can escort him. Report back to me in quantum monitoring as soon as you're able."

Cole thanks the admiral and stands at my side until the room empties. When it's just the two of us, I let my shoulders slump. Finally I'm going to get some answers.

"Captain, huh?" I say, slapping Cole on the shoulder. "How did that happen?"

Cole shrugs, looking awkward for the first time since he entered the room. "I was promoted."

I laugh. "Obviously." Why am I starting to feel awkward, too? "Congratulations."

"Thanks." He stuffs his hands in his pockets. "We all thought you were dead."

Still the same Cole—he gets right to the point—although something tells me he's not exactly the same as the last time I saw him. "I'm not, but speaking of people being dead, please tell me that my sister is okay."

Cole bristles at my question. "She isn't dead, Jasper."

I exhale, relieved that Addy's alive. Still, I need details, and Cole isn't spilling. "Ryan said she's with Marco."

Cole shakes his head. "Ryan can't keep his mouth shut."

This is ridiculous. I've been gone all this time and my best friend won't even tell me what happened to my own sister. The sense of relief I had at being left with Cole is quickly evaporating. "You need to be straight with me, Cole. I have to know what's going on."

"Fine, but only because I owe you. We all owe you. If you hadn't gotten that shield down on Alkalinia, none of us would be here right now."

Only because he *owes* me? How about because he's my friend? My pod mate? "What's the situation with Addy, Cole? You need to tell me!"

He drags his foot across the floor. Is he really that uncomfortable about breaking confidentiality? She's *my* sister! Don't I have a right to know?

"She's joined the Resistance, Jasper," he finally says, "a rebel group based on Gulaga—mostly Tunnelers and disgruntled Earthlings. They're believed to be led by Jon Waters."

"Addy is with Waters?" Last time I saw her, Addy had never even met our former fearless leader. I can't believe she's with him on Gulaga. "And Marco's there, too?"

Cole glances anxiously at the door. "That's what our intelligence reports say."

When Mira and I were rescued on the Gulagan tundra, we discovered that Waters was friends with the Wackies, a group of Tunneler rebels who opposed Earth Force's control of their planet. Addy and Marco must be with them now, too. "So, Waters joined forces with Barrick and the Wackies and formed the Resistance? Are they rebelling against Earth Force? I mean, what are they *resisting?*"

Cole flicks his gaze around the room, looking anywhere but at me. "I can't say any more, Jasper. All of this is well outside your clearance. It's for your own protection. The less you know, the less likely you'll be caught up in a security sweep."

He's shutting me out? I curl my fingers into fists. "Secrets are for my safety? Why do I have a hard time believing that?"

"We've had leaks. We suspect there's a mole within the higher ranks of the Force. You don't want to be the subject of an investigation."

I can't believe this. My best friend is completely stonewalling me. "It would've been tough for me to leak information from the rift, don't you think?"

"No one is immune," Coles says, either ignoring or not catching on to my sarcasm.

"We made a pact on Gulaga not to keep secrets!" My voice shakes. I'm barely keeping it together. "It's all about the pod, remember?"

Cole stares at me, expressionless. "Our pod was disbanded."

I close my eyes. This is going nowhere. Since I left Alkalinia a few hours ago, Cole became Earth Force boss man, Mira left with the Youli, and Marco and Addy joined up with the Wackies. Who does that even leave? I take a deep breath. "What about Lucy? Is she okay? Or is that above my clearance level, too?"

Cole rolls his eyes. Apparently, we've landed on a topic he's allowed to talk about. "Lucy's fine. She's here. I'm sure she'll find you the moment she hears you've arrived at the space station." He takes a step toward the door. "We should move along. The admiral expects me by her side soon."

That's it? That's all he's going to tell me? I want my friend back. I want my *life* back. "So, you're not just a captain, you're like a really important captain, aren't you?"

"I'm the chief military strategist."

"In one year you went from cadet to chief military strategist?" Wow. To say I missed a lot would be a serious understatement. I shrug, not really knowing what else to say. "You always were the master at *Evolution of Combat*."

The bed I'm in is incredibly comfortable. It's almost as comfortable as the couches in our souped-up common room on Alkalinia, which was no more than virtual reality meant to keep us happy and stuffed and distracted so the Alks could pump us up with reptilian venom and knock us out.

My body is beyond tired. Every time I close my eyes and start to fade, my leg jerks or a shiver runs up my arm. I'm so exhausted I can't even get my body coordinated enough to sleep.

Plus, I can't turn my brain off. I keep thinking about the fact that I lost a year of my life in that horrible rift. I've only been back at the space station a few hours, and from what I can tell, everything has changed.

Every time I stop my mind from spiraling over my lost time, I zero right back in on Mira's odd behavior in the rift. My brain is on repeat, replaying her final words.

I'm leaving with the Youli.

I have to.

It's my choice.

I can't go with you.

I don't want to.

What did she mean? Did she want to leave with the Youli? Was it really her choice? Or was that part of the deal and Mira chose to shield me from it? Maybe she knew I'd never agree to let the Youli help us escape the rift if it meant Mira couldn't come with us.

If that was her reasoning, she was right.

But what if she really meant exactly what she said? She chose to go with the Youli. She said she didn't want to come with me.

Maybe the only reason I refuse to believe what she said is because it hurts too much.

When I finally manage to doze off, there's pounding at my door. I bolt upright, convinced that I'm back in Alkalinia.

Light pours into the room and something crashes onto my bed. I'm about to fend off the intruder when I realize the high-pitched voice could only be Lucy's.

"Oh my God, it's true!" she yelps. "I half thought that arrogant Cole Thompson was playing mind games with me when he confirmed the rumor that you'd returned from the dead! Oh, Jasper, not a day has gone by that you haven't been in my thoughts. You are one of the true good people in the galaxy! And to think you were almost lost forever!" With this last line, she flings herself at me, knocking us both back onto my bed.

Such drama! At least Lucy hasn't changed.

"Good to see you, too, Lucy," I say, carefully extracting myself from her hug without making her mad. Lucy can be touchy. I flip the light switch by my bed so the room is illuminated by more than just the light from the hall. "What time is it?"

"Oh, I'm so sorry. You must be exhausted. I didn't even think about how much you needed rest. I just heard first thing that you were here, and I needed to lay my own eyes on you to believe it."

Lucy looks . . . strange. Her braids and ribbons are gone. Her hair is smoothed back and secured in a knot at her neck.

She's wearing all sorts of makeup, and her lashes are so huge it looks like she's got spiders crawling out of her eyeballs.

"Um, Lucy, really, what time is it?"

"It's just past 0600."

Wow. I feel like my head just hit the pillow, and now it's already morning.

"Is it true?" Lucy asks. "Were you really stuck in the rift? And were you only gone for a few hours?"

I nod. "Two nights ago, you and I were hanging out on the couch in our Alkalinian common room."

Lucy shivers. "Don't even say the name of that horrid place! Until this morning, I thought you and Mira died there, and that I was partially to blame."

More drama. "How were you to blame?"

Lucy blinks. "Oh, you know, if I weren't so annoyed at your sister and her good-for-nothing boyfriend, maybe I could have been more helpful."

She must be talking about Marco, but boyfriend? Well, it's not like I didn't see that coming. "Come on, Lucy, that wouldn't have made any difference. The Youli were coming, no matter what we did."

"I suppose." She turns her head. A dangly diamond earring reflects the light of my bedside lamp.

It's probably a bad idea to stay on the subject of Addy and Marco given that Lucy's feelings about them don't appear to have changed, but I have to find out what she knows. "So, my sister and Marco are with Waters and the Wackies on Gulaga?"

Lucy looks around, then kicks the door closed with her foot. Fortunately, she loves to gossip, so her annoyance fades. "That's the scoop. They've joined the Resistance. Although it's on the hush hush, of course. Everything's on the hush hush around here. Word is, we have a mole." She squeezes my hand. "I'm sorry, Jasper. I'm sure you were hoping to see Addy. I can't say I'm a big fan of hers, but she was awfully broken up about your death. We all were. At the funeral, we cried in each other's arms."

"Wait. What funeral?"

"Your funeral. They had a service for you back on Earth. I delivered one of the eulogies. Mine was really spectacular—the best, by far, if I do say so myself. I may have to reenact it for you. Wouldn't that be fun? You can hear how I remember you before you even die. Actually, I'm sure we have a vid recording of it in the press archives. I'll make sure to have it retrieved this morning."

My heart clenches. I can't believe Addy had to go through that. She had to mourn a lost brother. She was already pretty anti–Earth Force by the time she reached Alkalinia. My apparent death was more than enough to push her over the edge. No wonder she bailed on Earth Force and joined up with Waters and the Resistance.

"What about my parents?" I ask.

"They were at your funeral, too, of course."

I cover my eyes with my hand. My parents held a funeral for me? I can't even imagine what that did to them. I have to contact them today. I don't care what Earth Force and its ridiculous confidentiality rules say, I can't let my parents keep thinking I'm dead.

"Speaking of death," Lucy says, "is Mira . . . ?"

"She's alive."

Lucy exhales. "Oh, thank goodness. Where is she? I'll go visit her next."

"She's not here."

Lucy looks at me quizzically.

"It's complicated. I'm sure the admiral is going to ban me from talking about this once we finish our debrief, so I might as well tell you now. The Youli rescued us from the rift, and now they have Mira."

Lucy's eyes go wide. "The Youli? I don't understand. Why would they rescue you?"

"I'm not sure, really. Waters always hinted that the Youli weren't all bad."

Lucy looks at me sideways. "How can you say that with all that's happened? Actually, I guess you don't know all that's happened. Let's just say that the war has escalated. And Earth Force has informed the public."

My eyes widen. There were rumors, sure, but now it's official knowledge. Our planet is at war. I wonder what things are like back home.

I shake my head. "I'm desperate, Lucy. I missed so much. You have to fill me in on everything. So now everyone knows about the Youli?"

"They do. I've made sure of it." Lucy smiles, bats her spider eyelashes, and tips her head to the side, freakishly like Sheek. "You're looking at the face of Earth Force—the new and improved *feminine* face."

So the comparison to Sheek was actually real? For Lucy, this must be a dream come true. She wanted to see her name on the webs ever since I met her. But how did she go from cadet to the face of Earth Force in a year? I have so many questions. "No more Sheek?"

Lucy snorts. "Oh, that clown is still around. But my ratings are sky-high. I have to think his days are numbered." She does that weird Sheek smile again and looks at me expectantly.

"Congrats. I'm sure you're great."

"Oh, I am. Speaking of which, I need to read my morning briefing notes. I bet things will be a bit chaotic over in the press room since we've raised to red alert, not to mention the unexpected return of the greatest celebrities in the history of Earth! And you, of course. We've got to determine the spin, right?"

With that, she delivers yet another Sheek smile. Then she pushes off the bed and disappears out of the room before I can answer, and before I can press her for more information about the past year.

When the door closes, I turn my light back off and throw the blanket over my head. Maybe if I burrow down I can catch another hour of sleep. Or at least maybe I can push away the thoughts that are fighting for attention in my mind.

Cole is chief military strategist and Lucy is the new face of Earth Force. What else has changed while I've been gone?

Do my parents know Addy's gone AWOL? Or do they think she's dead, too?

Why on earth did Mira leave me? What did the Youli say that made her choose to go?

I thought the only thing they wanted was peace.

The message!

I bolt up in bed.

How could I have forgotten about the message? So much has happened since I arrived at the space station that I didn't even think about speaking to Admiral Eames about the Youli's message.

I need to find the admiral right away! Giving her the message may be the only way to get Mira back. If Mira wants to come back.

Flipping the light switch, I rummage around on the floor for my shoes then dash to the bathroom. Actually, *dash* is too strong a word. I quickly wobble to the bathroom. My legs barely feel like they're holding me up. Dark circles rim my eyes. I look pretty much what you'd expect someone who's gone through a battle, an alien rescue, and multidimensional time travel on half a night of sleep would look like—which is to say, horrible. I splash some cold water on my face then try to pat down my hair.

Once I'm dressed, I jet out of my room and instantly realize I have no idea where I am. I didn't pay attention when Cole walked us here last night, and I basically have no innate sense of direction. My internal compass is so horrible I stranded Mira and me in that VR torture chamber on Alkalinia last night. Or I guess I should say last year. We were lucky we made it out.

I take off down the hall, following the silver stripe that guides the mini spider crawlers. Hopefully that will get me out of the officers' quarters at least.

As I track the stripe around the corner, I think about my lost year and everything I learned from Cole and Lucy since I got back last night. What else did I miss? I wish Marco was here. He would have no problem filling me in, security clearance or not. I can't believe—

"Hey!" a girl's voice calls.

I stop and look up. A small girl with curly brown hair that falls just below her chin is pancaked against the wall next to the silver stripe.

She puts her hands on her hips. "You nearly plowed me down, Jasper Adams!"

"WATCH WHERE YOU'RE GOING!" THE GIRL snaps.

"Sorry," I mumble. "I'm kind of lost. How do you know my name?"

She tilts her head and narrows her eyes at me. She must be confused how someone bright enough to be an Earth Force officer could be dumb enough to get lost at the space station. "Everyone knows your name. Your face has been plastered all across the planet for the last six months, not to mention flashed repeatedly on every web station."

"What?" I can't make sense of anything this girl just said. I take a closer look at her. She looks vaguely familiar. "Do I know you?"

"Not really. I heard you showed up last night. I work with Lucy, and she talks about you all the time." She glances down the hall before adding, "And I know your sister."

"Addy? Have you heard from her?"

The girl quickly looks around again like she's making sure no one heard me. Her eyes are so dark blue they almost look purple. "Of course not. We were juniors together. I didn't really know Addy until after the battle."

"The Battle of the Alkalinian Seat, where I supposedly perished?"

"That's the one, although apparently you didn't."

We stand there staring at each other. I'm not sure what to say. I can't seem to do much other than look at her eyes. I've never seen anyone with purple eyes before.

She blinks, and I remember why I'm here in the first place. "I need to see the admiral. Any chance you know where I can find her?"

The girl steps away from the wall, forcing me to backpedal.

"She's probably finishing up morning briefing," she says. "I'm headed that way." She waves her hand to herd me along, then takes off at a brisk pace.

"What's your name?" I ask, jogging beside her. If this girl works with Lucy, she must have access to lots of Earth Force information.

"Jayne."

"Are you like another face of Earth Force?" As soon as the words leave my lips, heat rises in my cheeks. I don't want her to think I'm saying she looks like she should be the face of Earth Force, although she kind of does, especially with the purple eyes.

She laughs. "No, that's not my thing, although I do work in public relations. Leave the cameras for Lucy and Max. I'm a copywriter. I compose what they read over the teleprompter."

"Did you just call Maximilian Sheek *Max*? He lets you call him that?"

"Of course not, but I don't see him anywhere around here, do you?"

When I don't answer, she takes off walking again. "Let's go, Jasper! I can't be late. This is going to be a big news day. Haven't you heard? The famous lost aeronauts and the Earth Force poster boy returned from the dead."

I know she's talking about me, but it doesn't feel real. Since when am I news? And the whole *returned from the dead* thing, well, that's going to take some time to sink in.

Jayne is fast. In fact, it's amazing how fast she can walk without breaking into a run. I'm half out of breath when we get to the chute cube. She holds the door and gestures with her hand. "You first."

"That's okay. You go."

"I insist. I've had way too many cadets crash into me in the tube. Something about building a human chain. We just met. I'm not ready for you to grab my ankles."

"Who said anything . . . Forget it. I'll go." Sliding past her into the cube, I stand on the chute grate with my arms folded across my chest. What's her problem with a human chain? If my pod mates were here, we'd be fighting over who got to be chain leader.

Actually, now that Cole is the military strategy god or whatever his title is, maybe he wouldn't be so quick to goof off with me, a lowly cadet. And I bet Lucy wouldn't risk messing up her new hairdo and perfect makeup.

The chute activates, and I'm sucked in. Jayne seems all right and all, but she makes me realize how much I miss the way things used to be. And from what I can tell so far, things used to be very different from how things are now.

I press my eyes closed and let the wind rush across my skin. For a moment at least, I'm anywhere I want to be. Or maybe I should say, any *when* I want to be.

As I'm dumped into the landing trough, I slam back to the here and now.

Jayne whisks in behind me.

When we exit the chute cube, she starts down the hall to the right. The hallway ends in a T. The new hall to the left is crowded with people talking and rushing between rooms. To the right, a guard stands post.

"The press room is that way," Jayne says, tipping her head to the left. "Admiral Eames is down there." She nods at the guard.

"Thanks for showing me the way," I say. "I'll see you around."

"No problem. And yes, you will. I'm sure we'll be seeing lots of each other." She turns and heads up the hall, leaving me to brave Admiral Eames solo.

The guard escorts me the rest of the way to the admiral's briefing room. My palms start to sweat. Now that I'm about to see the admiral, I'm freaked. What am I going to tell her? Sure, I have a message to deliver, but what am I actually going to say? I can't exactly waltz in and say, *Peace, peace, peace,* like the Youli. That would go absolutely nowhere.

Not to mention, what am I going to tell her about Mira? I'm still not sure how I feel about the Youli, but I know how I feel about Mira. Delivering the message and cooperating with the Youli may be the only way I'll ever see her again.

I have to stay focused on my goal: bringing Mira home. That is, if she wants to come home.

We stop in front of a door. The guard points at a small bench against the wall as he speaks into his com link.

I sit down and bend over my knees, trying to shut out the hum of the florescent lights so I can come up with a plan for what to say to the admiral. When I finally push back up, the guard is no longer there. It's just me on the bench. That must mean I'm supposed to wait.

Yesterday I told the admiral that the Youli took Mira. There's no doubt she'll want me to elaborate when we talk. I could set the record straight, explain that Mira chose to go with the Youli. It's not as if I lied last night. Saying that the Youli took Mira doesn't mean it wasn't her choice. After all, the Youli had to take her, because Mira didn't know how to get out of the rift on her own. So I was technically being completely honest. Maybe the admiral would be more likely to meet with the Youli if she knew Mira had gone with them of her own free will. Maybe Mira's choice to trust the Youli would convince the admiral to trust them, too.

Somehow I doubt that.

Odds are, if I tell the admiral the truth, she'll think Mira is a traitor. She may even suspect me of being a double agent since everyone knows how close Mira and I are. I might be locked in the cell block and interrogated, especially with security so tight like Cole said. Earth Force may never trust me again. And that's not the worst of it. If I tell the truth, Mira may never be able to come home.

Maybe I shouldn't deliver the message.

The truth is, I'm not sure what to do. I wish Mira were here. She'd help me through this. She might not tell me what to do, but she'd support me as I figured it out. She'd help me find the meeting and didn't even plan for this question? I am such an idiot. It's basically impossible to answer without talking about my brain patch, and I really don't want the admiral to know about that. "Umm . . ."

"We know about the Youli patches implanted in yours and Officer Matheson's brain stems."

"You do?"

"Yes. And if we didn't, you were going to inform me about them in response to my question about how you communicated with the Youli, I presume." Without waiting for my confirmation, she continues, "Let's get to the point. What's the message?"

Peace. Peace. Peace.

The word rings in my mind just as it did in the rift. I can almost hear the deep voice of the Youli speaking in my brain: *Tell your people we wish to meet and discuss the requirements for your planet's entry into the Intragalactic Council. This is our gesture of peace.*

"The Youli want to talk about reaching a peace deal and Earth's entry into the Intragalactic Council," I tell her.

She laughs and shakes her head. "A peace deal? You can't be serious."

"I'm totally serious. They kept saying, *Peace, peace, peace.* They really meant it."

"And you're suddenly an excellent judge of Youli character?"

strength to push aside my stress with all the changes from my missing year and persuade the admiral to push for peace.

Of course, the fact that Mira *isn't* here is one of the main reasons I'm sitting on this bench right now. I bury my head in my hands. My life is a mess.

Thanks, Mira. Thanks a lot for leaving me.

The door opens, and I jerk up. I have no idea how long I've been sitting on this bench. Next to me, Denver Reddy exits the admiral's briefing room. His eyes are puffy. He looks like he didn't sleep at all last night.

"I wish you'd reconsider, Cora," he says to the person on the other side of the door, who must be the admiral. "And if you do, you know where to find me." He pulls the door shut, leans against the frame, and closes his eyes.

He's obviously upset. It's kind of awkward just sitting here. I try to clear my throat to tip him off that he's not alone, but my spit goes down the wrong pipe, and I end up in a coughing fit.

Denver pulls himself together. "You okay, kid?"

I nod between coughs.

"You waiting to talk to the boss?"

I nod again as I get the coughing under control.

"Careful. She's in a mood, if you know what I mean."

Great. Just what I need. "Thanks for the heads-up. How's the reentry going?"

He shrugs. "Strange. Life kept going without me. I guess everything about that is pretty messed up. Got to go. I'm getting briefed on recent history in five minutes."

Denver takes off down the hall. Recent history? I probably need to attend that briefing, too, at least the part that covers the past year. Denver's right about one thing. Everything is pretty messed up.

"Come on in, Jasper." Admiral Eames leans against the doorframe.

I jump to my feet and raise my hand in salute. She barely seems to notice. She just disappears back into the room, which must mean she expects me to follow her.

I enter the briefing room and realize it's the same room where we had the meeting last night. Geez. My sense of direction really is awful. I had no idea that's where I was, and I certainly couldn't have made it back here without Jayne's help.

The room looks a lot different today. The lights are dimmed, and the only person present other than me is the admiral. I've never seen Admiral Eames without her entourage. Now suddenly I'm having a one-on-one meeting. This whole return from the rift experience feels like a dream. Or maybe a nightmare.

She nods at the chair beside her. I pull back the seat and perch on the edge, my back as straight as a board.

The admiral looks even more tired than Denver. I wonder if he's one of the reasons why. I don't know what the[ir rela]tionship was before he was lost in the rift, but it's clea[r they] were close. It must be super weird for her to see him a[t] this time. She's lived more than a dozen years longe[r than] him. She's fought more wars, commanded more mis[sions,] watched more soldiers die.

"At ease, Jasper. It's just us."

I let my shoulders fall forward, and I scoot back i[n my] chair. Crossing my hands on the table, I tap my th[umbs] together as I try to figure out what to do next.

Admiral Eames raises her eyebrows. "You were wa[iting] outside my office, Jasper. I'm assuming you wished to [speak] with me."

"Oh, right. Sorry." Okay, now I need to lay it all out. "[I] thought I'd follow up about my time in the rift—you k[now,] maybe elaborate on some of the stuff we talked about [last] night." I twirl my thumbs in a circle to keep focused. I'm [still] not sure how much to say.

The admiral nods. "Great, please go ahead."

"Well, the thing is, the Youli asked me to give you a mess[age.]"

She tilts her head to the side. "You communicated w[ith] the Youli?"

"Yep. I mean, yes, sir."

She narrows her eyes at me. "How?"

Inside, I kick myself. I had all morning to prepare for t[his]

"Well, not exactly—and I know they're, like, our mortal enemies and all—but they were really convincing. And not only that, but they rescued us. There's no way we could have escaped the rift without the Youli's help."

The admiral's expression is blank. I can't tell whether I'm managing to convince her of the Youli's commitment to peace. I need to make sure she believes me. It may be the only way to bring Mira home.

There has to be a way to reach her. But this is Admiral Eames, unreadable, and pretty much unreachable. The only time I've ever seen a crack in her exterior is last night. "They brought Denver back! He'd still be in the rift if it weren't for the Youli!"

Admiral Eames folds her hands in her lap and takes a deep breath.

Something tells me that was the wrong thing to say. I shouldn't have brought up Denver.

She locks eyes with me and says slowly, "Don't presume a thing about Captain Reddy, am I understood?"

My shoulders sink under the weight of her stare. "Yes, sir. What I mean is, the Youli said they wanted to talk peace, and to prove it, they rescued us from the rift."

"I see." The admiral steeples her fingers on the table. "What else?" Her voice is sharp and icy.

"Sir?"

"What else did you want to tell me? For example, what happened to Officer Matheson? This time, I want specifics."

"Well . . . she . . ."

"Last night you said the Youli took her."

"That's right." What do I say? How do I convince her that the Youli want to cooperate? That Mira didn't betray her people?

"You need to flesh that out, Jasper. What exactly happened?"

"I'm not sure. I think that was part of the deal. They get us out of the rift, but Mira goes with them."

"She's their hostage?"

"Yeah, I guess so."

"You think we should trust our enemy who took your friend hostage? That doesn't make sense to me, Jasper. Is there something I'm missing?"

"No." As I say the word, the hope I'd held in my heart for Mira's safe return starts to seep out. This was my one shot to get the admiral's help, and I blew it. The way she just summed up the scenario—the suggestion that we should trust an enemy who took one of our soldiers hostage—even sounds ridiculous to me.

Admiral Eames stands. "I don't think there's anything left to say on the matter." She crosses to the door and opens it, leaving no question that our meeting is over. "You'd do well to remember, Officer Adams, that disloyalty to the Force is a grave offense. Thank you for your service." She walks out, leaving me alone in her dimly lit briefing room.

Like Denver said, everything is pretty messed up, and I just made things a lot worse.

I DON'T KNOW HOW LONG I STAY IN THE
admiral's briefing room, but eventually I realize it's probably not the greatest idea to be sitting here on my own.
Someone's bound to come in eventually, and when they do
they'll want to know why I'm here, and I have no explanation other than I've had no energy to move since the
admiral left.

I stumble into the hall. My legs feel like jelly. At first I
think I'm just exhausted (which I am), but I begin to wonder whether it's a side effect of my travels through the rift.
Like maybe my body didn't get put back together 100 percent correctly, or maybe hanging suspended in time and then

jumping a whole year ahead just messes you up. I'll have to ask the old aeronauts how they're feeling. Their time jump was fifteen times as long as mine, so if jelly legs are a side effect, they would definitely have them.

My mind replays my conversation with the admiral. I can't believe how inept I was. Nothing I said made the admiral pause for even a moment to consider whether the Youli could be reaching out with a genuine gesture of peace. Or maybe she doesn't want to believe it. Either way, we're no closer to bringing Mira home than we were last night.

When I get to the fork in the hall, the guard nods. I still have no idea where I am. I didn't pay any attention when I was walking here this morning with Jayne. But I do know where Jayne is. She turned left for the press room when I turned right to meet with the admiral. That means if I walk straight I should run into Jayne, which hopefully means I'll also run into Lucy. And if there's one person who might be able to help me with the Mira situation, it's Lucy.

Just like this morning, tons of people buzz around the press hall reading their tablets, chatting excitedly with other officers, most of them paying zero attention to me. Some of them look up and do this weird double take when they see me, but I just keep walking.

At the end of the hall, a wide door opens to a huge room filled with dozens of monitors mounted on every wall. I head

THE HEROES RETURN

in, hoping to spot Lucy. What I see instead is my face on at least half of the screens.

"Why is my—"

"There you are!" Lucy collides with me from the side, pulling me into a tight hug. Instead of letting me go, she sort of unravels, still gripping me by my arm and unfurling her other arm wide. "Excuse me! Excuse me! All eyes and ears over here! Everyone, this is Jasper, although of course all of you know that. Jasper, this is everyone!"

This morning I thought something was different with Lucy, but now there's no mistaking. First off, she's taller—like a *lot* taller. I'm basically looking at her eye to eye. And it's not because she's grown that much. She's wearing shoes that rise up on spikes in the back. High heels, I think they're called. Second, she's wearing tons of makeup, even more than this morning. The black spider eyelashes compete for my attention with her raspberry-pink lips. And her hair is pulled back into a tight knot. Not even her uniform is the standard issue. Sure, it's still the Earth Force uniform, but it's custom-made or something. It looks more high fashion than military.

And that smell! She smells like . . . roses!

"What's with the perfume?" I ask. "You getting beauty tips from Florine?"

A couple of laughs escape around the room. Others avert their eyes so they don't look like they're eavesdropping.

MONICA TESLER

Lucy glares at me. But a second later, she waves her hand, and her smile returns. She snuggles up against me. "Oh, you silly boy! I've missed you so much! Now let's head to my office, where we can have a private chat." She links her arm in mine and pulls me away from the crowd of press officers.

I glance around the room and spot Jayne in the back corner. She's sitting at a desk against the wall watching me and Lucy like everyone else in the room. When I smile, she shakes her head and gives a small wave.

Lucy leads me to a back hall. We pass an enormous office with a large desk that appears to float in the middle of the room. On the back wall, a huge painting hangs. It's the face of Maximilian Sheek, four times, each face a different color.

"Is that Sheek's office? Not much for modesty, huh?"

"Oh, that's his office, all right. He never makes it here until after lunch, though. Unless he has appearances, of course."

The next office is smaller, but not by much. Lucy pushes the door open and leads me in. Everything in the office is pink. Pink lacquer desk, pink desk chair covered in pink feathers, pink faux-fur rug, pink wallpaper with pink stripes, pink flowers in a pink vase, pink paper with pink pens, which I'm sure have pink ink.

"Well, what do you think?" she asks, twirling around.

"It's . . . pink. Is this stuff for real? It kind of reminds me of the VR in Alkalinia."

She slaps my hand. "That's a nasty thing to say. Of course it's real. I decorated myself."

"Why? I mean, why do they let you have all this stuff? And why do you need it?"

Lucy frowns. "I told you this morning, Jasper, I'm the new face of Earth Force. It's only fitting that I have an office that reflects that."

"So Earth Force's new look is pink?"

Lucy huffs. "No. This is *my* look. It's important to have a signature style, don't you think?"

"A what style?" I want to plug my nose. Her whole office reeks of roses.

"Signature. Look, Jasper, I know you've been gone a long time, and a lot has happened while you were away, but you need to understand I'm a very important person now."

"That's one of the things I want to talk to you about," I say. "You're right, I've been gone a long time, but not *that* long. How did you become the new face of Earth Force in such a short time? And how did Cole rise in the ranks so quickly?"

"Are you suggesting I don't deserve to be the face of Earth Force?"

"No, Lucy. As you always said, you were destined to be a web star. Really." Hopefully, if I tell her what I know she wants to hear, she'll answer my questions.

Lucy's lips lift in a small, unimpressed smile. "That's sweet,

Jasper. Now I know we have a lot of catching up to do, but let's get through the talking points first, shall we?" She nods at her pink guest chair, expecting me to sit. "The way I see it, the heart of the story is your hero quest. It's just amazing that someone our age—a Bounder—was the one to rescue Earth's most famous aeronauts. It really speaks to how special and important the Bounders are, wouldn't you agree?"

I have no idea what Lucy is going on about. "Talking points?"

"Yes, of course. We'll be making spin decisions imminently, and I thought we could chat first. Your inside perspective could be very helpful in creating the narrative."

"What narrative?"

She rolls her eyes. "The rescue of the lost aeronauts, of course! And you as the hero of the homecoming story! Our very own poster boy returned from the dead! You always wanted to be popular, Jasper. It's like this story is your destiny. Not to mention, it's the hugest news since I came into the position. It couldn't have come at a better time."

Jayne called me poster boy, too. "What do you mean, *poster boy?* And why is now such a good time for this news?" And why did she say I always wanted to be popular?

She waves a hand. "Oh, nothing we can't handle. Just that someone out there has been leaking information. Things can get ugly quick if we don't have control of the message."

That must be the mole Cole mentioned. "What are the leaks about?"

"You may not know this, Jasper, but Earth Force informed the public about the Youli conflict. In fact, that's what most of our press focus is about, that and the Bounders. It's very important that the public have an accurate impression of how critical Earth Force's efforts are for planetary prosperity and security."

"What about the Bounders?" Before we even left Earth for our last tour of duty, there were rumors and information leaks about the Bounders. An Earth Force officer came to our apartment and questioned Addy and me. Addy was furious. She almost joined the protestors at the Bounder launch.

Lucy gives me that fake smile again. I wonder if it's part of her signature style. "There's been some minimal backlash about Earth Force withholding information about the Bounders from the public."

As in keeping the reason for the Bounder Baby Breeding program a secret for more than thirteen years? "Minimal backlash? Are you kidding? Lucy, this is me. Jasper. We've had countless talks about how awful it was for Earth Force to keep those secrets, how they even kept our true mission a secret from us!"

"Now, really"—that smile again—"countless? I recall it coming up one or two times. But what's important is how they've handled the information once disclosed, don't you think? Not to mention that the Bounders have proven themselves invaluable in the ongoing war efforts. The public knows that many of us have risen in the ranks faster than any of the other aeronauts."

"Is that why they promoted you and Cole so—"

"Oh, I hate to interrupt, but my first daily report is about to stream. Let's watch."

She flicks her wrist at the pink wall and it morphs into a giant screen bearing the Earth Force insignia.

The insignia fades into Lucy's giant face. On the screen, she smiles and tips her head, kind of like the way Sheek always does. Then she says, "I'm Captain Lucy Dugan, and I invite you to face facts." She turns her head to the side, then glances back at the camera, batting her enormous eyelashes.

"That's my signature line," she tells me. "Get it? *Face* facts—with me as the new face of the Force. Pretty clever, right?"

The screen shifts to an image of the space station, with Lucy's voice talking over it. "Make sure to tune in later today as we bring you a breaking story that's years in the making."

"Does that blush make my face look too angular?" she asks me.

"That what?"

She waves a hand at me. "Forget it."

On the screen, the image shifts to Lucy again. She's

standing in front of a backdrop with the Earth Force insignia. She continues to hype the story breaking later today. It must be the rescue of the lost aeronauts.

The door cracks open and Jayne pops her head in. Lucy doesn't seem to notice; she's too focused on her giant face. Jayne winks at me.

"Excuse me, Captain Dugan?" Jayne says.

Lucy averts her eyes from the screen long enough to see Jayne. "What is it?" she asks impatiently.

"The image meeting is about to commence. Reddy and the other aeronauts are already in the conference room."

"Oh yes, thank you," she says, eyes still on the screen. "Is this being recorded?"

"Of course," Jayne answers. "We have the original footage we shot this morning, and we're recording the web stream as you previously requested."

Lucy extends her hand toward the screen then pauses. She gazes at her image for another second. Then she flicks her wrist and the giant Lucy disappears.

She stands. "Thank you very much, Jayne," she says without a glance in Jayne's direction. Jayne backs out of the room.

Lucy flashes a smile at me that might not be fake. "Come here, you!" She waves me over and plants a kiss on both cheeks. "We'll talk more later, okay?"

"Sure," I say to Lucy's back. She's already half out the door, and I'm left standing alone in the smelly pink room.

What happened?

I didn't get an answer to any of my questions. I never had a chance to mention Mira. I couldn't even slip in a plea to let me contact my parents.

Maybe our return is huge news, but this homecoming sucks.

Once I get out of Lucy's pink palace, my stomach starts growling. I haven't eaten anything since I arrived at the space station. In fact, I haven't eaten anything in a year if we're talking Earth time, and for weeks before that I was eating virtual Alk food. I don't even know what that stuff really was.

I need to brave the mess hall. I ask Jayne to walk me there, but she's too busy. She grabs another press officer and has him take me. Before we go, another officer snaps a dozen pictures of me against a wall with the Earth Force insignia.

My stomach is practically seizing by the time the first officer drops me off at the mess hall door. I'm greeted by the smell of day-old hot dogs. It's still disgusting, but at least some things about this place haven't changed.

As soon as I walk in, Ryan spots me. He rushes to my side and pulls me over to a table filled with familiar faces: Meggi, Annette, Desmond, Orla and Aela, even Hakim and Randall. Before I reach them, everyone at the table is on their feet clapping. Meggi runs over and wraps her arms around me. Even Hakim shakes my hand, which is weird because I can't even look at him without seeing his old pal Regis.

"When Ryan told us you were back, we could hardly believe it," Meggi says.

They give me a seat and insist I tell them what happened.

I'm sure the admiral is going to put a gag order on me soon. The true story of the rift will be classified above my own security clearance level. But as of now, no one's told me to keep quiet.

"Let me get some food first. I promise to tell you everything you want to know about the rift as long as you fill me in on everything I missed this past year."

Now I'll finally get some real answers, not rosy pink spin.

After I've choked down a grilled cheese and a couple of yogurt squeezies, I launch into the tale. As I talk, cadets from other tables gather round. The crowd hangs on every word I say.

When I reach the part where we find the lost aeronauts in the rift, Meggi reaches over and squeezes my hand. "You really are a hero, Jasper."

That's what Lucy said. Maybe she and Meggi are right. Maybe I *am* a hero.

I smile at Meggi, kick my feet up on the orange table, and go on with the story. There will be plenty of time to catch up on what I missed later.

JUST AS I'M DESCRIBING MY BOUND TO
the Ezone with the lost aeronauts, the Bounders' com links
start beeping.

"Welp, I guess that's it for lunch," Ryan says, shoving
another huge bite of tater tots into his already-full mouth.

Meggi dabs her lips with a napkin, then stands with her
tray. "It's so great to see you, Jasper. I can't wait to talk more
later!"

"Wait a minute!" I swing my legs off the table. "Where are
you guys going? I have tons of questions!"

"Duty calls." Annette's face is as expressionless as always.
"That much hasn't changed."

I stand. "Seriously, where are you off to?"

"There's a captains' briefing," Hakim explains as I follow the Bounders to the tray line. I can't believe he's friends with my friends! At least Regis is still gone.

"You guys are all captains?"

"Yep," Ryan says, his mouth still full with his last bite of tater tots. "No more pod leaders, no more classes, no more kid time. We're full-fledged officers of the Force now."

"What does that even mean?"

"Pod patrol, military engagements, bounding drills—there's no time for much else," Meggi says. She and Ryan hang back, letting the other Bounders exit the mess hall first. They promise to meet up later and fill me in on what I missed. For now, I ask them to drop me at the suction chute leading to the sensory gym.

"I suppose Cole's going to be at this briefing, too?" I ask, trying not to sound too annoyed.

"He'll probably be leading the briefing," Meggi says.

"Why?" Ryan asks. "You hoping to talk to him? Good luck."

"What's that supposed to mean?"

Ryan sneers. "Only that Cole doesn't have time for the little people."

Meggi glares at Ryan then smiles sympathetically at me. "It's not like that, Jasper. Cole's just very busy these days. The best time to catch him is first thing in the morning. He wakes up super early and heads down for breakfast."

"Come on, Meggi," Ryan says. "Cole is all business these days. You should have heard his lecture about confidentiality when he found out I'd told Jasper about Addy and Marco." Ryan looks around, making sure no one heard him, then shakes his head at me. "Thanks for ratting me out, by the way."

"Really? You got in trouble for that? Sorry."

"Forget it. Just promise me you'll keep what I tell you between friends from now on."

I nod at Ryan as he and Meggi leave me at the suction chute and hurry up the hall to their briefing.

I can't believe Ryan got in trouble for telling me about my own sister. Wouldn't Cole want me to know about Addy? If Ryan hadn't tipped me off, would Cole have kept that from me?

Plus, how on earth can *keep things between friends* not include Cole?

I activate the chute and close my eyes as I'm sucked in. The wind plasters my hair to my forehead, and my hands to my sides. I try to lose myself in the rush of the chute, forget about the disaster that's my life right about now. But there's no escaping my new reality.

Me, Jasper Adams, apparent poster boy of the Bounders

(whatever that means), but otherwise useless and clueless. Sister? Missing. Friends? Busy. Life? Stolen.

That's what it feels like, anyway, like the last year was stolen from me, and all I'm left with are questions and that infuriating Youli message.

The structure that houses the sensory gym is deserted. The lights are dimmed, and all the doors in the hall are shut. It's like no one's been here in a long time. Actually, that's probably true. The main things on this side of the structure are the gym and the pod hall. It doesn't seem like the Bounders have time for the gym anymore, and they're apparently way past the need for pod leader lessons. Practically all the Bounders are captains now. Another thing I missed: a big Earth Force promotion.

I stop by the door to the pod hall and lean my eye to the scanner. A flicker of hope waves in my chest as I wait, only to hear the sour beep denying me entrance. How long ago did I first enter the pod hall? Jasper time: less than two years. Real time: way more.

I continue down the hall to the sensory gym. When I enter, the memories nearly overwhelm me. I can almost hear Mira playing piano. I close my eyes and imagine holding my clarinet in my hands, harmonizing with Mira's powerful melodies.

But there's no music today. I slowly walk to the ball pit in the corner, climb in, sink down, and disappear.

I let myself drift until I fall asleep, my mind skipping from one stressful dream to the next. Eventually, the sound of footsteps shakes me awake.

"You're a very hard person to find," a girl's voice calls.

So much for disappearing. I awkwardly push myself up through the balls to find Jayne staring back at me.

"I've never heard that before," I say. "In fact, I'm the one who's usually lost."

She crosses her arms and stares at me with her purple eyes, like she's deciding whether to believe me.

Believe me, Jayne, I'm directionally challenged.

I lie back in the ball pit, wishing I could return to disappearing. I don't have the energy to deal with people right now. "So, you found me. What do you want?"

"Geez, don't sound so thrilled." Jayne sits on the edge of the ball pit. "What's wrong?"

I shake my head. "It's nothing."

She gives me the side-eye. "It's obviously something. Talk to me. I'm a good listener."

Maybe I *will* feel better if I talk to someone. I heft myself out of the pit and sit next to her on the edge. "It's strange coming back." I stare at my shoes and force myself to keep talking. "For everyone here, life went on. They have new friends, new roles, new responsibilities. Sure, they're happy I'm back, but there's no place for me in their lives anymore."

Jayne puts her hand on my shoulder. I can feel the heat of her palm through my shirt. "I wouldn't say that, Jasper. It takes time for everyone to adjust. You included."

"I know, it's just . . ." I bite my lip, not exactly sure how to express what I'm feeling. "I'm used to certain people being around, people who know me almost better than I know myself. When they're not here, it's harder."

"Addy."

"Yeah . . . and—"

"Mira."

I nod.

"You guys were—"

"No. I mean, yes. I mean, sort of." I shake my head. "It's hard to explain."

"I was going to say 'close.'"

"Oh. Yeah, we were close."

"You know what I think you need?" Jayne pops up and shoves my shoulders, launching me back into the ball pit. Laughing, she says, "Some sensory playtime."

By the time I get my feet under me, Jayne is already across the gym, jumping on the trampoline. She hops across the springs, hurls herself in the air, and drops into the pit beside me.

"That wasn't nice!" I say with a smile. I pick up a ball in each hand and throw them at her.

"Hey!" Jayne bats the balls away then pegs me with one.

"You've got a good arm," I say, "but you won't hit me twice."

I dodge and duck the balls she hurls at me, then dive backward into the pit, letting the balls cradle my body. Jayne showers an armful of balls on my head. Then she spins around and falls beside me, giggling.

"You were right," I say. "This is what I needed." I like being with Jayne. It's easy. It's fun. And I don't need to worry about her reading my thoughts.

She stops laughing. "I'm glad, because we've got to go now."

I almost forgot that she was looking for me when she came in here. "Where?"

"To see the admiral."

By the time Jayne and I arrive at the auditorium, the first several rows are filled. Lucy is on the front stage with Maximilian Sheek. She glares at Jayne when we walk in. Jayne rushes to check in with Lucy, then takes a reserved seat near the front. From the looks of it, the entire public relations department has assembled for this meeting.

Also, all the old aeronauts are here. I slide into an empty seat next to Bai Liu.

She nods at me. "Finally a familiar face, or at least a face that hasn't aged fifteen years."

I never thought Bai Liu would think of *me* as familiar. I

guess, in a way, we're in this together. What's going on?" I ask her. "Another debrief?" I scan the room for the admiral but don't spot her.

"Hardly," Bai says, rolling her eyes. When I look at her quizzically, she adds, "You mean you haven't heard?"

"Heard what?"

The door opens before she can answer. The admiral enters, flanked on either side by Cole and Ridders. Everyone in the auditorium stands at attention. They march straight down the aisle and take seats in the front row.

Lucy approaches the podium with a humongous fake smile on her face. "Thank you all so much for coming. I'm pleased to formally announce the Lost Heroes Homecoming Tour."

The screen behind her fills with a huge graphic that reminds me of old-school video games. The letters zoom onto the screen from the left and right in bold colors. Then behind the letters, a swirling sphere comes into focus. When it slows down, I can see that it's Earth.

Old photos zoom across the image, freeze for a second in the center, then zoom away, replaced by another. They're all pictures of the lost aeronauts. Most of them are famous photos that have been all over the webs for years.

"The tour will travel to eight major sites on Earth," Lucy says. "The publicity campaign is already well under way. The public reaction to today's announcement of the lost heroes'

MONICA TESLER

return has already been record-setting. We'll be rolling out spots on the webs about the tour starting tomorrow. We expect turnout at the rallies to be huge, well into the tens of thousands at every location. And, of course, press coverage will be constant. In addition to EFAN filming at the rallies, we'll have cameramen with us all the time so that we can piece together a fantastic behind-the-scenes special."

Sheek pulls the mic from Lucy. Even though it's clear she's the one who put this all together, he's not about to let her take the whole spotlight. "I'll be hosting the rallies, of course."

Lucy grabs the mic back from Sheek. "We'll be cohosting them. We're not the highlight attraction, though." She turns around to look at the screen.

This is obviously a cue to whomever is running the video, because when Lucy turns, the image morphs into the face of Denver Reddy.

"I give to you . . . your lost heroes!" Lucy says with a flourish of her arm.

The audience claps as the screen moves from one lost aeronaut to the next.

Jayne catches my eye from the front. I get why she needed to be here, but why me? I would much rather be in the sensory gym than under the fluorescent lights of the auditorium.

Lucy's been talking through the whole presentation, describing each aeronaut, their home city, their greatest accomplishments. ". . . last but certainly not least . . . ," she's saying.

The screen behind her morphs into a giant picture of my face. I'm staring off to the side and look a lot younger than I am now. I have no idea where or when it was taken. The image is sort of faded in the background with these words on top: PROTECTING OUR PLANET COMES AT A PRICE.

"We can't forget the youngest hero on the Lost Heroes Homecoming Tour," Lucy continues, "Jasper Adams!"

The screen image spins. When it stops, a new picture of me smiles back. It's one of the pictures they took of me this morning in the press room. This time the words OUR HERO COMES HOME! overlay the image.

"Hero? *Me?*" I blurt out.

"Of course!" Lucy says through gritted teeth. "Although you obviously have some work to do in playing the part. Fear not, we've onboarded stylists, and I'll personally be training all of you on line delivery and stage presence beginning first thing tomorrow."

I can't believe this. They're sending me to Earth on a PR tour? How am I going to convince the admiral to talk to the Youli if I'm halfway across the galaxy?

Lucy goes on and on about the tour, but I'm not capable of listening. Everything is happening too fast. It's like the count-down for a bound that's not in my control.

Next thing I know, everyone is getting out of their seats and shuffling toward the door.

Denver claps me on the shoulder as he walks up the aisle. "Back to the future, kid. We'll be home before we know it."

"Huh?"

"You're a real zone-out, aren't you?" Bai asks as she slides by me to join Denver. "They aren't wasting time with this Lost Heroes Homecoming Tour. Our ship leaves the day after next at 0800."

"Let's go, kid," Denver says. "They need us at a secondary briefing, stat. Apparently, we need lessons on how to be heroes."

THE SECONDARY BRIEFING FOR ME AND
the lost aeronauts takes place in a large training room where
I'm pretty sure I took quantum technology with Ridders during my first tour of duty. It's basically a repeat of what was
said during the first briefing with some extra info about the
tour and our schedule for the next twenty-four hours. Midway through, plebes roll in carts of food. At first I'm pumped
because senior officer cuisine is a heck of a lot better than tofu
dogs, but then I realize I'm missing dinner in the mess hall.
I was supposed to meet up with Meggi and Ryan. They were
going to fill me in on my lost year.

"Why do I get the feeling they don't want to let us loose

at the space station?" Bai asks during our meal break.

"Because they don't want to let us loose at the space station," Denver says.

"You really think so?" I ask. "Why?"

"Information control," Bai says. "I told Den he asked too many questions during our recent history lesson this morning."

Denver shrugs. "I couldn't help it. They got it all wrong about the Tunneler treaty. Who knows what other crap they were feeding us?"

Crap? That doesn't sound too officer-like, especially when talking about the Earth Force party line. "What do you think they'd do if I tried to leave?"

"Go for it, kid." Bai nods at the door. "Be the guinea pig."

I push aside my soy nuggets and head for the door. A female officer steps in front of me. "Can I help you, Officer Adams?"

"I just need to run to the mess hall," I say. "I told my friends I'd meet them for dinner, and I want to let them know I'm not going to make it."

She smiles. "Who are your friends? I'll make sure they get the message."

"That's okay. I'll only be a minute." I dodge to the side and try to reach the door.

She's faster than me. Her body blocks the exit. "We're getting ready to resume, Officer Adams. Your friends will understand."

I back away from the door and return to the table.

As I slink into my seat, Denver leans over. "Told ya, kid."

After the briefing, we're escorted to our rooms and informed that a guard will arrive in the morning to take us to our next prep session for the Lost Heroes Homecoming Tour.

Denver and Bai were right: Earth Force is keeping tabs on us. They won't let us out of their sight. I have only slightly more freedom than the caged Youli prisoner we discovered here during our first tour of duty.

I try my door handle. At least they haven't gone so far as to lock us in our rooms. I think about heading out now and tracking down Ryan. His quarters are probably close. But the truth is, I probably only have one shot at getting out and getting answers. I need to maximize my chances.

My best chance at real answers and real results is Cole.

I set my alarm for 0445. Meggi said Cole was up early. Hopefully his version of early is earlier than the time the guard arrives at my door. And hopefully, he's willing to help out an old friend. I need answers about what happened over the last year. I have to talk to my parents. With all the press coverage, they must know by now that I'm not dead. Still, I'm sure they'd feel a lot better hearing it from me. Plus, I've got to convince Cole to persuade the admiral to talk to the Youli. Mira's future depends on it.

The next morning, I make it out of my room and to the

mess hall door without running into anyone. Two minutes later, Cole cruises down the hall in a fast, efficient clip. He's focused on the tablet he's holding. I'm betting he's going to blow right by me.

"Cole!"

He abruptly stops and jerks his head in my direction. "Jasper. Sorry, I didn't see you. What are you doing here? Why are you awake so early?"

I follow him into the mess hall. "Why are *you* up so early? I heard you eat at this time every day."

"I'm very busy, and I find the best way to maximize—"

"Forget it," I interrupt. "I didn't really mean for you to answer that." He's moving like a machine. We're already halfway through the buffet line. He stocks his plate with highly practical, protein-packed foods, like fluffed tofu and veggie nutripatties and dried fruit chunks. My plate is empty. I grab a few tater tots and a leftover yogurt squeezie from last night's dinner and tail after Cole.

"Anyway," I continue, "we haven't had a chance to catch up. I was hoping we could have breakfast together." We exit the food line and head into the seating area.

Cole stops. He stares at his plate in one hand and his tablet in the other. "I usually read the overnight briefing material during breakfast and then go directly to the fitness room."

"Does that mean 'no'?"

He stays frozen a moment longer then turns and walks toward a table near a porthole. "Let's go," he calls. "I'll skip the fitness room this morning, but I'm still on a tight schedule."

I slide into the seat across from him. "Thanks for making time for me. I know you're like a really important person these days." An awkward laugh sneaks out of my throat, and I can't think of what else to say. What is this? I'm feeling insecure around Cole? I can't afford to let that happen. Too much is at stake in this conversation.

"It's not like that," Cole says. "I function better when I stick to a schedule, that's all."

His words help me relax a little, and I toss a mushy tot into my mouth. "The food's better. At least they have choices now."

"I haven't noticed," he says. "I've gotten used to the fluffed tofu. It doesn't taste like much, but it keeps me full until lunch."

"Cool. Very efficient."

"Are you settling in?" he asks after swallowing a huge bite of tofu.

It's such a strange question, like something you'd ask a houseguest who came for an extended vacation.

"Sure. The officer digs are a real upgrade, although I'm sure that's not a permanent assignment."

"I'll see what I can do." Cole finishes his tofu and moves on to the veggie nutripatties. "I may be able to have your accommodations level permanently elevated."

"Don't worry about that," I say. "The dorm is fine. Real[...]

Cole nods and glances at his watch.

This breakfast definitely has a ticking clock. I need [...] prioritize. I can probably get someone else to fill in t[...] blanks about my missing time. And Lucy said we'd hav[...] visiting hours for friends and family during the Lost Heroe[...] Homecoming Tour, so I know I'll get a chance to talk to m[...] parents soon. My first priority has to be Mira. I need to ge[...] to the Youli's message, for her sake. "There *is* something you[...] can do for me."

Cole raises his eyebrows and mumbles, "*Hmmm,*" through his food-filled mouth.

"I need you to talk to the admiral."

He sets his fork on his plate and slowly finishes chewing. Then he takes a large gulp from his mug filled with electrolyte-probiotic water. After placing his mug on the table, he turns his gaze on me. "Jasper, you're a friend. I'm happy to listen. But you should know before you say anything that I don't practice favoritism."

Of course he doesn't. It's Cole, after all. "I would never ask you unless it was extremely important."

Cole nods for me to go ahead.

I take a deep breath. "The Youli have a message for the admiral, and—"

"You mean *peace*?" Cole whispers. "They want Earth Force

to meet for peace talks and discuss Earth's entrance to the Intragalactic Council?"

"Basically, yeah. Who told you?"

Cole rolls his eyes. "I'm the admiral's chief military strategist. I know everything. She told me yesterday afternoon. She also told me her answer: an unequivocal *no*. I agree with her wholeheartedly."

I clench my fists beneath the table. This is not going well. I have to get things back on track. "Wait a second. Hear me out. When Mira and I—"

"No. You won't change my mind. All that *peace, peace, peace* talk—the Youli said the same thing to you on their ship when we were placing the degradation patch, remember? And since then they've tried to annihilate us multiple times."

"I know you're busy, Cole, but if you just consider—"

"This has nothing to do with me being busy." Cole stands. "Come with me."

He doesn't give me a chance to respond before pushing back from the table, taking his plate to the dishwasher, and heading for the exit. I stuff the uneaten yogurt squeezie into my pocket and dash after him.

"Where are we going?" I ask once I catch up.

"My quarters. I have something to show you."

"Are you sure we can't talk about this?" I jog to keep pace with his brisk walk. He's even faster than Jayne.

Cole scans in all directions. "Certainly not in the hallway. Wait until we get to my room. Things will be a lot clearer."

We speed walk the rest of the way to the officers' quarters, and I follow Cole to the last room on the hall. He flashes his eye at the lens pad, and the door swings open.

Cole's room is huge, easily twice the size of mine. Half of the room is set up as a Spartan living space—bed, bureau, trunk—without any decoration or touch of color. I suspect Cole hasn't changed a thing since the day he was assigned these quarters.

The other half of the room, though, is something else entirely.

The walls aren't really walls but seamless screens, each one filled with data and images. Multiple projections float in the space unanchored. One is clearly Earth. It rotates on an axis, spinning by Americana East, Eurasia, and all the other mega cities visible from space.

A long, black table stretches across the room. A single chair sits behind it. The table is piled high with papers, but I can see through a gap in the clutter that the table itself is a computer console.

"Rufus," Cole says.

Uh . . . what? I'm about to ask him what he's talking about, when the room itself answers.

"Welcome back, Captain. Your morning briefing is ready."

"Thanks, Rufus," Cole says.

"You're most welcome, Captain," the voice says.

"Wait a second," I say, "Rufus is your computer? And it calls you *Captain*?"

Cole colors red and shrugs. I bet I'm the only person besides him who's ever been in here. "Rufus was the name of my avatar on my very first combat game, *Junkyard Dog Fights*."

"You never told me you played *Junkyard*."

Cole smiles, and for a moment, it's just like old times. "Of course I did. This one time, I tricked this old hound into burying his gold bone in my yard. He nearly bit my head off. In fact—"

"Captain!" Rufus interrupts. "I must remind you that your morning briefing begins in fifteen minutes."

Cole stuffs his hands in his pockets. "Anyway, that's enough about that. Let me show you why I brought you here. Rufus, run a summary vid of Youli conflicts over the last twelve months."

"Processing, Captain."

The projections fade, and the entire wall in front of us fills with an underwater image of Alkalinia. A flood of emotion washes over me. We almost died in that horrible poison sea. I brace myself against the doorframe and force myself to watch. "Where'd this vid come from?"

"We have recording devices in all the bounding ships, and many of the combat officers have cameras mounted on their helmets. I just asked Rufus to pull together a montage. I want you to see what the rest of the Youli were up to while those guys paid you a visit in the rift and asked you to deliver their message."

The video skims through one horrifying scene after another. Youli firing at Earth Force ships. Earth Force officers drowning in the Alkalinian sea. Others being seized by their atoms and ripped apart by the Youli inside the Alk port.

"The Youli in the rift told us there was division in their ranks," I say. "The degradation patch we planted caused mega damage and created a splinter in their society. How do we know the Youli who did this represent the rest of their people?"

"Keep watching," Cole says. "Ask yourself what the right call is here: Gamble the safety of your people on what the Youli told you, or defend your planet? You can't choose both, Jasper."

The image pulls away from Alkalinia into open space. As the camera zooms in on a remote bounding base, a Youli vessel materializes on-screen and starts firing. Half a dozen Earth Force officers are left dead on the bounding deck. Then it shifts to an image of the Paleo Planet and a pair of tourist hovercrafts under attack. More violence. More death. All at the hands of the Youli.

The scene shifts again, and now the space station comes into view. I take a deep breath. What on earth happened here?

But then the screen goes blank. "Captain! I must insist you leave immediately for your briefing! The admiral will not tolerate tardiness!"

"Thanks, Rufus," Cole says as he grabs his tablet. "Back to your question, Jasper. No, I won't talk to the admiral and try to convince her to engage the Youli in peace talks. I won't because I don't think we should, and hopefully now you don't either."

My mind scrambles to find something else to say, some fact or follow-up that will prolong the discussion, the one ticket I may have to seeing Mira again. Maybe that's the only way. "What about Mira?"

Cole drops his gaze and shuffles some papers on the table. "Earth Force doesn't negotiate with its enemies, Jasper, not even when a hostage is involved. Mira knew the risks when she joined Earth Force."

"It's not like she had any choice about joining Earth Force, Cole! It's not like any of us had any choice!"

Cole gathers up the papers and stacks them in a neat pile. "I don't see how that's relevant. Now if you'll excuse me, I need to get to my morning meeting with the admiral."

How can he do this to me? How can he do this to Mira? "You don't see how it's *relevant*? Come on, Cole! We've spent hours talking about this! We didn't even know they were training us to be soldiers until midway through our first tour of duty!"

"Careful, Jasper." Cole grabs the door handle. "Disloyalty to the Force is a grave offense."

That's the same thing the admiral said to me yesterday.

"Rufus, I'm leaving," Cole says to his room computer. "Initiate all security protocols."

"Aye-aye, Captain."

He pulls the handle and stands at the threshold, waiting for me to exit before him.

I know once that door closes, my chance of finding Mira will practically vanish. I have to stall. "Can we meet up later? I need to know more about what I missed."

Cole stares past me into the hall. It's clear he wants me to go. "You have a full day of training for the tour, Jasper. I'm sure you'll be told everything you need to know about last year."

I rack my brain for something to keep him talking. "Where's Gedney? I can't wait to tell him about the rift. He'll freak out, right?"

"Gedney's on Earth."

"Cool. Maybe I'll see him on the tour. Plus, I need to talk to him about my gloves. They were lost on Alkalinia." Not to mention, if Cole won't intervene with the admiral, maybe Gedney will, for Mira's sake.

"I don't think you'll be needing your gloves anytime soon."

Wait . . . what? A Bounder with no gloves is basically useless. That confirms it. I've been totally sidelined.

"You've been through quite an ordeal, Jasper," Cole continues. "You need to focus on your recovery. Now I need to—"

"Okay, just one more thing. Can I please contact my parents? I have to let them know I'm okay. They think I'm dead, Cole. They had a funeral and everything."

Cole closes his eyes for a brief moment. "I know. I was there." He checks the time. "I'll see what I can do. Thanks for meeting me for breakfast, Jasper, but I really must go."

He waits until I'm fully out of his room then closes his door and tests the lock. Without another word, he turns and heads up the hallway, walking at the same fast, efficient pace as earlier this morning.

It's like the last hour didn't change a thing.

It's like he didn't just sell out his best friend.

AS I ROUND THE CORNER TO MY HALL, I
hear banging. It doesn't take long for me to realize that I'm
the cause of the banging—indirectly, of course. An officer
stands in front of my room pounding on the door.

He doesn't hear me coming. I'm only a few meters away
when he shouts, "Officer Adams, I really must insist that you
answer your door!"

"Hey," I say.

The officer jumps. "You scared me. . . . Wait a second . . .
you are Jasper Adams."

"Yeah, I . . . uh . . . woke up early and couldn't fall back to
sleep. So I took a walk."

"You were supposed to wait for your escort."

"I'm here. You're here. What's the big deal?"

The officer shakes his head like he can't find the words. "Just come with me."

I follow him down the hall to the chute cube. It's hard to shake what just happened with Cole, but I need to focus. Since Cole's a lost cause, Lucy is probably my closest contact to the admiral. "Is Captain Dugan running the training today?"

"The training we're late to? I have no idea."

It's clear this guy isn't looking to bond. Doesn't he know I'm a hero (for whatever that's worth)? If this morning's meeting with Cole is any measure, it's not worth much.

He drops me off at the same training room we met in yesterday. It's empty other than the lost aeronauts, a few low-level officers guarding the door, and a huge breakfast spread that reminds me way too much of the fake food on Alkalinia. The Alks filled us up on our favorites at every meal, but it was all virtual—some weird combo of chemical and neurosensory input that tricked our brains into thinking we were eating chocolate chip cookies. In reality, we were chowing down on snake food laced with venom. So now I can't eat anything without a bit of skepticism.

I push aside the nasty memories and fill my plate. Things may be rotten, but that's no reason to pass up donuts. I slip into a seat next to Denver.

"Thought you'd never show, kid." He steals a strawberry donut off my plate and takes a giant bite. "I forgot how good these were."

"I told you not to eat those things," Bai says to Denver.

"The kid's eating 'em."

"The kid's a teenager. He can eat anything."

Denver shoves the rest of the donut in his mouth and raises his hands like he never had it in the first place.

"Have you been here a long time?" I ask them.

"Long enough." Bai gives Denver a knowing look.

Denver finishes chewing then takes a long swig of juice. "Whatever you have to say, you can say in front of the kid, Bai. He knows who we're dealing with."

I'm not sure what we're talking about, but I'm curious. Maybe the lost aeronauts aren't such a dead end on info after all.

"Does this have anything to do with the guards not letting us out of their sight?" I ask.

"You have Denver to thank for that," Bai says. "Like I told you yesterday, he can't keep his mouth shut, especially when he thinks someone's got the facts wrong."

Denver waves his hand dismissively. "Ignore her, kid. We'd be on lockdown no matter what. The Force can't afford to have their precious Lost Heroes get a whiff of what's really going on around here."

The door bangs open and in walks Lucy and her PR entourage. Jayne comes in last, loaded up with tablets.

"Good morning, heroes!" Lucy says to the room. She circles the table, stopping to give each of us an air kiss (except for Denver—she gives him an actual kiss, and if he hadn't turned his head at the last minute, I'm pretty sure it would have been a big, juicy smack on the lips). Jayne follows Lucy, giving each of us a tablet.

Lucy takes her place at the head of the table. "Exciting news! We worked late into the night putting the finishing touches on the script for the Lost Heroes Homecoming Tour rallies. Everything is pretty and polished! Jayne, could you please load it up on the screen so we can follow along?"

Jayne fiddles with her own tablet, and soon the wall behind Lucy flickers and fills with the Earth Force insignia. Jayne slides her finger across the screen, and the giant EF is replaced with the graphic for the Lost Heroes Homecoming Tour.

"Fabulous," Lucy says. "First things first. Every show starts with a great story. And if I do say so myself, the story of your daring rescue is one of the best we've ever created. We've already circulated this vid clip to the webs." She nods at Jayne, and the room fills with the sound of a deep male voice announcing the return of the beloved lost aeronauts.

Denver shoots me a look. What's this all about? I shrug.

The voice-over continues, recounting the story of the

Incident at Bounding Base 51. So far, this is all old news (even if the news is a bit incomplete). The screen shows images of the old aeronauts waving good-bye from the bounding deck.

Then the screen flashes through headlines from the failed bound fifteen years ago. Finally, the images fade, and what is left is an image of a Youli bounding ship. The voice picks back up: "What we know now . . . what's been revealed by our heroes . . . is that the Incident at Bounding Base 51 wasn't a terrible mistake; it was an attack by our alien enemy."

Wow. The truth finally comes out. Well, kind of. Earth Force definitely isn't owning up to knowing about the Youli attack all those years ago.

"The Youli took our beloved aeronauts hostage," the voice-over continues.

Wait a second . . . *what?*

Next to me, Denver grips the edge of the table like he's about to launch himself up and over.

"Our dear aeronauts were held prisoner on the Youli home world for fifteen years. Then the miraculous happened. The Youli attacked again, this time taking two young Bounders hostage. But these Bounders were ready. They used their skills and wielded their advanced technology to thwart the Youli. One paid the ultimate price. The other, Jasper Adams, brought the lost aereonauts home."

Denver pushes to his feet. "I've heard enough. Turn it off!"

"Come on, Den." Lucy tips her head and smiles. "This story is absolutely riveting."

"That. Did. Not. Happen." Denver's jaw is clenched, and his hands are balled into fists.

I'm still playing the words back in my head. Finally, it all clicks into place. "Paid the ultimate price? Is part of the story that Mira died?"

Lucy's lips turn down, and I swear her eyes fill with tears. "I'm so sorry, Jasper."

I jump up next to Denver. "But it's not true! She's not dead! The Youli have her!"

The door to the conference room clicks shut. "It's true now."

I turn around. Denver spins so fast, he almost loses his balance. Neither of us knew Admiral Eames was standing at the door. She must have come in when the vid clip was playing.

"Cora, this is absurd!" Denver says. "I refuse to be a part of it!"

"You'll refer to me as *Admiral*," she replies, crossing the room to join Lucy at the front. "I know this is difficult, but it's necessary. We're at war, and one of our greatest weapons is propaganda. If we're to defeat the Youli, we need the support of our people. This story is how that support is secured."

"But why not go with the truth?" I ask.

"How do you suggest we do that?" Admiral Eames asks.

"How do we explain to the Earth people why these aeronauts haven't aged a day? They know the Youli have advanced technology. They'll blame it on our enemy. It's the easiest explanation."

"Tell them about the rift!" I say.

"Absolutely not. Knowledge that the rift exists is top-level security clearance only. We may be able to use the rift for our own military purposes at some point in the future. More important, however, is that our intelligence confirms not all the Youli know how the lost aeronauts got back. You were right about one thing, Officer Adams. There's division within the Youli ranks. We're not about to hand them secrets on a silver platter."

I can't believe they want us to tell this ridiculous lie! And I can't believe that almost everyone in the room is nodding in agreement, like what the admiral said makes perfect sense! How come I get the feeling that Denver and I and maybe Bai are the only ones who think this is a horrible idea? Why don't the other lost aeronauts speak up? Is following orders more important than the truth?

"What about Mira?" I ask.

Before the admiral can reply, Lucy hops up. "It's all about the narrative! All of Earth already knows you and Mira! Having you both be featured in this story—you as the young hero, and Mira as the martyr—just adds to the drama! They'll eat it up!"

"What do you mean they already know us?"

"Like I told you, you're our poster boy, Jasper! And Mira is our poster girl!" She waves a hand at Jayne. "Pull up the images."

Jayne pokes around on her tablet. First, the screen is filled with the image I saw yesterday of me with the words PROTECTING OUR PLANET COMES AT A PRICE superimposed over my face. The image slides to the left, and a second slides in beside it. It's a picture of Mira. Her long blond braid is pulled over her left shoulder, and she stares off to the side. These three words are printed on the bottom: BEAUTY. COURAGE. SACRIFICE.

I keep rereading the words beneath Mira's face, but they don't make any sense. "What are these?"

Lucy nods at Jayne. "They're part of our pro-Bounder propaganda campaign," Jayne says quietly. "These images have been all over the webs for close to a year. Physical posters were distributed across the planet."

Oh my God.

"And now you've returned from the dead!" Lucy claps her hands. "What a story!"

"Mira's not dead," I say.

"To us, she is," Admiral Eames says before leaving the room, closing the door just as firmly as when she arrived.

I'm still shaking when they wheel in the lunch carts.

"I need a break," I tell Lucy, who's squeezed into the space next to me so she can talk to Denver.

"Perfect timing, let's eat!" She calls Jayne over. "We're breaking for lunch. Please go get those updated numbers from the press room."

"Seriously, Lucy," I say. "I need to get out of here. Let me take a walk or something. Please!"

"Jasper can come with me," Jayne says.

Lucy grimaces. I'm sure she'll say no, but then she waves a hand at Jayne. "Fine, but don't be long."

"Thanks," I say to Jayne once we exit the room. She tries to make conversation as we walk through the halls, but I can't bring myself to talk much. If I do, I'll probably start screaming about how horrible the Force is, and then they'll either lock me up or haul me back to that training room and not let me leave until our passenger craft is loaded and ready to leave for Earth.

She stops at a chute cube and opens the door. I could have sworn this led to the structure with the sensory gym, not the one with the press room, but it's not like my sense of direction is at all reliable.

"After you," she says.

That's right. Jayne refuses to go first. Just one of many things that have annoyed me since I got to the space station two days ago.

When I arrive at the trough on the other side, I'm even more sure we're nowhere near the press room. As soon as I climb out, Jayne slides in behind me.

"Where are we going?" I ask.

Jayne grins. "He speaks."

I follow her out of the chute cube and down the hall at her usual fast clip. "Are you taking me to the sensory gym?"

Jayne smiles. "Nope."

She stops at the door to the pod hall. It buzzes open after scanning her eye. We walk into the dark hall. It smells faintly of dust and gym clothes.

I'm still super irritated, but being in the pod hall makes me feel at least a tiny bit better. "How long since anyone's been in here?"

She shrugs. "A while. Shortly after the Battle of the Alkalinian Seat, Admiral Eames promoted the Bounders and overhauled the training program. Now all bounding exercises mimic military engagements and are conducted in the hangar or off-site. This pod hall hasn't been used in months. Anyhow, I thought you'd enjoy visiting a familiar spot. Waters's pod room is where the magic started, right? It's where the all-star pod first bonded."

"If you say so." A week ago I would have agreed. Now, I don't know what to think. Our pod has been ripped apart. We stand on different sides of a huge chasm. Lucy and Cole feel like strangers. I don't know when I'll see Marco again. And I may never see Mira. As far as everybody else is concerned, she's dead.

We head to the last door in the hall, and Jayne stands aside to let me enter. At least our pod room hasn't changed. There's the same green grass carpet and starry sky ceiling. The familiar lava lamps and colored sticks line the shelves. Our bright beanbags dot the floor. I fling myself down on my favorite turquoise bag.

Jayne sits cross-legged in front of me. "Okay, I'm an open book."

"What?"

"I figure we have about thirty minutes before Lucy starts trying to track me down. I know you have questions about what you missed this past year. Fire away."

"Really? What about that data from the press room?"

Jayne grins. "I downloaded it directly to my tablet during our morning session. Now, what do you want to know?"

I can't believe Jayne is making this offer. It must be incredibly risky, especially with all the paranoia about the mole. "Why are you doing this? You could get in huge trouble."

Jayne leans forward, staring at me somberly with her purple eyes. "You're not wrong, but I think you deserve some answers. But if you want me to be one hundred percent honest, I'm doing it for Addy."

"My sister? Why?"

"We're friends, Jasper. Even now I consider her a friend. I know she'd want you to know the truth."

I smile. Jayne is totally right. How many times did Addy complain about me keeping things from her, especially when it came to Earth Force? "Addy always hated secrets. Okay, so what happened on Alkalinia? Who died?"

"The whole story would take too long, but you being the hero is not just part of the Earth Force narrative. If you hadn't gotten the shield down, we probably all would have died. As it was, all of the Bounders survived—except you and Mira, although we know now that you didn't die, you were just lost in the rift. Some of the more senior Earth Force officers weren't as lucky."

Jayne goes on to list many of the men and women who died that day. Some of the names sound familiar, but most of them were combat soldiers who I didn't really know. The one exception is Chief Auxiliary Officer Wade Johnson—Bad Breath. I'm certainly not happy that Bad Breath died, but I don't feel that awful, either. I'd rather it be him than one of the Bounders.

Still, I'd rather no one had to give their lives that day. If only I could have gotten that shield down earlier.

"You must have more questions," Jayne says.

Do I ever. "Why did my sister and Marco join the Resistance?"

"I'm not sure, but I have my suspicions. They jumped

ship after your funeral, immediately after we rolled out the war campaign. Sadly, I'm pretty sure the Force told your parents that Addy is now presumed dead, too, even though they know she's with the Resistance."

I cringe. I hate to think about Addy and my parents believing I was dead, sitting through my funeral. My parents had to do that twice? They thought they'd lost both of their kids? I can't dwell on that. We don't have much time, and there's a lot more I want to know.

"Tell me about the Resistance."

Jayne folds her hands in her lap and tips her gaze to the grass-green carpet. When she finally lifts her eyes, her face is unreadable. "The Resistance opposes Earth Force. They disagree with the Force's methods, their dominion over lesser developed planets, and the war with the Youli. They're pushing for Earth's entrance into the Intragalactic Council. Your old pod leader, Jon Waters, is at the helm, and a number of Bounders and Tunnelers have joined him."

That sounds a lot like the concerns Waters has hinted at since I met him during my first tour of duty. "The Force's methods . . . Do you mean all the secrecy?"

"That's certainly part of it."

Addy was already fired up about those issues before joining Earth Force. And the truth is, I care about them, too. "When the Force informed the public about the Youli War, did they also tell them about the Resistance? Was that part of the war campaign?"

"The Resistance? No. The Force hasn't publicly acknowledged the existence of the Resistance. They did inform the people of Earth about the Youli, but let's just say it wasn't the whole truth. Lots of things were coordinated with the announcement—yours and Mira's funeral, the propaganda campaign, the planetary curfews and lockdowns, the increased military presence, the criminalization of antiwar messaging."

"So what *did* Earth Force say about the war? And why did they say anything at all?"

"There were too many rumors running around that came way too close to the truth about the Youli and the Bounder Baby Breeding Program. Earth Force needed to take control of the message. They, or I guess we should say *we*, blamed the Battle of the Alkalinian Seat on the Youli, although we didn't give any details about the battle. The story is that we were engaged in a basic military operation and were ambushed. The Youli slaughtered our officers, including two young Bounders who died valiantly defending their people and their planet."

"Me and Mira."

Jayne nods. "As you heard earlier today, we've now changed the story up a bit. You and Mira were kidnapped and went on to rescue the lost aeronauts. But back then, we turned all the panic buttons up to full volume, informing the public that all of Earth Force's might would be put to defending the planet from the Youli. We scared the public into believing that an attack on Earth soil was imminent. That way, if the Resistance launched an operation, Earth Force could blame the Youli. And if there was no violence, well, then the Force's efforts were working and deserved full support."

Wow. They really plotted it all out. The story even makes sense to me, although there's barely an ounce of truth to it. The only fact they got right is that we're at war with the Youli. "You know, I never really understood why the Youli don't attack Earth, or at least knock us down a few notches in battle. They must have the ability to annihilate us."

Jayne again drops her gaze to the grassy carpet and bites her lip. Time stretches, and I think she's not going to say anything. Maybe I stepped over some invisible line that she's not willing to cross.

"I don't know why, Jasper," she finally says, "but I have suspicions. You're right: if the Youli wanted to defeat Earth, we wouldn't be here. Our planet would have been destroyed long before we were born. The Youli's attacks are little more than a big brother's slap on the wrist. I don't think they want to destroy us. It's just that there are rules in the galaxy, and Earth isn't playing by them."

It almost sounds like Jayne is sympathetic to the Youli's position—the *Resistance's* position. Could that be true?

Before I can ask, Jayne shrugs and laughs like her comment was nothing more than a joke. "But who says the Youli get to make the rules, right? We need to assert *our* rights. Our PR campaigns help unify our planet at a time of war. That's important."

I guess, but that sounds a lot like something Lucy might say. I'm not clear at all on what Jayne actually believes, but there's no time for that now.

She answers a few more questions about what happened over the past year, but soon she checks her wristlet. We need to head back.

"Wait!" I say when Jayne stands. "Before we go, there's something else. Until Earth Force announced the Lost Heroes Homecoming Tour, my parents thought I was dead. They must be desperate to talk to me. Can you help me contact them?"

Jayne scrunches up her face. "Hmmm . . . that's tricky. There's a strict ban on outside communication." She paces the room, clearly thinking. "You know what I can do? Let's record a vid message for your parents. I'll be able to send it to them later today via our PR channels. But we need to hurry—Lucy will be wondering where we are."

I close my eyes. "That would be great. Thank you so much!"

Jayne films me as I put on a happy face and smile for the camera, assuring my parents that I'm fine and looking forward to seeing them soon in Americana East, the third stop on the Lost Heroes Homecoming Tour.

On the way back, Jayne rides in front on the chute. That must mean she's starting to trust me. That we're friends. It doesn't change the fact that things totally suck, but it does make me smile for a second before I'm sucked into the chute.

IT'S IMPOSSIBLE TO RIDE ON A PASSENGER craft and not think about my pod mates. During my very first trip to the EarthBound Academy, I bonded with Cole and Lucy, chatting about the fierceness rankings of the famous aeronauts, hitting up plebes for snacks, comparing *Evolution of Combat* stats. Since then, every time I've ridden on one of these ships, I've been with my friends.

Today, it's me and the Earth Force propaganda machine.

At least we finally made the shift to FTL. Now everything out the window is a blur. Before, I had a clear view of the dozen gunner ships escorting our passenger craft to Earth. First stop on the Lost Heroes Homecoming Tour: Eurasia East.

Jayne tried to cheer me up, but I zoned out during her many attempts at small talk, and she quickly tired of my terrible mood.

How could my attitude not be terrible? My sister and one of my best friends are AWOL and rumored to be joined up with the Resistance. My other two best friends have moved on and moved over me in Earth Force. And then there's Mira— Mira, who didn't want to come back with me, who chose the Youli over me, who left me to deal with all this mess alone.

I close my eyes and try to shut out all the noise on the passenger craft.

Mira? Can you hear me? Where are you?

I open my mind as wide as I possibly can, all the while repeating my call for Mira like a beacon across the cosmos. A lonely, unheard cry in the dark.

Puke. I sound as dramatic as Lucy.

Then I sense a presence. *Mira?*

A finger jabs my shoulder. "Scoot, kid." Denver stands in the aisle staring down at me.

I unbuckle and slide over. I can't believe I thought I'd reached Mira. I must be losing my mind.

Denver plops onto the chair I just gave up. "I've got some questions for you."

"You mean about the tour?" I haven't paid attention to anything anyone's said about the tour since the first half of our training session yesterday, and I certainly haven't read the stack of materials Lucy hand delivered to me last night before I went to bed. "See, the thing is, I have the script, but I haven't had a chance to memorize the speaking parts that Lucy—that's Lucy Dugan, the assistant press secretary—gave me, and—"

"Forget the script. We won't follow that anyway, not if I can help it."

"Do you mean you plan to tell the truth?"

"Which truth?" Denver laughs and rolls his eyes. "I don't like it any more than you, kid, but it's what has to be. Our esteemed Admiral Eames had words with me last night. Apparently, planetary security depends on me toeing the party line. I don't particularly want to be court-martialed." His voice softens. "And, truth be told, I trust her, so I'll do as she asks. I suggest you do, too."

I nod. If anything has been made crystal clear to me over the last forty-eight hours, it's that I'm expected to follow orders.

Denver crosses his leg over the opposite knee. "I'm here because I want to talk about you."

"Umm . . . okay . . ." This has taken a turn for the strange.

"Here's the thing, kid. Our fellow officers have done an admirable job bringing me up to speed on recent history, and I've spent much of my downtime reading historical web reports, but I still have questions."

"And you think *I* have the answers?" The concept that anyone would think to come to me for answers about anything is almost laugh-out-loud funny. I bite my lip so I don't accidentally let a laugh slip.

"On this subject, yes," he says. "I don't understand what you do, as a Bounder, that is. I understand the science behind quantum bounding, of course. I was one of the original aeronauts. But bounding without a ship? That's all new to me. No one has been able to explain it to me in a way that makes sense. So I figured I'd ask a Bounder, and you're the only one I know."

"You must know Lucy."

"The PR princess? Sure, but I wasn't about to subject myself voluntarily to another round of her incessant talking."

This time, I do laugh out loud. "Yeah, Lucy can be chatty."

"That's an understatement." He scans the craft until he spots Lucy in the far corner talking to some of her staff. "Do you know her well?"

A small, sad smile settles on my face. "She was my pod mate. A few days ago she was quizzing me about a crush in our quarters in Alkalinia, although that was more than a year ago in Earth time. A lot has happened since then."

"You're telling me, kid." Denver sighs and shakes his head. "Don't take me down that road. It's a slippery slope filled with potholes and black ice and roadblocks. Back to my question.

What's this shipless bounding like? Do you just wave your gloved hands and—presto?"

"Not really." How do I explain bounding to someone who has no experience with the gloves? I think back to our first time in the Ezone. "You have to merge with the gloves in a way. They become part of you and make you bigger than yourself at the same time. It's like they amplify what's already there. When I use my gloves to tap into my deeper consciousness, the universe makes sense in a way I can't explain. And it's not just that I can see and understand at a heightened level, it's that I can actually manipulate matter like I *am* the universe."

"You're the master of the universe. *Right*."

"That's not what I mean. With the gloves, I can see what I'm made of. Literally. And I can use that knowledge to move myself, replicate myself, anywhere in the galaxy."

Denver's face is scrunched in thought. "So the gloves enable you to map and replicate atoms just like the computers on the bounding ships?"

"Yeah. Kind of." That's not how it works at all, really, but I guess it's as close as someone who has never experienced the gloves can come to understanding.

"And this is how the aliens—the Youli—magically appear places?"

"Basically," I say. "In fact, the glove technology came from them."

He sits back in his seat. "What do you mean?"

"If you ever thought your time in the rift was for nothing, you're wrong. It's above my clearance, but I think Earth Force took a Youli prisoner during the Incident at Bounding Base 51. It was after the Incident that they were able to develop the gloves. The gloves are made from Youli biotechnology."

Denver runs a hand through his hair. "That's a lot to take in. Why didn't I know this?"

"Maybe it's above your clearance level now, too."

He rolls his eyes. "A lot of things are above my clearance, and as we heard yesterday, I can't be sure anything I'm told is the truth. Never mind that now. Show me."

"Huh?"

"Show me how you bound."

I laugh. "No. Like I said, I need the gloves to bound. And even if I did have my gloves—which I don't, since they were lost on Alkalinia—I couldn't use them here. I'm sure they have bound detection activated and probably even a quantum scrambler. It's the primary defense against the Youli."

"Ah!" Denver nods. "That makes sense. If the green guys can't jump through space, it makes it a lot harder for them to sneak up on you. When are you getting new gloves?"

"I don't know." I'm sure Denver can hear the irritation in my voice. If there's one thing this conversation has brought into hyperfocus, it's the fact that I'm completely defenseless without my gloves. "I think the powers that be are worried that if I have my gloves I might be tempted to use them."

"Isn't that the whole point? You Bounders are the new front line against the Youli."

"Not while I'm on the Lost Heroes Homecoming Tour. My value as part of the Earth Force propaganda plan is more important." I cringe as soon as the words leave my mouth. Sure, Denver seems to be on the same page as me when it comes to all the Earth Force lies, but he's still one of the highest-regarded Earth Force officers of all time. I shouldn't risk bad-mouthing the Force to his face, especially now that Admiral Eames reminded him of his responsibilities. "Sorry. I shouldn't have said that."

Denver laughs. "Don't be, kid. You're exactly right. Your friend Lucy is the face of the greatest propaganda machine in the galaxy. I don't need level-one clearance to tell you that."

Despite my stubborn grumpiness, I can't help feeling happy when the image of Earth fills the front window of the craft. I'm going home.

Even though it hasn't been that long in Jasper time, it's been more than a year in Earth time, and now I can really feel how long it's been. I feel it in my bones and in my heart. It's like on some level my body registers the passage of time even though my mind can't. I hope Jayne got my message to

my parents. I want them to know that I'm really okay.

Once we descend through the cloud layer, the sprawling metropolis of Eurasia East can be seen in the distance. Even closer, though, is the famous Great Wall. It stretches over twenty thousand kilometers and has been around for thousands of years. It's even visible from space! Everyone in the craft is glued to the window.

We touch down at the aeroport to the north of the city. Our tour dates and locations have been widely publicized, but our arrival details have been kept under wraps, so there's not a lot of fanfare when we exit the passenger craft—unless you count all the starstruck ground officers who can't stop staring at the lost aeronauts. They usher us to a row of waiting hovercars.

Lucy disappears into the first hover with some of the senior PR officers. Jayne is left to direct the rest of us. She refers to her tablet and waves the old aeronauts into the hover behind Lucy. The rest of the PR staff takes the next hover, leaving Jayne and me behind with the last one in line.

"Looks like you're stuck with me," she says, ducking into the hover. I climb in after her.

We zoom through the streets of what's officially called Eurasia East, but which most people call Beijing after the old Chinese city that used to be here. It's less likely to be confused with Eurasia Central, where Moscow used to be, or Eurasia

West, where Paris used to be. In most ways, Beijing looks just like Americana East—tall skyscrapers on a grid, one after the next—but there are also some differences. The gardens in the green blocks have ponds and lots of rocks, and they've preserved some of their historic buildings and temples.

But that's not the only difference. There are guards strapped with weapons on every corner and armed hovers cruise the streets. It's nothing like the Americana East I remember, but if what Jayne told me in the pod room is true, it's probably like Americana East today.

Now Earth is "officially" at war, and it needs to look the part.

"I can't believe I'm here," I say to Jayne. "I'm not sure about this tour. I don't feel like much of a hero."

"You *are* a hero, Jasper," she says. "You took the shield down on Alkalinia. Like I told you before, if you hadn't done that, Earth Force would have been destroyed. All of the Bounders would have died."

"I guess." I fiddle with the control panel on the hover's central console.

"It's true," Jayne continues. "Thanks to you, we dealt a huge blow to the Youli and the Alks. Just as important, we wiped out the Alks' venom stockpile. Without those black-market sales, the Alks are no longer a factor on the intra-galactic scene."

I hit one of the buttons on the console, and the windows in the back of the hover shade to dark gray. "Admiral Eames put so much stock in our alliance with the Alkalinians. It must have been a big blow to us, too."

"True, but the Alks sold us out, Jasper. There was no avoiding that. Plus, we took captives and were able to secure a ton of intelligence." Jayne hits another button on the console, and a soundproof divider rolls up between the passenger and driver compartments. "You may not know this, but the degradation patch your pod placed on the Youli vessel worked. It caused tons of confusion with the Youli's organic communications systems, and it drove a wedge within their society. Apparently, they don't see with one mind anymore."

In other words, there's division within their ranks, just like the Youli told us in the rift. Cole wanted me to question whether that was true, or whether it really mattered. This information is definitely above my clearance level. I'm lucky Jayne is willing to bend the rules. The question is: Why?

"Oh, look!" She points out the window. "See the crowd? They're here for the heroes, Jasper. They're here for *you!*"

Up ahead, the entire city block is mobbed with people. The nucleus of the crowd is a tall building bearing the Earth Force Insignia above its main entrance. That must be where we're headed.

As our hovers approach, the crowds go wild, cheering and

shouting. They push against a blockade manned by rows of guards, all with their weapons drawn. Spectators spill to the sides of the blockade, and as our hovers part the crowd, people slam against the car, pounding on the windows, banging on the hood.

At first, I instinctively recoil and cover my head. Slowly I lower my hands and stare as desperate faces press against the windows, eager for a glimpse inside our hover. The guards push them back, clearing a path.

We glide to a stop behind the other hovers in a barricaded area in front of the building. The crowd swarms around us. Lots of people hold placards in the air. Close to half of them are posters of me—the old ones and the new ones. They wave my face in the air and scream at the hovers.

My hands shake. "I don't know if I can do this."

Jayne grins. "Get ready to be famous, Jasper Adams!" She opens the door and steps out of the hover.

"It's Jasper!" A spectator spots me in the hover and jumps the barricade. A guard dives for her, but she's too fast.

Shouts rise up and crystallize in a chant: "Jasper! Jasper! Jasper!"

The guard stops her with an electric pulse and slams her to the ground.

"Stop!" I shout, hurrying out of the hover, but I can't even hear myself over the crowd.

Another girl hops the barricade, even though she must have seen what happened to the first. She lunges for me, throwing her arms around my neck. Guards pulls her off and drag her away, but not before she slips a piece of paper in my hand.

Earth Force officers take me by the arms and rush me to the building entrance. The noise level never dips until I'm safely inside the Earth Force headquarters.

Once I'm through the revolving doors, Lucy runs over. "Oh my goodness! This is amazing, isn't it? I knew the tour would draw crowds, but I never expected quite this amount of hoopla right at the start. What do you think? Are you enjoying being a hero?"

"It's kind of intense," I say. "How did they know we would be here? I thought only our tour dates were released."

Lucy winks. "Let's just say I thought we needed a teaser for the webs to generate buzz. Jayne did an excellent job at letting a little detail of our schedule slip out, don't you think? Did you see the cameras? I hope they caught some footage of my face. Your face, too, of course. It was just so crowded. Ha! I never imagined that being too crowded could be a problem."

When Lucy moves on to talk to someone else, I unfold the paper the girl slipped me outside. It's her web address and a handwritten note: *Message me.* The words are ringed by pink hearts.

Meanwhile, guards escort a team of cameramen in through a side door.

I fold the paper back up and stuff it in my pocket. I weave through the lobby to avoid the cameramen and look for Jayne. She's standing with some of the lost aeronauts. When she sees me, she waves me over.

She finishes talking to Bai Liu, then traces her finger down her tablet screen. "Here you are, Jasper, room 3217. That's on the thirty-second floor, just down the hall from me, actually. I'm in room 3210, so feel free to stop by if you need anything. Oh, by the way, I asked Earth Force to provide you with some toiletries and a fresh set of uniforms. The trunk should already be in your room. I'm sorry all your personal effects on Alkalinia were lost."

I shrug. Most of what I lost was Earth Force stuff anyway. The only things I really miss are my gloves.

"A guard will be by with your tablet," she continues. "It has the schedule for the tour already loaded. You'll see we have rehearsal tomorrow morning first thing. Don't be late! The lock for your room should be preprogrammed with your lens signature. See you bright and early!" She points me to the elevator and turns to help the other lost aeronauts, who are waiting for their room assignments.

The lift dings and opens. I step inside, and the doors close, leaving me pleasantly alone. After the trip from the space station and the crowds outside, I could use some alone time. I exit on the thirty-second floor and follow the hall until I reach room 3217. When I tip my eye to the scanner, the door buzzes open.

I walk in and look around. There's a small kitchenette and table in front of me and a room with a couch and a large window to the left. Then I realize someone's sitting on the couch. Did I get the room wrong?

I'm about to double-check when the person stands.

"Hello, Jasper."

It takes a few seconds for me to process, and then—

"Gedney!"

I PRACTICALLY HURDLE THE COUCH TO get to Gedney and give him a hug. He feels frail and familiar. Even though I'm used to seeing him in his lab clothes, he couldn't look more Gedney than now in an old brown coat that smells of peppermint and old books.

"What are you doing here?" I ask as we sit on the couch.

"I came to see you, of course." He pats my shoulder. "I've been worried about you, son." Leaning close, he adds in a conspiratorial tone, "And you know I couldn't resist the chance to talk to someone who's traveled to the rift and back."

Gedney was the one who'd theorized that the rift existed.

He told us about it in Alkalinia. It's not a surprise that he wants to hear about the rift from someone who's actually been there.

He winks. "Not to mention, I thought you may have a need for these." Opening his worn leather briefcase, he withdraws a small black sack and hands it to me.

"What's this?" I loosen the drawstring and reach inside. "Oh yes!" I'd know that gauzy material anywhere. I pull the gloves from the bag. "How did you find them?"

"These aren't your original gloves, I'm afraid," Gedney says. "Those were lost on Alkalinia. In a thousand years, once that ocean finally detoxifies, some fisherman will be in for a surprise when she pulls those up from the depths. I got to work on the new ones as soon as I heard you were back. I made some for Mira, as well, but I understand she wasn't so lucky."

How much should I tell Gedney about what happened to Mira? He knows about the rift, so he knows the Earth Force narrative is fiction. Even though he definitely doesn't have the clearance level for the truth, I can't let him think that Mira is dead. "Well, that's not exactly true."

He raises a hand. "You don't need to say another word, son. I already had my suspicions, and I certainly didn't come here to put you in an awkward position." Leaning back against the couch cushions, he changes the subject. "My blood sugar is a bit low. I snooped around before you arrived and found a fully stocked pantry and refrigerator. How about you pour us a glass of juice and fill me in on the rift?"

Gedney and I spend the next hour talking. He asks a million questions about the rift. I don't know the answers to most of them, like *what was the temperature?* (kind of cool, I guess), *was there water?* (the air felt damp and it was foggy, so maybe), and *did you know while you were there that you were experiencing a different time progression?* (yeah, once we found the lost aeronauts, but that's because they told us they'd only been there two days). No matter how many half answers I give, he always has another question. I don't think I've ever seen him more excited. It must be pretty cool when one of your most out-there theories ends up being true.

As I'm describing the mushy ground and the all-consuming grayness of the rift for at least the twentieth time, an enormous yawn swallows the last of my words.

Gedney puts his hands on his knees and slowly stands. I think he's even more hunched over than the last time I saw him. "It's best I let you get some rest. I'm sure they have your schedule filled."

I roll my eyes. "That's an understatement. We have rehearsal for the rallies first thing tomorrow morning, and I heard a rumor about a stylist appointment." I've been ignoring that tidbit. The last thing I want to do is be styled. I'm not even sure what that means, but I know it will be awful.

Gedney laughs. "Better you than me, son." He holds the edge of the couch for support and lowers his voice. "Jasper, before I go, there's one thing I want to discuss."

I lean closer to him. Whatever he wants to talk about sounds serious.

"As I said before," he says, "I don't want to put you in a compromising position, but there is something you should know." He waits until he's sure I'm paying attention before continuing. "Despite the many warnings to the contrary, Earth Force is not currently using a quantum scrambler on the planet's surface. They've been disabled. The Force is hoping to catch the mole red-handed (or red-gloved, if you prefer the literal), and their intelligence just revealed the culprit is likely to be on Earth at the present moment."

Why is he telling me this? As I raise my eyebrows, Gedney lowers his gaze to the black sack on my lap.

"Oh! So I can use my gloves?"

"Exactly," he whispers. "There are, however, quantum detection sensors everywhere. That much of the excessive security is the absolute truth, although the reasons have not as much to do with the war effort as they claim. So if you were to use your gloves to travel somewhere discreetly, you would want to make sure you were in a private location, somewhere you could complete your port and bound before you were identified, perhaps somewhere underground where quantum detection sensors can't quite reach. Don't spread that last piece of information around. Not many know about the sensors' limitations."

"Okay . . ." What exactly is he trying to tell me?

"And one more thing: I'm traveling from here directly back to my labs. You remember them, don't you?"

"Of course I do." How could I forget? We stayed at his labs for an entire week practicing with the BPS before our second tour of duty.

"Good. Then presumably you also recall exactly where they're located."

Before I can reply, Gedney starts for the door. Before he steps out, he turns back to me and places his hand on my shoulder. "It was great to see you, Jasper. Take care of yourself. You are one of a kind. One of the *best* kind."

The door closes behind him.

I pour another glass of juice and return to the couch. It's quiet aside from the occasional hum from the lift as it passes by the thirty-second floor. I hold my new gloves in my hands, trailing my fingers across the gauzy fabric.

What was Gedney talking about? I mean, *do I remember exactly where his laboratory is located?* Why would he ask me that? It must have been a message or have some kind of layered meaning.

Wait a second . . . that's it! He must have been asking if

I remembered the lab's exact location so that I'd be able to bound there!

But why would I need to bound there?

I'm not sure, but I'm happy to have the option.

I stuff my gloves safely back into the black drawstring bag. I need to keep these safe. And quiet.

At exactly 0600 the next morning, every light in my room turns on and Florine Statton shouts, "Time to get up! Time to get up, puhleeeeze!"

What on earth? I must be having a nightmare. I squish my pillow over my head.

"Officer Adams, wake up, puh-leeeze! It's time to get up!"

If I'm not having a nightmare, that means Florine Statton is in my room.

"Get up, Officer Adams!"

I bolt up in bed and scan the room. There's no sign of anyone—definitely not Florine.

"I sense you are still in bed, Officer Adams. I must insist that you get up!" The words seem to come from the room itself.

No Florine. No whiff of roses (although that could be Lucy these days). But still, that voice!

Oh! I get it. This must be like Cole's room. Florine Statton is the voice of the room's computer.

I drop my feet to the floor.

"Officer Adams, get—"

"Shut up!" I shout. "I'm getting up." Florine must really be slipping in popularity if she's stooped to doing voice-overs for guest room computer systems. Lucy has truly taken her place as the face of Earth Force.

"Very well, Mr. Adams. You are expected downstairs in fifty-four minutes."

That means I could have slept for at least another half hour. "Hey, Florine!"

"Yes, Jasper Adams?"

"Tomorrow I only need twenty minutes to get ready, okay?"

"That will require an override."

The Force even controls when I sleep? Great.

I drag myself to the bathroom. After a hot shower, I dig through the trunk Jayne had delivered for me. It's filled with a full set of Earth Force uniforms—dress, dailies, shoes, even a new Earth Force coat. There's also a brand-new blast pack. I can't wait to use that!

I hold up the dress uniform. It looks huge, at least a size bigger than the one I used last tour. I head back to the bathroom and stand in front of the mirror. Am I really that much taller? I turn my head from side to side. My skin's not the greatest these days. There's a kind of nasty pimple on my nose. Other than that, I look exactly how I've always looked. Except maybe my jaw's a bit pointier. And maybe my shoulders are a bit wider. I drag my fingers through my messy, wet hair.

After I get dressed, I pour a glass of juice from my fridge and sit down at the small kitchen table. It's only 0615.

"Hey, Florine!"

"How may I be of service, Officer Adams?"

Florine Statton asking what she can do for *me*? I could definitely get used to this room computer. "Make that fifteen minutes."

"Noted, Officer Adams."

"So can I get that override?"

"You will need to clear that with your superiors."

Terrific. I'll have to ask Jayne if I can sleep in. It seems like I shouldn't have to ask permission for that. "Fine. Turn off . . . or . . . whatever it is you do when I'm not here. I'm going to find some breakfast."

"Understood. Have a great day, Officer Adams."

"Thanks. You, too." Geez. Now I'm talking to a computer. And not just any computer, a Florine Statton computer. I'm worse than Cole.

I pound the rest of my juice, grab my new blast pack, and am halfway out the door before I stop. Earth Force is so focused on catching the mole that I wouldn't put it past them to search rooms. I shouldn't leave my gloves here. I head back to my bedroom and extract the gloves from their soft pouch. I stuff them in a side pocket of my blast pack.

Wait . . . what if they search my blast pack? I take the gloves out of the pack and lay them on my bed. If there's anything to take from Gedney's visit, it's that these gloves might prove to be very important. Where should I put them to make sure they stay safe? I pull up my pant legs and slip one glove into each sock. It's not the most comfortable solution, but at least they're safe.

I open my door and nearly collide with Bai Liu, who's sprinting down the hall in shorts and a tank top. Her muscles are enormous. I better stay on Bai's good side.

"Morning," she says when we reach the elevator bank. "Figured I'd head out for a run before breakfast to see how much the place has changed."

"This is where you're from?" I ask.

The elevator dings, and the doors peel back.

She nods as we walk on. "It's surreal. I feel like I've been gone six months, but in reality, I haven't set foot here in fifteen years."

That must be strange. I feel pretty weird about missing a whole year. The lost aeronauts have been gone longer than I've been alive. "Do you have family coming to the visiting hour before the rally tonight?"

Bai's shoulders droop, and she stares at her shoes. "Sort of.

My mother died when I was young, and apparently my father died while I was in the rift. My wife remarried. She's coming, but I don't know if I'd call her family anymore."

I watch the numbers count down on the elevator panel. "I'm sorry."

We ride the rest of the way in silence. There's not much to say. I've been so focused on myself, I never fully realized how bittersweet this homecoming must be for the lost aeronauts. Life went on without them. Even for the ones whose *welcome homes* are better than Bai's, there's no getting around the fact that they've missed a huge chunk of life.

Bai gets off at the ground floor, and I continue on to the basement where the dining hall is located. I'm starving, and for once I feel pretty confident about what I might find to eat. After all, we're on Earth.

The dining hall is basically deserted. I head to the kitchen line and take a peek. There are noodles, tofu pudding, and three different kinds of steamed buns. I'm guessing those are traditional Eurasian foods. There's also a large vat of rice porridge with toppings like dried fruits, nuts, and honey. A huge pan of fluffed tofu sits under a heat lamp (no surprise there—Earth Force loves its fluffed tofu, the galaxy's most efficient food source). Next to the tofu, something delicious catches my eye: pancakes. I toss a steamed bun on my plate and then heap on a stack of pancakes with butter and maple syrup.

I find a table in the corner and dig in. Shivers run through my body when the sugary syrup hits my taste buds. You'd think I hadn't eaten in a year, which is kind of true. Even the greatest food will never taste quite as good as it used to, though, not after Alkalinia.

I get the feeling that someone is staring at me. I take a break from the pancakes and look around. Sure enough, an EFAN cameraman is headed my way, his lens already locked on my face. He stops on the other side of the table and adjusts his zoom lens.

"You really expect me to eat while you're filming?"

No response.

"Did you film me asking that?" Ugh. This is going to ruin a perfectly good breakfast.

"Get lost!" Jayne's bright voice calls behind me. When the cameraman doesn't react, she shoves her press badge in his face until he lowers the camera and heads to the food line where others are starting to line up for breakfast.

"Thanks," I say, covering my mouth filled with the giant bite I took while she was getting rid of the cameraman.

"Sure." She sets her tablet down on the table. "Aren't you an early riser!"

Something's different with her hair. She's tied it on the side. And she's painted her eyelids so that her eyes look even more purple. They must loosen up the Earth Force dress code for press events. She looks pretty, not that I care or anything.

"Actually, I'm not an early riser at all," I tell her. "My room computer woke me up. By the way, do they all sound like Florine Statton?"

She laughs. "Apparently, yes. Earth Force upgraded their system a few weeks ago."

"Upgrade? I'm afraid of what the computers must have sounded like before. I asked for a snooze tomorrow, but Florine said I had to get authorization."

Jayne taps on her tablet. "I'll make sure to green-light your snooze since it's clear you can get ready on the fast track."

"What's on the agenda today?"

She tips her head up. "Rehearsal, styling, and then the big rally tonight! Plus a bit of interrogation thrown in for good measure."

"Interrogation?"

"There was another intelligence leak last night. The webs are rattling with news that Earth Force has been holding back information about the aeronauts' rescue."

"You mean they know about the lost time?"

"Only rumors. You don't need to worry. They know you're not the mole. You were stuck in the rift during most of the leaks."

The smell of roses nearly makes me choke on my pancakes. "Good morning, sunshine!" Lucy plants a kiss on my cheek.

"You're just the guy I'm looking for." She slides into the seat across from me. "Are those script changes uploaded?" she asks Jayne in a much less friendly tone.

Jayne and Lucy talk briefly about the script, and then Jayne hurries out of the dining hall, leaving me and Lucy alone at the table.

"You were looking for me?" I remind Lucy. I'm ready for seconds on pancakes, but Lucy will consider it a major snub if I leave before she says what she came to say.

"Oh yes!" She leans close. I hold my breath. I don't know what's with the overdose of perfume, but she has to be taking tips from Florine (the real Florine, not the computerized version). "I saw you talking to Denver on the flight yesterday. Did he say anything about me?"

What is this about? Lucy always has an agenda with these types of questions. I think back to the ride and my conversation with Denver. "Actually, yes."

She bites her lip. "Oh my God, what was it?"

Hmmm . . . Denver and I were talking about how Lucy never shuts up. "I kind of forget."

She grabs my hand. "Think, Jasper. What did he say?"

"Not much, really. He asked me if I knew you, and I told him we used to be pod mates."

"He asked about me?" When I nod, she leans even closer. "Okay, Jasper, this is not your forte, but I need some advice. I know in some ways Denver is a lot older than me. But in other ways, he's not that much older. In fact, he was younger than Sheek is now when he went missing. So even though there's a bit of an age difference, it's not terrible, do you think?"

I have no idea what she's asking. "Do I think what?"

"Me and Denver?"

"You and Denver, what?"

She slaps my arm. "Me and Denver together. You know, as a couple. What do you think?"

I burst out laughing. "You're joking, right?"

Lucy glares at me. I guess she wasn't joking.

"Sorry," I stammer. "I must be one of those people who looks at his age the other way. He's a lot older than you, Lucy."

Lucy stands and puts her hands on her hips. "I disagree. Remember, Jasper, I have a lot more life experience than you. While you were in the rift, I was moving up the ranks of Earth Force. We stand on opposite ends of a vast maturity gap." She turns and walks across the dining hall to where the EFAN crew is filming.

I'm pretty sure Lucy just insulted me, but I don't care. I like the view from this side of the maturity gap. At least I'm free to get some more pancakes. I'm going to need them. This is lining up to be a very long day.

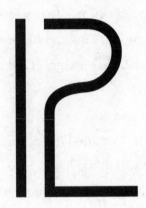

12

"PLACES!" LUCY SHOUTS. "PLACES, PLEASE!"

We've already run through the script for today's rally three times. I'm practically asleep on my feet. I got up too early thanks to Computer Florine, and the sugar crash from this morning's maple syrup definitely isn't helping.

"Haven't we been through this enough?" Denver asks, walking to the other side of the Earth Force conference room where we've been practicing. "And where's Max?"

Sheek, Lucy, Denver, and I are the only ones who have speaking roles at the rally. Since Sheek is a no-show (something Lucy won't shut up about), Jayne is reading his lines.

"I guess he's okay with looking like an idiot in front of

millions," Lucy replies, "but I'm not. As I always say, practice makes perfect. In fact, when I was one of the leads in the Pacific Players performance of *Dear Evan Hansen* . . ." I tune Lucy out. I've found I can use her excessive talking time to catch a short snooze.

When I open my eyes, Lucy has Denver by the hand and is walking him back to the group. "What do you say, Den? You want to be at your best tonight, don't you?"

Den? I'm convinced Lucy has extended this rehearsal just so she can spend more time with Denver.

Jayne rolls her eyes. She must have reached the same conclusion.

"One more time," Denver says. "That's it. And no more talking. Stick to the script."

Somehow Lucy turns one more time into five more times. Our rehearsal runs so late we have no break before lunch and then the mandatory Earth Force security training.

I try to hide in the back during training, but I'm not so lucky. After the introduction, we're divided into small groups, and the lost aeronauts and I are sent to a breakaway room.

The young officer assigned to us is clearly overwhelmed.

"Is this really necessary?" Bai asks for the second time. Her bad mood hangs in the air like a dark cloud. She must be nervous about the visitation hour immediately after the training.

"Just give us the basics," Denver says to the officer. "All of us went through the security training protocol back at the space station, except maybe the kid, not to mention all of us were thoroughly trained fifteen years ago, when we joined the Force."

I pretend not to understand that *the kid* means me. The last thing I need is a one-on-one training session.

"The security protocol has changed," the officer says. "First, it's important that you review the updated, official Earth Force rules and positions that have been uploaded to your tablets. For example, you are not allowed to talk to your friends and family about the rift, including any mention of the time differential. Stick to the official narrative at all times."

"What am I supposed to say when my ex-wife asks why I haven't aged a day in fifteen years?" Bai asks.

The officer ignores Bai's totally legitimate question and continues reading from his notes. "Second, Earth Force wants to remind you of your confidentiality obligations. When you took your oath, you agreed to follow orders, and that includes complying with all rules pertaining to your security clearance."

"We all know there's a mole," Denver says, "and we all know it's not us. We've been lost in the rift for fifteen years, remember?" He nods at me. "Even the kid's been gone for a year."

I sink deeper into my chair, trying to disappear.

"Third," the security officer continues, "it's imperative that you follow all security precautions in place for the rallies. We are on high alert for a potential incident. Consider this an official warning."

"What kind of incident?" Bai asks.

"We have reason to believe there could be an attack by domestic terrorists."

I sit up. "You mean the Resistance?"

All eyes in the room turn in my direction. So much for disappearing.

How do I explain why I know about the Resistance without spotlighting myself for the security team? "Umm . . . I overheard one of the officers at the space station mention the Resistance. I thought maybe that's what you were talking about."

"That subject is above your clearance level," the officer says. He makes a note on his tablet, probably flagging me for future interrogations.

I don't care too much, because I'm thinking about the Resistance and what his warning might mean. I'm sure I'm the only one here who's excited about the possibility of domestic terrorism. It might help me find out exactly what's going on with my sister.

The hovers drop us off at a large, heavily guarded tower that looks exactly like every other large tower we've passed on our way here. On the outside.

When we walk in, my eyes go wide. It's like walking into Lucy's office times a billion. Everything is either gold or pink and totally over the top. The reception area has five enormous, glittering chandeliers hanging from the ceilings. The floor is covered in a pink plush rug with a twirly gold pattern. Right in the middle of the room is a circular gold desk with a pink robot receptionist.

As soon as we walk in, the robot greets us. Guess whose voice it is? That's right. Florine Statton. Not only is Florine my room computer, she's the pink robot. She must be really desperate for work.

"Greetings and welcome to the Style Gallery. Your design is our desire. How may I assist you?"

Jayne registers our arrival and seconds later we're escorted down the hall to a large room that's just as pink as the first. The ceiling is domed, and the walls are rimmed with pink plush sofas complete with pink pillows with gold tassels. I take a seat next to Denver on the closest sofa to the door, unrealistically hoping I can make a fast getaway.

Lucy is buzzing around, talking a mile a minute, giving a tour of the dome room for the EFAN cameras. She's as excited as I've ever seen her. It's like the Style Gallery was made for Lucy.

"Yoo-hoo!" Lucy calls from the center of the room. She holds her arms to the side and twirls. "Isn't this place fantastic?

You are in for a real treat! We have something super special planned for all of you! The Style Gallery helped *me* find my signature style when I became the fresh face of Earth Force. And today my stylist friends will help you find yours! As they say, your design is their desire!"

I'm pretty sure my dread levels reach record heights. Signature style? No thanks.

The next thing I know, the stylists walk in. They're all wearing pale pink pants and tight shirts striped in pink and gold. Lucy greets each of them with a triple air kiss.

"Is this for real?" Denver whispers beside me during the kissing. "Or is EFAN filming this for a candid camera show?"

"I wish. Knowing Lucy, this is as real as it gets."

Lucy squeals with delight and claps her hands. "I'm just so excited! Each of you have been assigned to one of these fantabulous stylists, who has already developed your signature glam plan! So when they call your name, come on up!"

This is a nightmare. As in, I'm pretty much convinced I'm asleep right now. My sleeping brain has mashed up pod selection from my first tour of duty with my recent visit to Lucy's pink office. That's the only explanation for the horror that's unfolding in front of me.

I pinch my forearm. It hurts. And I don't wake up.

One of the stylists steps forward. She has jet-black hair cut short to her scalp. "Bai Liu?"

Bai tentatively stands. Lucy introduces the pair, and they head off through one of the side doors. Two more aeronauts are called and exit with their stylists.

The next stylist to step forward is actually not one but two. They're virtually indistinguishable from each other. They're both tall and thin with warm brown skin and gold spiky hair that matches the tassels on the pillows.

"We have . . . ," the one on the left starts.

". . . the poster boy himself . . . ," the one on the right continues.

". . . Jasper Adams!" the one on the left finishes.

Great. Double trouble.

Denver slaps my back. "Go get 'em, kid."

I slowly walk across the wide room to where my stylists are waiting.

"Hi, Jasper!" they both say together.

"I'm Nev!"

"And I'm Dev!"

I look from one to the other and back again. "Let me guess, you're twins?"

They exchange a glance and turn back to me with wide smiles. "Bingo!" they say at the same time then erupt in giggles.

"It's obvious we're twins," one of them says, "but still, everyone has to put it out there."

I've already given up telling them apart.

"Right this way, Jasper," the other says, taking me by the arm and leading me through a side door into another room.

"Welcome to our pink palace!" they say together once the door closes behind us.

Palace is the right word. There is even more opulence in here than out there, if that's possible. More pink. More gold. More crystal. Mirrors line all the walls and the ceiling, so there aren't just two, but more like a thousand Devs and Nevs staring back at me. There's a pink table with shelves of perfumes above. There's a gold sink with gold hairbrushes and curling wands and several more styling devices I don't have the names for. There are carts piled high with makeup and hair dye and feathers and other fancy stuff.

In the center of the room is a large, pink, cushioned chaise on gold wheels.

"Will you do us the honors, Jasper?" one of the twins says, gesturing at the chaise.

"Uh, sure . . ."

"It's Dev." The twin points to a small *D* monogrammed over the heart on his shirt. I hadn't noticed it before.

"And I'm Nev," the other twin says, pointing to a monogrammed *N*.

I climb up on the chaise and sink into the soft cushions. It's so comfortable, I almost forget how pink everything is. Almost.

"What's your scent preference?" Dev asks.

"Huh?"

"Scents, aroma, perfume," Nev says. "Shall we try rose?"

I'd almost choked on Lucy's rose perfume. "Definitely not."

"Let's go with lavender," Dev says. "It's classic and relaxing."

Nev nods and retrieves a small glass bottle from the shelf. The next thing I know, lavender-infused mist is blowing through the room.

"So, Jasper," Dev says. At least I think it's Dev. I lost track of them and can't see the monogram from the chaise. "We have to ask. What's with the super-duper security?"

"It was awful," Nev says. "They questioned us all day yesterday. We didn't even get our aeronaut assignment until this morning. Can you imagine? They expected us to come up with a whole glam plan for you in just one morning!"

"There's a mole," I say. "And by the way, I'm not in need of a glam plan."

"You *so* are," Dev says.

"A mole?" Nev asks. "Do tell more."

"I'm not really supposed to talk about it," I say, remembering today's security training. "They've had problems with information leaks, and they're pretty sure there's someone on the inside. Until they find the mole, everyone's a suspect. Well, everyone but me and the lost aeronauts. We definitely weren't leaking information from the rift."

"We like to call it a spa nap," Nev says. "Most of our clients love it! So rejuvenating!"

I do feel refreshed. . . .

"Never mind that," Dev says, spinning my chair to face a giant mirror. "Voilà!"

It's me, obviously. But it's like me plus.

My skin has this healthy golden glow. My hair is shorter and styled in that intentionally messy look that most of the guys on the webs wear. My eyes seem to sparkle.

"Am I wearing makeup?"

"Just a bit of bronzer."

"And some clear mascara."

"Really just a touch to bring out your natural beauty."

Oh, geez. I don't know what's worse—the fact that I'm wearing makeup or the reality that I actually look pretty good with it.

"Just in time," Lucy says. "The hovers will be arriving any minute to drive us to the rally. The crowds have been gathering since last night. There are thousands there already, all waiting for a glimpse of our heroes." She squeezes my shoulder. "What do you think of that, Mr. Hero?"

I'm not used to being called a hero. Especially since I don't feel like much of one. "They've been there since last night? Do you mean they camped out?"

"Of course! What did you expect? The return of the lost aeronauts is probably the biggest story of their lifetimes."

"If only they knew the whole story," I say without really thinking.

As soon as the words slip from my mouth, Lucy's eyes bug out and she glances sideways at Nev and Dev. "Now, now don't be so dramatic, Jasper. Time to go!" She grabs me by the hand and drags me out of the chair. She blows good-bye kisses at Nev and Dev as she steers me out of the room. I mumble some thanks and jog alongside Lucy. She's a really fast walker.

"Me? Dramatic?" I say as soon as it's just us. "That's a bit of a role reversal, huh?"

Lucy stops cold. I almost trip and send us both tumbling.

"You need to think before you speak, Jasper. After all I've done for you, the least you could do is keep your mouth shut."

"What do you mean 'all you've done for me'?"

Lucy startles. "Is that a joke? I've made you into a huge superstar, Jasper, possibly more of a star than me. All you have to do is smile and say your lines. Simple. But for some reason nothing seems to be simple with you these days."

She spins on her heels and continues down the hall. I have to race to catch up.

Now I'm mad. "What's that supposed to mean?"

"Isn't this what you wanted? To be popular? Now when

you finally get what you want you keep running your mouth with all this anti–Earth Force blah, blah, blah. Do you know what happens to people who do that? No, you don't know, because you never hear from them again."

"That's what you think of me? That I just want to be popular?"

"Don't you? When Regis targeted you during our first tour of duty, and everyone started talking about you and Mira, you kept saying how you thought it would be different. How you got to the Academy and things were just as bad for you as they'd been on Earth. Don't you remember? The day you showed up Regis in the blast pack relay race was the best day of your life."

"No, it wasn't."

"It was *then*, don't deny it. And ever since, you've loved being the hero—defeating the Youli on the Paleo Planet, planting the degradation patch on the Youli vessel, taking down the shield in Alkalinia. Now you're a hero on an even grander scale. Admit it. You love it. So enjoy your popularity. And stop trying to screw it up!"

Lucy takes off down the hall, leaving me alone. She must assume I'll follow her, which I suppose I will eventually, but I can't manage to move my feet. I'm rooted to the spot as Lucy's words replay in mind. Is that what I wanted? To be popular? It seems so silly and shallow. But could she be right?

A memory flashes. I'm on the air rail the day before I leave for the EarthBound Academy. I've just met a Tunneler for the first time. I'm staring out the window and daydreaming about my trip to space, about finally finding a place where I fit.

Then I miss my stop, and my stuff spills out of my backpack right in front of Will Stevens and Dilly Epstein. Will laughs and calls me a B-wad.

At that moment, my greatest wish was to show them who I really was. A Bounder, soon to blast off and train to be an aeronaut, just like the ones on the posters, the most popular people in the galaxy.

Now *I'm* the poster boy.

As they say, be careful what you wish for.

"JASPER! THERE YOU ARE!" JAYNE RUNS
down the hall. "They're loading the hovers. Everyone's there
but you. We don't want to be late for the rally. Come on!"

She grabs my hand and drags me through the hall even
faster than Lucy. She leads us down two sets of stairs to a
parking garage where the hovers wait. An Earth Force officer
opens the rear door of the last hover, and Jayne and I slide in.
Seconds later, we're rolling.

Out the front window, I can make out our procession as we
drive up the ramp. At the front is an armored hover with the
Earth Force insignia and flashing lights.

The doors to the hover garage open, and the noise swells.

At first, I can't tell what it is, but then I realize it's scream-ing. Officers on foot hold back the crowd so our caravan can cut a path. There are so many people, I can't see where the crowd ends.

"There are thousands of people out there," I say to Jayne.

"Just wait until we get to the rally."

I press the window button, and the glass slides down. The screams intensify, and the crowd pushes against the barricade.

"We love you, Jasper!" someone shouts.

I lock eyes with a girl holding a gigantic poster. It's the new one with my face on it, but instead of the Earth Force text, the words JASPER, WILL YOU MARRY ME? are printed over my face. When she realizes I'm looking at her, she grabs her friend and starts crying.

"Can you put up your window?" Jayne asks. "We have a whole evening of this ahead of us, and I'd like a moment to catch my breath before the insanity begins again."

I roll up the glass and turn around in my seat. The noise from the crowd is still intense. I can't believe there are so many people here for us: the lost aeronauts and me. Like Lucy said, I'm beyond popular. I'm a hero.

"You okay?" Jayne asks.

"Yeah, it's just kind of bizarre."

Jayne shrugs. "It's in line with what we expected."

"Why do they even care about me?"

"We told them to, that's why. That's how propaganda works. We control the message. We hyped you and now they love you, just like Sheek, just like Lucy."

"That's it?"

"Well, it helps that you're cute."

I look at Jayne, but she's tapping on her tablet.

My face warms. Jayne thinks I'm cute? Does she think I'm cute in a propaganda way or in a cute-cute way?

Definitely a propaganda way. It's her job.

Still, she thinks I'm cute in one way or another. A smile pushes at the corner of my lips.

"Why did they make Lucy the new face of Earth Force?" I ask.

Jayne glances up from her tablet. "Isn't it obvious? It's the same reason they're hyping you now. The Force is doing everything it can to change public opinion about the Bounder Baby Breeding Program. That's been one of the most damaging leaks. Having Lucy in front of the cameras helps. It puts a friendly, pro-Force face on the Bounders."

That makes sense, I guess. I wonder who leaked the real reason Earth Force bred the Bounders after they'd managed to keep it a secret all these years. Whoever the mole is, they must be working for the Resistance.

Once we clear the crowd, the hovers make good time. Before long, our caravan slows. We're approaching the rally site, a huge open square in the center of the city, once called Tiananmen Square. The square is packed, but what really strikes me is the military presence. Earth Force officers are everywhere. Armored hovers form a solid barricade corralling the thousands of spectators. Guards stand atop the hovers, weapons drawn, scanning the crowds.

An elevated stage is set up at the gates to the ancient Forbidden City. Scaffolding surrounds the stage, and at least a hundred Earth Force officers are stationed on top.

Our hovers glide into a side building. Officers scan the vehicles top to bottom and flash mirrors beneath. They must be inspecting for bombs, or maybe even stowaways. Next, our hover passes through a sensor arch to confirm no listening devices or other electronic trackers were placed on the hovers.

I suppose the extra security should make me feel safe, but all it does is make me more nervous.

Finally we're given the signal to unload.

"You ready?" Jayne asks.

"Let me put on my hero face." I give her my best Maximilian Sheek impression.

She bursts out laughing. "Try for a more natural look, golden boy."

"Golden boy?"

"I don't know what those silly stylists did to you, but your skin is practically glowing."

The car door opens, and a guard leans down. "Each of you has a personal escort. Stay with them at all times and walk quickly. At my signal, exit the vehicle and proceed with your escort directly to the staging area."

Jayne smiles back at me before climbing out of the hover. I take a deep breath and follow her out. When we reach the door to the staging area, the guard hands me off to another Earth Force officer. She smiles and ushers me along. I follow Jayne and the lost aeronauts to a room directly beneath the stage. It's set up as a lounge with plush green couches and peacock-blue recliners. A bar and buffet line the back wall.

I'm about to head for the buffet when the officer grabs my arm.

"Hey, Jasper," she whispers. "My daughter is a huge fan. Would you mind a quick autograph?" She pulls a wristlet from her pocket.

"Um, sure." I grab the wristlet and press my thumb onto the screen. A second later, the screen reads: "Identified: Jasper Adams."

The woman beams. "Thank you so much. This will make her day!"

I nod and head to the buffet where Denver is piling buffalo chicken wings onto his plate. "Hey, kid," he says as I step beside him. "I can't get enough of these. Sure, I only felt like

I was in the rift for two days, but I'm pretty sure my stomach knows I was gone for fifteen years."

I grab some food and sit down in one of the recliners. While running my lines for the rally in my head, I devour a quesadilla and half a dozen sugar cookies with colored sprinkles, most of the time with an EFAN camera poked at my face.

Time passes, and I start to get nervous. What's the hold up? If I have to wait any longer, I'm going to forget everything I'm supposed to say. Then I'll look like a moron in front of all those people, not to mention the millions watching on the webs.

Maybe the delay is because of the terrorist threat. Could the Resistance be planning something for today's rally?

Just then, Jayne claps her hands. When she has everyone's attention, she says, "Okay, the security sweep has concluded and we're good to go. Captains Dugan and Sheek will kick off the event and introduce you like we've rehearsed. Then Captain Reddy and Officer Adams will join them at the front of the stage. Make sure to enter in the correct order so that you'll be lined up with your onstage seat. Denver, Jasper? Are both of you ready?"

Denver gives Jayne a thumbs-up. "I was born ready."

I nod, although I don't feel a bit ready. In fact, I'm worried the food I just ate will make a repeat appearance onstage.

"Okay then, let's go," Jayne says.

She waves the aeronauts out of the staging room. "You okay?" she asks, linking her arm with mine and guiding me from the room.

"Maybe? Where's Lucy?"

"She's already in the wings. She always worries that Max will try to upstage her, so she's making sure he doesn't ruin her entrance." We turn a corner and head up the stairs.

"That sounds like Lucy. And like Sheek."

She smiles. "You'll be great."

Up ahead, I can see the stage. The other aeronauts are taking their positions in the wings.

"I don't know."

"I do. And they do." Jayne coaxes me ahead and nods at the stage and the crowd beyond.

I can only see a tiny portion of the crowd from where I'm standing, but it's packed. Everyone is on their feet, clapping and whistling and shouting for us to come onstage. The air smells of sweat and excitement.

"You're sure there's no risk of an attack?"

"Trust me. I'm sure." She nods at the stage. "It's almost time."

Next thing I know, Lucy is walking across the stage from the other side, and Max glides by me to meet Lucy in the middle. The crowd roars. The sound alone nearly knocks me off my feet.

They clasp hands and walk together to the front of the stage. This is really happening.

"Welcome to the Lost Heroes Homecoming Tour!" Lucy says, waving her hand in the air.

More screams and claps and wails. The EFAN cameras pan the crowds then refocus on the stage.

I want to cover my ears.

"You know you're our first stop, right?" Sheek asks the crowd.

Even louder.

"That's because Eurasia East knows how to throw a party!"

The crowd swells in a sea of noise. I can barely hear myself think.

"You sure like your parties, Officer Dugan."

"As do you, Officer Sheek."

Their onstage banter goes on for a few more minutes. Then Jayne is tapping my shoulder and steering me into line in front of the lost aeronauts. She raises a hand and whispers, "We're a go, folks." Then she leans forward and kisses me on the cheek. "You'll be great!"

Lucy's voice rings out our cue. "Now welcome Jasper Adams and the lost aeronauts!"

Sheek and Lucy part and turn to face us. Jayne gives me a gentle push, and my feet start moving across the stage, just as we practiced in rehearsal. I focus on my breath like Mom used to make me do when I was nervous. Eight steps. Now I turn and wave at the crowd. Another breath and . . .

Oh. My. God.

I stop moving.

The crowd goes back as far as I can see. And they're screaming. For us. For me.

Denver places a hand on my shoulder. "Keep going, kid. You're doing great."

I suck in air and force my feet to move. I focus on the chair waiting for me across the stage. If I can make it there, I'll let myself look again.

I get to my chair and sink down. Denver slides in beside me. The other aeronauts fall in behind him.

Sheek is saying something, and Lucy is laughing. It's a joke they rehearsed, the joke that comes right before they introduce me and Denver.

And now they're turning and smiling at us—our cue to stand.

Denver nods at me as he rises. "Just follow my lead, kid."

When I walk past Lucy, she squeezes my wrist. "Remember, enjoy it!"

And then I'm standing in front with Denver, all the cameras pointed right at us, just a meter of stage between us and the screaming masses.

"Thank you so much for coming out today!" Denver says.

"One of the things that kept us going all those years is knowing you were pulling for us!"

The crowd erupts in applause. Denver keeps running through the script. It's almost my turn to talk.

". . . thanks to this kid right here, Jasper Adams."

The crowd roars. I stare out at the sea of faces. A girl in the front row catches my eye. For a second, I think it's Addy. I do a double take. She's grabbing her friend's arm and screaming.

Of course it's not Addy. What would Addy think of all this? She'd hate it. She'd call it for what it is: another piece of Earth Force propaganda.

But Addy's not here. I'm here, for better or worse. So, like Lucy said, I might as well enjoy it.

I've missed my cue. I can almost hear Lucy silently screaming at me from behind. Fortunately, Denver was the face of Earth Force before Lucy was even born, so he knows how to get us back on track.

He swings his arm across my back. Then he balls his other fist and gives my shoulder a gentle punch. "Don't be shy, kid. They want to hear the story. Tell them how you saved us. Tell them how you brought us home." Denver sounds so genuine. No one would ever guess how hard he argued against the lie I'm about to tell.

The crowd roars again, and then they're shouting my name, over and over. My nerves start to fade as I'm lifted by

MONICA TESLER

the wave of their chant. I feel like I'm floating high above the crowd. They're calling to me. All I have to do is give them what they want.

I glance to the side and see Jayne. She's chanting my name, too.

Raising my hands to the sides to quiet the crowd, I take a deep breath, and then speak my line. "I was just doing my duty."

This obvious attempt at modesty stokes the crowd even more. They clap and cheer and chant my name even louder.

Denver waves them down again and says to me, "Tell them what happened, Jasper."

I launch into the carefully rehearsed story about how Earth Force was ambushed by our alien enemy. The attack was swift and deadly. The Youli executed all of our superiors and took Mira and me hostage. While imprisoned by the Youli, we made a startling discovery. The lost aeronauts from the Incident at Bounding Base 51 weren't dead, they were being held captive. Mira and I formulated a plan to break them out and bring them home. The mission was successful, but Mira paid the ultimate price. She was killed by the Youli during our heroic escape.

Behind me, a giant screen displays Mira's face, the one from the posters. It's meant to elicit sympathy from the crowd. I can't bear to look at it. If I do, I doubt I'll be able to keep up this farce.

Denver takes over, recounting their shock at our arrival. He describes how unexpected it was to be rescued after all that time, and especially by kids.

As Denver talks, I start to relax. I gaze out at the crowd, at the thousands of faces staring up at me, looking at me like I'm the hero Earth Force wants me to be.

"We owe so much to this Bounder," Denver is saying, clapping his hand on my shoulder. "It is my honor to serve with him."

"The honor is all mine," I tell the crowd. "I grew up worshipping these men and women, our lost aeronauts. They're the reason I wanted to serve in Earth Force. I am so grateful I could bring our heroes home!"

The crowd goes wild. Lucy leans over and whispers in my ear, "You're fabulous! A natural! They love you!"

Our story is fiction, but there's nothing fake about the smile spreading across my face. I wave at the crowd as Lucy, Sheek, and Denver say some parting words. Lucy grabs my hand and leads me to the wings, officially ending our first rally of the Lost Heroes Homecoming Tour. As soon as I step offstage, I'm desperate to do it again.

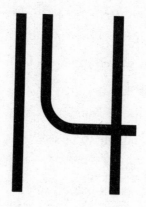

I CAN'T RELAX. I TRY EVERYTHING TO
distract myself—web shows, snacks, a nap—but I can't keep
my mind off today's rally. I can see the crowd, hear them
chant my name. *Hear* isn't quite the right word. It's like I can
feel them calling for me. I throw on my street clothes and
creep down the hall to Jayne's room.

I lightly knock. No answer. I'm about to head back to my
room when the door swings open. Jayne is wearing black
shorts and a purple T-shirt. The front of her hair is piled on
top of her head with a stylus stuck through to keep it in place.

"Hey," she says. "Everything okay?"

"Yeah, I just . . . Sorry to bother you."

"Oh, no bother. You can come in, just hold on a second." She closes the door so it's almost shut and heads back to her room.

I press on the door to sneak a peek at her room. Jayne is at her computer, collapsing a transmission projection. I only see it for a second, but something looks familiar about the location of the transmission.

She heads back to the door and waves. "Come on in."

"Who were you talking to?" I ask.

"No one important."

"Where was the transmission from?"

"The space station."

That did *not* look like the space station.

As if Jayne can read my suspicions, she adds, "I was just going over some details for the next stops on our tour."

That must have been it. "The Americanas, home of Lucy Dugan."

"Not like she'd let any of us forget it."

"Coming home to Americana West as the face of Earth Force? I honestly think Lucy's been dreaming of this her whole life. I hope it's as great as she's expecting it to be. And okay, I'll admit it, I'm pretty excited about our stop in Americana East."

Something dark crosses Jayne's face, but she quickly turns away. She grabs her projection screen and tucks it inside the pack she always carries.

I wonder why she doesn't have a blast pack like the rest of

the Bounders. Does she even know how to use one? What about the gloves? In fact, why isn't she training now? I understand why Earth Force wants Lucy and me to be on this tour—Bounder propaganda and all—but what about Jayne?

"How come you're not training with the other Bounders?"

"That question came from nowhere." Jayne pulls the stylus out, and her hair falls in curls around her face. "I used to think your mind was blank when you had a zone-out moment, but I guess it's just jumping through random topics."

I shrug. "Pretty much. Really, though, how did you get this job? Why does Earth Force have you stationed in communications rather than defense?"

"I'm kind of Lucy's understudy, actually," she says, taking a seat on the edge of her bed. "Lucy's job isn't without some risks, and I'm prepped to step in if anything happens."

"You mean a Resistance attack?" I know it's risky to ask, but Jayne brought it up when we talked in the pod room.

She scrunches up her face like she's thinking, probably deciding how much to tell me. "The Resistance is gaining strength. There are lots of people out there who would love to see Earth Force fall. That's what this tour is all about. The Force has to generate support for the war and keep people rallied around their cause."

"So Lucy's job is dangerous?" I ask, sitting down next to Jayne.

"Yes, and we have a long list of death threats to prove it." She places her hand on top of mine. "You're probably targeted, too."

"Well, that takes my mood down a few notches." Not really. I'm too focused on the feel of Jayne's hand over mine. Her fingers are warm and solid. She feels so different than Mira. Mira's hands are always cold.

Jayne jumps up and claps. "That means we need to do something fun. I'm sick of working all the time. We're in an amazing place. Let's explore!"

"You mean, like, leave the building?"

"Exactly. It's time we took an actual tour of Eurasia East. But first, hold on." Jayne runs over to her trunk and rummages through her things. When she comes back, she's holding a hat and a pair of sunglasses. "For you."

"You want me to wear those glasses? It will be dark out soon."

"I know, but people might recognize you otherwise."

"In this?" I look down at my gray sweatpants and Americana East futbol tee. I was psyched when I found them at the bottom of the trunk Jayne had sent to my room.

"You're a celebrity, Jasper! No one will have a clue who I am, so I don't have to worry about it."

I take the hat and glasses from Jayne and put them on in front of the mirror. I look ridiculous. The hat is orange. If you ask me, it makes me stand out more than blend in, and not in a good way. Plus, I would never pick these sunglasses. They're humongous. I basically look like an orange-headed bug.

"Let's go!" Jayne is already at the door.

We head down the hall and take the elevator to the lowest floor of the parking levels. That way we can skate around the area where the hovers are parked and walk out the exit ramp, hopefully avoiding the EFAN cameras, not to mention the Earth Force guards. With all the paranoia about the mole these days, they definitely wouldn't let us out to roam around Eurasia East on our own.

When we reach the top of the ramp, it's clear there's still a crowd outside. I'm guessing there will be until the guards enforce curfew. We find a side door. No one notices Jayne and me slip outside, hang a left, and head to the end of the block.

Jayne illuminates her wristlet. "If we take the air rail, we can make it to the Summer Palace in twenty minutes."

She grabs my hand and takes off running. Her grip is strong. Life pulses through Jayne. She's vibrant and grounded and more real than most people. When I'm with her, I feel confident, like everything will go our way as long as she's in charge. I can see why she connected with Addy.

We weave through the streets, trying to avoid the armed guards on every corner. When we can't avoid passing them,

I put on the hat and glasses and keep my head down, hoping they don't look too closely at us. When we finally make it the air rail stop and through the metal detectors, I slip the glasses back on and pull the brim of my hat down low. We blend into the crowd. I don't know if I've ever felt like I fit in this much in public. Before the EarthBound Academy, I was basically a nobody, but I still always felt like everybody was looking at me, like they could tell what a loser I was with just a glance.

When the next rail car arrives, we climb on and find seats. We plant our feet on the clear, plastic floor. Eurasia East spreads beneath us. It looks a lot like Americana East. Rows and rows of high rises. Still, it beats being stuck in my room with Florine Statton.

"I can't believe we're out," I say. "I was feeling pretty cooped up on the Lost Heroes Homecoming Tour."

"Not enough excitement for the big celebrity, huh?"

"Cut it out. I'm hardly a celebrity." I know that's the right thing to say, but the truth is, I *am* starting to feel like a celebrity, and I love hearing Jayne say it.

"You sure?" She pulls the glasses off my face and the hat off my head. "Just wait."

I roll my eyes. What exactly does she think is going to happen? I'm not even wearing my uniform.

At the next stop, the doors slide open and a crowd of people spill in. They fill up the other end of the rail car. Before long, one of the girls catches my eye. She whispers something to the girl next to her, and then they're both staring.

Soon, their whole group of friends is gawking at me. They giggle and steal glances.

The first girl to spot me heads in our direction. She's older than me by a few years and incredibly beautiful. She has midnight hair that hangs to her waist. Her face is a perfect oval, and her lips are painted rose red. A girl like her would never have noticed me before I returned from the rift.

"Excuse me," she asks with a shaky voice, "are you Jasper Adams?"

Before I can answer, Jayne pipes in. "Yes, he is, and I'm his publicist. Can I help you?" Her voice is so snooty and businesslike. She kind of sounds like Florine Statton.

The girl twirls her hair around her finger. "Oh no, nothing. Sorry to bother you." She glances back at her friends, then takes a deep breath. "It's just . . . can I have your autograph?" She lifts her wristlet.

"Sure." I press my thumb onto the screen. Identified: Jasper Adams.

"Oh my God!" she claps her hands and smiles. "Thank you so much!"

She runs back to her group. They giggle and squeal when she shows them my thumbprint.

"What did I tell you?" Jayne says as the air rail pulls into the next station. She hands me the hat and glasses. "This is our stop."

I follow her off the air rail, and we dash through the crowded platform. We hurry down a few city blocks until we reach a heavily guarded, brightly colored gate with ancient Chinese lettering across the top.

"How are we going to get in?" I ask.

"Leave it to me," Jayne says.

She marches up to the guards and whips her tablet out of her pack. "We're here from the Earth Force public relations department," she says, showing the guards something on her tablet. "We're scouting sites for next year's rally, and we need immediate admittance to the grounds."

The guards laugh. "Sure you are. Go home, little girl. It's almost curfew."

Jayne waves me over. "Take off the hat and glasses," she says to me then turns to the guards. "Don't you know who he is?"

The guards don't respond, but they don't mock her, either.

"Run his face through recognition. Or don't, and I'll report you directly to the admiral tomorrow."

The main guard is clearly mad at being called out by a "little girl," but he flashes his scanner at my face. Once it registers, he straightens and raises his hand in salute. "I . . . I'm sorry I didn't recognize you immediately, Officer Adams.

It's an honor to meet you. Right this way." He escorts Jayne and me to the gate. "Take as long as you need. I'll personally ensure that no one else is admitted."

Once we're inside the grounds of the Summer Palace and out of earshot of the guards, I stop Jayne. "You could have let me in on your plan."

She grins. "I could have, but that wouldn't have been as fun."

I follow her along the path leading deeper into the grounds. "This place is amazing." The Summer Palace sits on a wide lake surrounded by gardens. The buildings are all pre-served in the classic Chinese architecture. The colorful, tiered structures look straight out of a fairy tale. In all my days in Americana East and even my days in space, I've never seen a human-made place that was as beautiful as this.

We walk down a long, outdoor corridor with magnificent painted ceilings. Everything is quiet except the gentle lapping of the water against the boats in the lake. Jayne and I slow down and exhale all the drama of the day, all the stress of the tour, all the expectations of the Force.

Jayne cuts off the path, but I continue, enjoying a few moments of peace.

Peace.

I haven't even thought about the Youli message today. What am I supposed to do with it anyway? Admiral Eames won't listen. Even Cole brushed me aside.

I keep walking. Soon, I'm looking at my own face. One of the old propaganda posters is tacked up on a pillar.

PROTECTING OUR PLANET COMES AT A PRICE.

Mira's face stares back from the next pillar. I stop in front of it.

Why did you leave me, Mira?

How many times have I asked that question? I'm no closer to an answer.

Or maybe I am. Maybe it's time I accepted Mira's own words. She didn't want to stay with me.

No, she *left* me. She left me to deal with all the aftermath of our lost year, and our torn-apart pod, and that ridiculous Youli message. Alone.

"Jasper!" I hear Jayne call.

I cut away from the path, and follow her voice through the trees to a garden hidden away from the lakeshore. The garden is ringed by pale, flat stones that reflect the moonlight.

"Over here," she calls.

I follow her voice to a small stone bench. She's perched on one side, staring at the sky. I sit down next to her. There's barely enough room for both of us. She leans over, ever so slightly, and our shoulders touch.

"This place is magical," she says.

"I know," I say. "It's like they transported it from another age."

"An age before space travel."

"An age without aliens."

"An age with no war."

"There's always been war," I say. "Don't you play *Evolution of Combat*?"

"Fine, then at least no alien wars." Jayne hops off the bench and sits cross-legged on the ground in front of me. "You've been through so much, Jasper. How are you doing? Really?"

I shrug. "I'm okay." I'm not going to unload my inner thoughts on Jayne anymore. I'd rather her think of me as Jasper Adams, hero, not Jasper Adams, sad and sappy dork who misses his friends. Plus, I'm starting to like this hero stuff.

"Have you been thinking about your sister?" she presses.

I guess I'm not getting out of it. "On and off. Our next stop after West is Americana East. I'll see my parents, and they're going to ask about Addy. I was supposed to look after her, you know. Great job I did at that."

Jayne places her hand on my knee. "You were saving all the Bounders and a good chunk of Earth Force. I'd say that's a pretty good explanation. Plus, you technically did save your sister."

"But I can't tell them that, can I?" My parents can't know the truth about Addy. Earth Force doesn't want anyone except level-one clearance officers to know about the Resistance. I'm definitely not allowed to talk about it with my parents.

Jayne doesn't answer. She knows what the confidentiality rules are, and she knows there's nothing I can do about it. Instead, she extends her hand.

I help her up. We stand facing each other. I should probably drop her hand, but I don't. She doesn't drop mine, either. Even in the faint light of the garden, her purple eyes shine. They're dark like the midnight sky and filled with magic like the moon.

Jayne turns her head like she can hear my thoughts and they're making her blush. But the amazing thing is, she didn't hear my thoughts. She can't. She doesn't know I was thinking about her beautiful eyes. She doesn't know I was thinking about her at all in *that way.* Which means I don't feel like a floundering mess the way I do with Mira.

The thing I love most about Mira—our intimate connection—is the thing I'm most happy is missing with Jayne. I can think about anything I want when I'm with her, and my thoughts remain my own.

Mira's face from the poster flashes through my mind, but I push it away. Remember, Jasper, Mira chose to leave. That's what she wanted. It's time I accepted that. It's time I stop looking to the past and start seeing what's right in front of me.

Jayne squeezes my hands, then pulls me deeper into the garden. The trees part, and we spill into a small clearing

MONICA TESLER

with a lotus pond. She drops my palm and kneels in front of a perfect flower. She lifts its wet, glistening petals in her fingers.

"Do you ever wonder if Addy has it right?" she whispers.

Her question takes me by surprise. I know what it sounds like she's asking—do I support the Resistance—but can that really be? Jayne works in Earth Force public relations. She knows what's expected. She knows the risk of disloyalty to the Force. I trust Jayne, but if I misinterpret her question, I could be putting both of us at risk.

I decide the safest thing to do is turn the question around. "Do you?"

"Forget I asked." Jayne stands and wipes her hands on her shorts.

But I'm not willing to forget it, risk or not. I wonder all the time whether Addy and Marco and Waters are right. Not to mention Barrick and the Wackies who saved Mira and me back on Gulaga.

"No, really," I say, grabbing her hand, "I want to know what you think about the Resistance. It's hard for me to dismiss something that Addy feels so passionately about."

She pulls her hand loose. "We should go. We need to get back before curfew." She turns and starts to walk away.

I must have said too much. As I follow Jayne out of the garden, the air hangs heavy, like there are words between us still clawing to get out. We walk in silence past the gate guards and back toward the air rail station.

Then something shifts, and the tension in the air seeps away. Jayne skips ahead, then spins back and smiles, beckoning for me to catch up. As we near the crowd waiting for the next air rail car, she squeezes my arm and cozies up against me. "Oh, Jasper! Can I have your autograph?"

I shrug her off. "Shut up."

"Don't forget your hat and glasses," she says. "I'm too tired to fend off your admirers on the way back."

THE NEXT MORNING, FLORINE WAKES ME
up at 0545.

"I thought we discussed this!" I grumble, pulling the blanket over my head. "I'm low-maintenance. Let me sleep!"

"Get up, Jasper Adams! You are required to board the hover bound to the Eurasia East aeroport in fifteen minutes."

I bolt up. Jayne must have overridden the computer with a new wake-up time. That means I need to hurry.

I take a two-minute shower and stuff my gear into my trunk. Water trickles off my hair as I bend to pull the Earth Force–issued tight navy socks over my damp feet. Just as I drag my trunk into the hall, building management comes by with a huge, rolling cart to collect the luggage for the Lost Heroes Homecoming Tour. A few minutes later, I dash to the elevator then sprint through the dining hall and grab a handful of yogurt squeezies to suck down in the hover.

The aeronauts are already loaded into their vehicles when I race into the garage. A flock of EFAN cameramen turn their lenses on me as I bolt toward Jayne, who's standing in front of the last hover in line, tapping into her tablet. Terrific. There's going to be web coverage of me and my wet hair. I guess that's what Lucy meant when she said she wants them to catch us in our natural environment. Hopefully, these natural moments end up on the editing room floor.

"Nice of you to join us," Jayne says when I skid to a halt by her side.

I smile. "You kept me out late last night."

Jayne shushes me as we board. She's dressed in her Earth Force uniform, but I can still picture her in shorts and a purple tee pulling the orange hat over my head and dragging me out exploring. She said people would recognize me, and she was right. I can hardly believe that girl asked me for my autograph. That would never have happened to the old Jasper Adams. I guess it's time to accept that the new Jasper Adams—the *hero* Jasper Adams—is here to stay.

"Good morning, sunshine," Lucy coos as I climb onto the hover. Other than Jayne and me, Lucy is the only one on board.

Why on earth is Lucy riding with us? She usually insists on sitting with Denver and Max.

"We're heading home!" She squeezes her hands together and lifts them to her chest. "Americana, here we come! Just think of it, Jasper, we spent so many days dreaming of returning as celebrities, just like the aeronauts before us, and here we are! The day has finally arrived!" She pats the cushioned bench beside her, expecting me to scoot close. "Let's review our lines for the West rally. They're a bit more elaborate than our Eurasia East script, and I know you struggled with that one."

"I didn't struggle." I almost add that she may have me convinced I was once on a popularity quest, but I certainly didn't spend my days dreaming of becoming an Americana West superstar. That's signature Lucy.

Lucy smiles. "Oh, I'm not trying to make you feel bad. I know the stage is not your natural calling like it is mine. But we're on a very tight timetable. The rally's tonight, shortly after we arrive. The Americana West event is going to be huge and lots of important people are going to be there. And they're planning to film the Lost Heroes Homecoming Tour web special tonight, so it's really key that you have your part down, okay?"

It's not like I have a choice, so I just nod Lucy on.

"Great. So, when Sheek and I finish our introductions . . ."

I try to focus on what Lucy's saying—or at least I kind of do—but my mind won't stay put. I'm back onstage at last night's rally, the cheers swelling, the crowd pulsing with excitement. Are they really expecting the Americana West rally to be even bigger? Lucy's wrong. I *am* a natural. Once I settled in last night, I could have stayed onstage forever, riding the wave of elation, giving my fans exactly what they called for.

"Ow!" I pull my foot back in pain. Given the strategic placement of Jayne's shoe on the hover floor, it's clear she just stomped on my big toe. "Why'd you do that?"

Jayne just smiles and flicks her eyes at Lucy, who is glaring at me. The hover is stopped, and the Eurasia East aeroport is visible in the distance.

That was a very quick trip. I definitely zoned out.

"I *said*, do you think you have them down now?" Lucy says through gritted teeth.

She must still be talking about our lines for the Americana West rally.

"Definitely." It's always best to be definitive around Lucy. "You don't need to worry about me for a second. Jayne ran lines with me last night."

The muscles in Lucy's face relax. "Excellent. Come directly to the on-air salon once you board. Nev and Dev are waiting." She opens the door and disappears from the hover.

"Nev and Dev? *Again?*" I say to Lucy's back. She ignores me and keeps walking. "I never agreed to that!"

"Actually, you did," Jayne says. "You nodded yes to all of Lucy's questions while your mind was somewhere else."

"Great. What else did I agree to?"

"Nothing you could have gotten out of, so don't worry."

"Thanks for getting my attention at the end, but you didn't need to disfigure my foot in the process."

"You're welcome," she replies, ignoring the second half of my sentence. "Why did you lie about us running lines last night?"

"I thought it would get Lucy off my back, and it looks like it did. Why does it matter? We were together last night, weren't we?"

Jayne's lips press together in a thin line. "Yes, obviously, but that was supposed to be a secret."

"I thought us sneaking out was a secret, not us spending time together. What are you so worried about?"

"Nothing. It just wasn't on the schedule, that's all." She points at the door. "Let's go."

"Why do I get the feeling you don't want anyone to notice us alone together?"

"Don't be ridiculous. I'm worried if I get out of the hover first, you'll space and forget to unload."

"Touché." I climb out of the hover behind her. "Where are we anyway?"

"Our security team advised we use a different route to get to the aeroport. We'll take the pneumatic pipeline the rest of the way."

Jayne nods at a raised platform where the rest of our group is gathering. A long pipe extends from the platform all the way to the aeroport. In the distance, the sun rises over the Eurasia East skyline.

Something wasn't right about that exchange with Jayne, but I'm not going to waste my time trying to figure it out. If she's worried about spending time with me, who cares? These days, there are plenty of people who would kill for a few minutes with Jasper Adams.

I follow the old aeronauts onto the pipe platform. The solid doors slide back to reveal an open passenger capsule. We stream in single file, having to duck to avoid hitting the capsule's roof. I take a seat behind Bai. Seconds later, the doors slide closed and the chairs recline until we're nearly lying down. Claustrophobia creeps into my chest. I knew I wouldn't be a fan of the narrow, windowless capsule. The ceiling panel opens above me. It holds a VR visor. I pull it over my face and blink through the channels until I land on the Paleo Planet safari. That should be distracting enough to keep me from hyperventilating on the short ride to the aeroport.

The sound of an air generator fills the capsule followed by the strong sensation of forward propulsion. The VR screen flashes on, and I'm walking through the high grass, scoping a saber cat in the distance. It's so lifelike. I wonder if Cole has this visor. Playing *Evolution* on this would be outrageous.

A flock of fuchsia birds dips low to drink from the river in the distance. That might be the watering hole we visited. The place where we first battled the Youli. It took every bit of our skill to protect the other Bounders. We worked well together—me, Cole, Lucy, Marco, Mira—even when Marco decided to kamikaze the Youli on the ridge and got himself flung into a herd of mammoths. I ended up having to jump off a Youli ship as it prepared to bound.

I wonder where Marco is right now. Is Addy with him? Are they safe?

What about Mira? She could be anywhere in the galaxy right now.

I push Mira from my mind. I can't afford to get distracted before the big rally tonight. Plus, who needs Mira when there are thousands of people who are desperate just to see me onstage?

I turn off the VR headset and close my eyes.

Then I'm at the rally, gazing out at the sea of faces stretching back as far as I can see, all of them chanting my name.

There's an Earth Force officer standing at the door to the jet as we board. I recognize her from the security briefing at the space station. She's stopping everyone as they pass.

"Please place tablets and wristlets in the bin and line your bags against the wall," she says, gesturing to a circular black basket beside her. "This is a security scan. All your belongings will be returned to you upon landing."

"Are you kidding?" I ask. "I was going to play *Evolution* during the flight."

The officer raises her eyebrow. "Comply with orders, Officer Adams."

So she outranks me. So what? Doesn't me being one of the heroes on the Lost Heroes Homecoming Tour count for anything?

"Don't worry, kid," Denver says from up ahead. "You'll be spending your whole trip in styling."

The whole trip? I roll my eyes. "I thought we already went through that."

Denver shrugs. "I don't get involved in those decisions, kid. Ask your friend Lucy."

No thanks. Maybe I'll try hiding out in a corner and hope they forget about me.

I hand my tablet to the officer and lean my blast pack against the wall. I'm glad I decided to shove my gloves in my socks rather than leave them zipped in my pack. I have no idea what would happen if they discovered the gloves during the security sweep, although I can't imagine it would be good.

I follow Denver toward the passenger cabin. "What's with the security scan? They didn't do this on our other flights."

"Not sure, but it probably has something to do with the mole. I overheard some chatter this morning that we moved to red alert on the risk of a possible domestic terror event, and they think the mole is directly involved."

That must be why they rerouted us this morning. "Do they think the mole is someone on the tour?"

"Maybe? Like I said, if you want details, ask your chatty friend. My days of being in the know are in the past. Fifteen years in the past, to be exact."

I don't even get a chance to hide because Dev and Nev swoop in as soon as Denver and I step into the cabin.

"Oooh! There you are!" Dev's lavender sweater vest has a cursive *D* on the heart.

"You were fabulous at the rally!" Nev's wearing a matching vest but in lemon yellow. "You've never looked better!"

"But you will!" Dev says. "We have an enhanced glam plan ready to roll out for tonight's rally!"

"Right this way, Jasper," Nev says.

They each grab my hand, and we walk in a chain down the cabin aisle and into a back hallway. They lead me to a small room that they've done up as a salon. Everything is draped in pink cloth, and the room smells like roses. Lucy would love it.

"It's nothing compared to our salon at the Style Gallery," Nev says, "but we make do, don't we, Dev?"

"Most definitely. We would do anything for our young, handsome, oh-so-popular poster boy." Nev winks and smiles.

I force a smile. Why did they have to make everything smell like roses? "Got any of those purple eye pads?" If I have to endure this style session, I might as well sleep through it.

When I wake up, the captain is announcing our arrival at the Americana West aeronautical port. Dev spins me around in their styling chair to face a giant, rhinestone-rimmed mirror. My skin is radiant honey like last time. My hair still has that messy style, but now it's amped up with streaks of actual gold. They've done something different with my eyes, too, so they look deep and penetrating.

"So, what do you think?" Nev asks.

"I kind of look like a superhero," I reply, already picturing myself on the grand stage in Americana West.

"You're our golden boy!" Dev says. "Now hurry back to your seat and strap in before we land."

AFTER TOUCHING DOWN AT THE AEROPORT,
ten kilometers off the shores of Americana West, we take an
elevator deep below the surface of the water and board a sub-
terranean transport, another ride with no windows. (Are they
trying to push my claustrophobia buttons? They're lucky I
don't puke!) The transport takes us right to the main hub of
Americana West, where they're holding the rally. From there,
we're escorted in a private air rail car to the rally site, where
the crowds already number in the tens of thousands and are
growing by the minute.

The air rail station stands high above the city, so when
the rail car doors open, the glamorous city spreads before us.

What was once known as the Las Vegas strip is now the central metropolis of Americana West, and the people of West have gone to great lengths to preserve the historic city.

Down on the left is a giant pyramid reaching almost as high as the air rail. Behind it is an enormous, colorful castle, and behind that, an old city skyline. On the right is the space-themed Quantum Tower, the tallest building in Americana West and the last attraction to be built on the strip. At the base of the Quantum is where the rally stage is set up. Farther ahead, a replica of the famous Eiffel Tower in Eurasia West stands next to an enormous hot air balloon. Interspersed among the sites are huge, decadent buildings with mirrored glass and cascading fountains and too many pools to count.

I can't wait to go exploring. Hopefully, Jayne is game again tonight.

Every meter of open space on the strip is jammed with people waiting for the rally or Earth Force officers ensuring their protection—at least, that's the party line.

I take a deep breath. It's still hard to believe they're all here to see us. To see me.

Lucy scoots beside me and wraps her arms around my waist. She's so excited, it feels like electricity is radiating from her skin. It's like this place was made for Lucy, and today is her grand homecoming.

How did we end up here? It seems like yesterday we were

taking the passenger craft to the EarthBound Academy for our first tour of duty. Lucy, Cole, and I were debating who was the coolest quantum aeronaut ever.

Now could it possibly be *me*?

As soon as the thought pops into my mind, I shake my head. Don't be ridiculous, Jasper. My brain buzzes in a way that reminds me of Mira laughing, probably because that's exactly what she would be doing if she could peek inside my mind right now.

But she can't. Because Mira's not here. Mira's not anywhere where she can reach me. She left me with that ridiculous Youli message that Admiral Eames didn't even want to hear.

Why do I keep letting her into my head? Mira chose to leave.

Mira chose to leave *me*.

Out there, spreading across the landmarks of Las Vegas, are tens of thousands of people who came to see *me*. Last night, Jayne chose to hang out with *me*. I may be clueless most of the time, but it's pretty clear how Jayne feels, even if she doesn't want anyone else to know.

I ball my hands into fists. Mira's not the only one with a choice. I can't keep choosing to stay in the past, obsessing over someone who chose to leave me. I need to descend to the stage and greet the thousands of screaming fans calling my name.

The choice is obvious, easy. So why does it feel so hard?

An EFAN cameraman taps me on the shoulder. Lucy squares us both to the lens and flashes a megawatt smile. Before I know it, I'm answering questions about what it feels like to be a hero and what words of wisdom I have for kids who want to grow up to be a quantum aeronaut someday, just like me.

We're herded along and vetted by security (there's still the mole to worry about, after all, not to mention the show Earth Force needs to put on to keep up planetary panic) and next thing I know we're backstage listening to the calls of the crowd.

This is it. Showtime.

Jayne squeezes my shoulder and nods: my entrance cue.

Then I'm standing onstage soaking up all the adoration.

After the rally, they usher us into the Quantum Tower and escort us to our rooms. Fortunately, my room isn't haunted by the voice of Florine Statton. The Quantum rooms are super modern, with furniture and tech that disappears into the floors and ceiling and walls when not in use. When I first walk in, I think I'm back in the VR chamber in Alkalinia because the room is totally empty. But then I happen to say out loud, "There isn't even a bed," and the wall shifts, and out drops a king-size mattress draped in silk.

I entertain myself for a good fifteen minutes shouting things at my room and watching them appear. I quickly learn that every surface can also serve as a web monitor, so soon I'm surrounded by replay images of the rally. My own face stares back at me from every direction. I have to admit, I look really good with the gold threads in my hair.

Jasper Adams, golden boy.

Soon, though, I get antsy. I'm still riding high from the energy of the crowds. I need to do something. It's time to find Jayne and explore Americana West.

When I step out of my room, Jayne is halfway down the hall, heading to her room. Perfect timing. I sprint after her.

Jayne must not hear me coming, because she doesn't even glance back. She seems totally absorbed in her thoughts, which is far more like me than Jayne.

I slam into the wall beside her, seconds before she reaches her door. "Boo!"

She jumps and lets out a little yelp. "Geez, Jasper! You scared me!"

I lean against the doorframe and tip my chin to the side the way I've seen Sheek do it a million times. If it works for him, why not for the golden boy?

She looks at me and bites her lip. Then she checks the time on her wristlet. "What's up?"

I give her my best golden boy smile. "Thought we could go exploring again, like in Eurasia East—just you and me. What do you say?"

Jayne scans the hall. "I can't. I've got work to do."

What? That's not cool. I cross my hands against my chest. "I thought we had the rest of the day off?"

She shakes her head. "Not me. Lucy has me working on a special project."

Something about this is suspicious. I narrow my eyes. "What kind of special project?"

Jayne presses her lips together. "The *none of your business* kind." She twists her doorknob and pushes past me into her room.

"What's the problem?" I ask, stepping in after her.

Jayne turns and blocks my way. A forced smile spreads across her face, and her voice comes out super sweet. "Look, Jasper, I'm sorry. I'm just in a bad mood because I have to work. We'll probably have some time tomorrow morning during the family and friends visitation hour. Maybe we can sneak out then. Sound good?"

As she talks, she places her hand on my shoulder. I don't realize it until I'm back in the hall, but she pretty much pushes me out of her room.

"Fine," I say in a way that's supposed to let her know it's really not fine at all.

I expect Jayne to keep talking—at least try to make me feel a bit better—but instead she shuts the door in my face.

I lean against the wall, my cheeks burning. Why did I pose

at her door like that? Who do I think I am? Some web star from West? Jasper Adams, golden boy, is just a fictional character. A character Jayne helped create! She probably thinks I'm a total dork. No wonder she doesn't want anything to do with me.

I shuffle down the hall to my room. I open my own door only to find my face staring back at me from all the web screens, a frozen image from the rally earlier today. Actually, I am a web star now, and if Jayne wants to blow me off, that's her loss.

"Bed!" I call to my room, standing clear as the mattress falls from the wall. I fling myself onto the silk sheets.

This sucks. It seems like everyone in West wants to be with me except Jayne.

What is she up to anyway?

She said she has to work on a secret project for Lucy. She's pretty conscientious when it comes to work, and Lucy is pretty demanding. It's probably true. Jayne's just busy.

Still, I can't shake the feeling that there was something more to Jayne's behavior. It's like she was trying to get rid of me as quickly as possible. But why?

Down the hall, the lift bell buzzes.

On a hunch, I hop up from the bed and pull the door handle just in time to see Jayne disappearing into the lift.

Secret project for Lucy . . . right.

Jayne lied.

I know it's a huge breach of trust, but I make a split-second decision to follow her. I grab the hat and glasses Jayne gave me back in Eurasia East, then dash out of my room and down the hall. I make it off the lift on the ground floor just in time to see her disappear around a corner and duck into a stairwell at the end of a back hallway.

She must be up to something.

I race to catch up and descend the stairs to the parking levels two at a time. I ease open the basement door, fingers crossed that she doesn't see me. I make it into the garage just in time to see Jayne jogging up the loading ramp.

Soon I'm tailing after her along the Las Vegas strip. I pull my hat low and slip on the sunglasses, even though it's getting dark. The city is coming alive. Everything shines with brilliant neon lights, and the crowds surge. I don't look strange at all in my sunglasses. Most of the West folks are oddly dressed—hair dyed purple or pink or turquoise, metallic clothes, lots of bright accessories. This place explains a lot about Lucy. I mean, no wonder she wants to be a star. Half the people in West seem to think they're stars whether they are or not.

There's no curfew in Americana West—something about how the city was built on a foundation of nighttime entertainment. Instead, the city is now under lockdown since the Youli war was announced. No one can enter or depart Americana West from dusk until dawn. There are also checkpoints throughout the city. In order to pass through, you need to have your eye lens scanned. Then you're uploaded into a tracker. Essentially, Earth Force watches your every move.

The weird thing is, Jayne doesn't hit a single checkpoint. Instead, we wind back and forth through streets and buildings, practically circling our steps, but slowly making our way . . . somewhere . . . without ever crossing a checkpoint. It's like she has a careful map of exactly how to avoid them.

She's hard to follow. I almost miss her hanging a left and heading for one of the classic buildings that looks more like it was transplanted from ancient Rome. I chase after her, past rows of fountains filled with sculptures of naked people shooting water out of their mouths. The ancient people of Americana West sure liked some odd stuff.

The inside of the building is just as weird and ornate as the outside. The floors are gold and slippery and filled with columns and busts with head wreaths of green leaves. Jayne leaves the main hall and darts through a crowded room filled with slot machines, all lit up with flashing lights. It instantly sends me into sensory overload.

I can't lose Jayne. I narrow my eyes to take in less of the lights and try to ignore the constant sound of clicking and bells and people shouting.

Up ahead, she turns right and picks up the pace. I follow her through a crowded hall packed with people and food.

Lines wind around the room with people piling plates full of Americana West delicacies.

My stomach grumbles, but I turn away from a banquet table stacked with cakes and pastries and keep my gaze glued to Jayne.

She ducks through double swinging doors that lead to the kitchen. When I follow her in a moment later, I nearly collide with a waiter in a tuxedo carrying champagne glasses stacked in a multitiered tower. He mutters some choice words at me, but I don't stop. On the other side of the kitchen, Jayne slips out the back door.

I make it to the door and slowly pull back the handle. It opens to an alley behind the building. I edge out as stealthily as possible, knowing that Jayne must be close.

Once I ease the door closed, I look around. Jayne is at the other end of the alley. I tiptoe behind a nearby dumpster that hopefully will give me some cover.

Jayne glances around anxiously and checks her wristlet.

What is she doing?

Seconds later, a figure emerges from the darkness.

I'm too far away to make out the details. There's another dumpster halfway between me and Jayne. If I stay low, I can probably make it there without them spotting me.

I crouch and scurry the distance to the second dumpster, crossing my fingers that Jayne and the mystery person don't hear me. I slide in behind the dumpster then carefully peek over. They're deep in conversation. I don't think they heard me.

I'm still too far away to hear what they're saying, but I have a much better view of what's happening. Jayne is talking to a guy with his back to me. He's dressed in dark canvas pants and a gray sweatshirt with the hood pulled over his head.

Who is that guy? Could he be part of Lucy's special project? Or is he a friend of Jayne's? Someone she'd rather spend time with than me? My chest tightens, but I shake it off. What is she up to? I need to know who that guy is.

Both Jayne and her mystery man activate their wristlets. They must be transferring data.

Jayne glances around. I duck. The next time I chance a glance, they're shaking hands. It looks like their meeting is over.

When they break apart, they shift positions so the man is faced in my direction. He starts heading my way, probably exiting at the other end of the alley.

I flatten myself against the wall and hope he doesn't see me. When he darts past, I get a good look at him.

He's not a man. He's a boy. My age. A face I'd know anywhere.

Regis.

17

I BARGE INTO JAYNE'S ROOM AT THE Quantum Tower. "I know it's you! You're the mole! I can hardly believe it, but I saw it with my own eyes! The only reason I'm telling you first is that I want to hear you say it. As soon as you do, I'm marching out of here and reporting you."

Panic flicks across Jayne's face, but only for an instant. "I have no idea what you're talking about." She turns back to her tablet and deactivates the projection. The table where she'd been working disappears into the wall.

"You're lying." I fold my arms tightly against my chest. "You know exactly what I'm talking about."

Jayne crosses the small room. "Look, Jasper, I don't know

what you think you saw, but you've got it all wrong."

"I'm not going to debate it with you, Jayne. You're the mole. As soon as I report you, I'm sure the Force will be able to confirm it. No one can cover all their tracks."

"Calm down. Let's talk about this. Couch!" A sofa rises up from the floor.

I retreat to the door. I'm about to walk out and go straight to the security officer, but I can't bring myself to leave without an answer. I spin around. "What I don't understand, Jayne, is how on earth can you work with him?"

"Who?" Jayne's voice is guarded, but it's clear she's starting to freak.

I spit out the name like it's poison on my lips. "Regis."

She closes her eyes and shakes her head. When she opens them, she whispers, "You followed me, didn't you?"

"I can't believe you, Jayne! He's the absolute worst! He's worse than the worst! He's the only cadet ever ejected from the EarthBound Academy!"

"Jasper, I've heard the stories. I know he was awful when he was in the Force, but he's changed. He's a good guy."

I choke out a laugh. I can't believe she's saying this. "Right. Regis, the epitome of good guy."

"I'm serious. I know he had some anger issues, but—"

"Some anger issues? Are you kidding me? He tried to *kill* me. Multiple times."

"Okay, some major behavioral issues. But he's getting help. And in the meantime, he's been a new-wave Resistance fighter for more than two years now."

"Regis is in the Resistance?" That can't be possible. Everything I know about the Resistance is contrary to what Regis stands for, unless he's just out for revenge against the Force for booting him from the Academy.

"Yes." Jayne tentatively touches my forearm. "I know I'm taking a chance here, Jasper, but I also know you're sympathetic to our cause."

"*Our* cause? So you're *in* the Resistance? You're not just selling secrets to the highest bidder?"

She scoffs. "Of course not! Your old pod leader, Jon Waters, is our top general. Your pod mate Marco Romero heads up the guerilla regiment. Addy is with us. I know that in your heart, *you* are with us, too. You said yourself that you have a hard time opposing something your sister feels so strongly about."

I sink to the couch. "That's not what I said. You're putting words in my mouth."

"I'm not. Marco told me you agreed that Earth was exploiting developing planets like Gulaga and the Paleo Planet. He said you'd want Earth to join the Intragalactic Council and abide by the code of planetary citizens. That's what the Resistance is fighting for." Jayne sits down beside me. "I know you, Jasper," she pleads. "I know you don't agree with what

Earth Force is doing. You hate having to go along with their lies. They're using you, Jasper."

I get it now. Jayne's not only the mole. She's not only working with Regis. She was ordered to convert me, to get close to me and turn me for the Resistance. Everything that's passed between us has been part of the Resistance's agenda.

"You don't know me," I say. "I'm just some ridiculous celebrity to you, like Sheek. You've spent this entire time leading me on so I'd eventually join your side." I square my jaw and stare her down. "That's it, right? You weren't going to spring it on me yet, but that's the plan, isn't it, Jayne?"

Jayne shakes her head. "It's not like that, Jasper. I like you. Really, I do."

"Sure." I scoot to the far end of the couch.

She reaches for my hand. "We're friends, Jasper."

"Right, friends." I pull my palm free.

"Yes, friends." Jayne's voice rises. "What did you think? I'm not out to steal somebody's boyfriend."

"What are you talking about?"

"I know about you and Mira, Jasper. Everyone knows."

Why is she talking about Mira? She has nothing to do with this! "Mira is not my girlfriend! How many times do I have to say that? And even if she were, she's halfway across the galaxy right now! She chose the Youli over me, okay? So I guess the joke's on me twice."

I bury my head in my hands. I can't believe this is happening. The few times I thought about joining the Resistance, this is not how I saw this moment going down. I envisioned Waters shaking my hand and welcoming me with Addy and Marco by his side. The last thing I pictured was Regis. I hate everything about him. How can we both stand for the same thing? How can Jayne stand to be around him? To be allied with him?

Plus, I still feel torn in two. I was destined to be in Earth Force since before I was born. Could I really oppose them? Fight for the other side? And what about the Youli? The images Cole showed me were powerful. The Youli has brought tremendous pain and suffering to our people. They aren't innocent. They may want peace, but they're not peaceful.

"Look, Jasper—"

"Don't even start. I don't want to hear any more of your lies. There's only one thing I want to know. Why were you meeting with Regis?"

"I can't tell you that," Jayne says quietly.

I push up from the couch, rage burning just beneath the surface of my skin. I'm sick of feeling like a pawn, to Earth Force, to Waters, and now even to Jayne. "Yes, you *can* tell me, and you *will*. If you don't, I'm turning you in."

Jayne stands and matches my gaze. Silence stretches between us. I don't break eye contact. She needs to know I won't yield on this.

Finally, her shoulders sink and she plops back down on the couch. "There's going to be an incident in Americana East," she whispers. "We're planting bombs—"

Bombs? "You can't! My parents are in Americana East! They'll be at the rally!"

"No one will get hurt. They're smoke bombs. Once they're detonated, the Resistance plans to grab one of the aeronauts."

It takes me a minute to process what she's saying. In my mind, I see my parents running scared in a cloud of smoke. "You mean you're going to take a hostage?"

"We don't look at it that way." From the way she says *we*, I can tell she believes in the Resistance, that she's dedicated to the cause. "We'll smuggle the aeronaut off the planet and over to Gulaga to connect with the Resistance."

"And you think this aeronaut is just going to go with you? Do your bidding?"

"We believe they will once they find out the whole truth about what Earth Force has been up to all these years."

"And you really think you can get them off the planet? How?"

"I don't know all the details, but I have confidence in the plan."

I laugh. "That makes one of us."

"Trust me."

I practically choke on another laugh. "*Trust* you? Really? You've been lying to me since the day we met."

"Sometimes deception is necessary, Jasper. Maybe I haven't been totally honest with you, but I haven't outright lied."

"Yes, you did! You lied today when you went to meet Regis!"

"Okay, fine, but only because it was absolutely necessary."

I used to think that secrets were justified sometimes. Mira and I kept our brain patches secret from the rest of our pod for most of our time on Gulaga. We did it at Waters's request, just like Jayne. "You sound like him," I tell her.

"Who?"

"Waters."

"He cares about you, Jasper."

"Right."

"Join us."

Jayne looks up at me. Despite the lies, I still feel the connection between us. I don't want to feel it, but it's there. Maybe she's being honest about us being friends. Maybe. All I know is I don't want to hurt her. If Earth Force finds out she's the mole, she'll be locked up and probably tortured.

"I need time to think," I tell Jayne.

"We don't have much time." She lets that sink in, then adds, "Joining us will help keep Addy safe, Jasper."

Now she's using my sister to justify her actions, to make me do what she wants? My eyes narrow, and I turn my head to the side. "What is this? A bribe? Blackmail?"

Jayne presses her lips together. "It's a fact, Jasper, plain and simple. Addy needs you. The Resistance needs you."

"Why do I need to choose sides? If the Resistance supports Earth's entry into the Intragalactic Council, they should try to persuade the admiral. If they were willing to compromise, I'm sure—"

"No." Jayne's eyes are cold, and her hands are clenched. "The Resistance won't compromise. We're done cowering before the Force."

I shake my head. Why doesn't anyone want to find a solution? Why is everyone so convinced that their way is the only way? "What do you want with *me,* then? You told me your plan, and it doesn't involve me."

"Go to Addy, Jasper. Join the Resistance in Gulaga."

"Oh sure, no problem. I'll just bound right over."

"You met with Gedney in Eurasia East, didn't you?"

How does she know that? "Wait . . . is Gedney in the Resistance, too?"

She doesn't answer my question. "If you met with Gedney, then you know what to do."

Huh? Oh . . . wait . . . when Gedney visited me in Eurasia, he asked if I remembered where his labs were located. Jayne must be saying I should go there first.

She takes a step back and crosses her arms against her

chest. "And Jasper, I'm sure Admiral Eames would be very interested to learn that Mira *chose* the Youli over you, like you said. That doesn't sound like a hostage situation now, does it? Of course, if what I've heard about your relationship is true, I'm sure you'd go to great lengths to protect Mira, even if she's not your girlfriend."

Now, *that is* blackmail.

In my small room on one of the highest floors of the Quantum Tower, I lie on my bed and slip the thin, gauzy material over my fingers. It's so tempting to tap in and feel the connection with the world around me. How fitting it would be to quantum bound in the very tower named for the technology. Of course, it's named after the quantum bounding ships that Earth developed through the normal course of technological advancement, not the bounding gloves that were developed based on stolen Youli technology.

Despite the temptation, I know I can't bound. Gedney said that Earth Force had quantum detection scanners in all the cities. If I even tapped in to the brain connection and started manipulating matter, a team of guards would rush in here and confiscate my gloves within minutes. I'm sure they'd arrest me. I doubt it would go much further than that, though. Admiral Eames would probably have a tough talk with me and send me back out on tour. They wouldn't dare disrupt the Lost Heroes Homecoming Tour, not with all the effort they've put into making me their star.

Instead, I close my eyes and feel the gauze against my skin. I told Jayne I needed time to think. The truth is, I'm confused, and not just about whether to join the Resistance. I'd do anything to have Mira here with me, to have her help me sort through all the chaos in my mind.

The familiar pain of Mira's absence stirs in my gut like a twisting knife. This time, though, instead of running from the pain, I face it.

I keep reliving our rescue from the rift as Mira leaving me, of Mira choosing the Youli over me, but is that just the story I keep telling myself? I've learned enough about stories from Earth Force to know that they're not always the truth.

I replay my moments with Mira in the rift—our relief that we'd survived the Battle of the Alkalinia Seat, the realization that we were trapped, the discovery of the lost aeronauts, the arrival of the Youli.

The more I think about it, the more I realize I have more questions than answers about why Mira left. Yes, she said it was her choice, that she wanted to go. But she also said she had to leave with the Youli, that it was *the only way*, whatever that means.

It's not like she rolled her eyes and said something like

I'm so sick of you, Jasper, that I decided to give up my friends, my planet, my entire life *to go live with our mortal enemy.*

What she did say is this: *You're the glue, Jasper. It has to be you. It's always been you.*

And while that's still pretty cryptic, it doesn't exactly sound like something someone would say as an explanation for why they just didn't want to hang out anymore.

That's simply not the truth.

This is the truth: ever since I escaped the rift, I've been having a giant pity party for myself. And while some of that is probably warranted—after all, Mira is missing, my sister is AWOL, all my friends moved on, and I lost a whole year—it's certainly not helping me move forward with my life.

So, time's up. No more pity party. I have to stop framing everything with me in the center. The world doesn't revolve around me, even if Earth Force would like the public to think so.

I'm not sure why Mira left, but what if . . . maybe . . . it wasn't because of me? What if it was because she believed in the Youli's message of peace and, for reasons I don't yet understand, her leaving was part of that?

Jayne's a Resistance fighter. Her actions aren't motivated by me. They're motivated by her cause. I don't have to look past the risks she's taking within Earth Force to see that.

Marco and Addy didn't abandon me. They thought I was dead. They joined the Resistance to fight for what they believe in, just like Jayne.

Cole and Lucy didn't leave me behind. They just got on with their lives.

And me? Is that my problem—that I can't get on with my life? Is part of me stuck in the limbo of the rift, wondering why all my friends have moved on?

Who would believe that? I've only been out of the rift a few weeks, and I'm already one of the biggest celebrities on the planet.

I rub my gloved hands together, feeling the friction of the material start to build, resisting the temptation to tap in. It's time I stop focusing on others' actions and motivations and turn the spotlight on my own. What do *I* want? What do *I* believe?

I'm still not sure who has it right. Earth Force wants to protect our planet, but their actions hurt others, and they keep the truth from the public. The Resistance wants Earth to become a better planetary citizen, but they're not willing to compromise to get there. The Youli say they want peace, but their actions don't add up.

Somewhere there's a middle ground, and I need to find it. I'm through with being someone else's pawn. It's time to seize control of my own narrative.

For now, that means I need to find my sister and reconnect with Marco.

I need to travel to Gulaga to engage with the Resistance.

I need to tell Waters about the Youli message and hope it's enough for him to see that peace is the only way forward, and we can't get there without compromise. Our future—the future of our planet—depends on it.

18

AS OUR CRAFT TOUCHES DOWN AT AMERICANA
East, my hands are shaking. Since the rift warped the passage
of time for me, I'll be seeing my parents sooner than I would
have if our third tour had gone as planned. But for my parents, it's been close to two years since we were together. They
spent most of that time thinking I was dead. Jayne told me
that the Force informed my parents that Addy was also missing in action and presumed dead. So even though I'm sure
they'll be excited to see me, they'll also want to hear about my
sister. At least Jayne was able to get them my video message
that we taped in the pod room.

Before we get off the craft, Jayne reviews the tour stop

itinerary with everyone. After the old aeronauts exit the cabin, she catches my eye. We haven't talked since last night. I know she wants to know what I'm thinking, whether I've made a decision about joining the Resistance, but I'm not ready to talk to her. Even though I've made my decision, I'm not ready to forgive her for lying to me.

I cut up a side aisle and head to the exit. Water shuttles wait to take us across the channel. It wasn't long ago that I rode in one with my family and listened to the protestors chant from their barges. Today a different kind of crowd greets us at the landing dock.

Just like at our last two stops, there are tons of people with posters, many of them with images of me and the lost aeronauts. I spot at least a dozen JASPER, WILL YOU MARRY ME? signs. Even if I'm kind of getting used to this celebrity stuff, those signs still make my cheeks warm.

In the middle of the crowd there's some jostling, and soon half a dozen new signs wave in the air: NO MORE WAR!, TELL THE TRUTH!, BOUNDERS HAVE RIGHTS! I bet some of the same protestors were on those water barges when we left for the Academy. Addy had wanted to join them. If only I could tell them what she's up to now. Addy would be their hero.

There's more chaos and confusion in the crowd, and soon the people part, admitting a group of guards with riot gear and raised shields. They zero in on the protestors, who hold their ground. Soon they're literally on the ground, tased and then cuffed.

I guess Jayne wasn't kidding when she told me antiwar messaging had been outlawed.

We're hurried off the shuttles and into hovers for the ride to the Earth Force complex, where we'll be staying. That's where I'll meet up with my parents later tonight during the family and friends visiting hour.

As we drive through the familiar streets of Americana East, I press my hand against the glass. We glide past the green block where Addy, Cole, and I caught our breath after taking the lift for a joyride. Two blocks to the left is my school. Above us, the air rail zooms by. How many times did I sit on a rail car and stare out to sea, waiting for the day I could finally leave for the Academy, the one place in the world where I thought I'd fit in?

Wow. I didn't know what I didn't know.

As soon as I unload from the hover in the garage, I chase down Lucy so I can escape from Jayne and her questioning eyes.

"Hey!" I dodge in front of Lucy and walk backward. "Do you think we can talk about the rally later?"

She narrows her eyes. "You've been doing everything you can to avoid talking to me about these rallies. What's changed?"

Aside from me not wanting to talk to Jayne right now? "I thought I might take on a bigger role. After all, this is my hometown."

Lucy flashes a megawatt smile and throws her arms around me. "Oh, Jasper, you make me so happy! I knew you'd embrace your role as a true celebrity! And I know just how to expand your speaking part. I hope Denver doesn't mind that we'll have to cut his comments short. He'll just have to deal. Tomorrow is your day, Jasper! We're going to make it extra special!"

She slips my hand under her arm and practically drags me across the garage to the lift as she keeps talking about her ideas to make me even more center stage. I glance back to make sure I'm far away from Jayne. Good, she's stuck talking to Sheek. That means she'll be tied up for a while. His list of demands for star treatment grows with each stop.

Once I'm given my room assignment, I take off, eager for some alone time. When I get to my room, I realize how exhausted I am from staying up half the night thinking about what to do. I plan to close my eyes for just a few minutes, but the next thing I know, the room computer is shouting at me.

"Jasper Adams, your guests have arrived. Please proceed to the lounge area."

The good news? The room computer doesn't sound a thing like Florine Statton.

MONICA TESLER

The bad news? I feel totally unprepared to see my parents.

I sit up in bed and look around my room. I don't even remember arriving here. In fact, my mind feels like mush. My palms are sweating. And my feet won't move. Why am I so nervous?

The last time I saw them, they were saying good-bye to me on the flight deck before I left on my third tour of duty. It was Addy's first trip to the EarthBound Academy. My parents asked only one thing of me: to watch over my sister.

How did that go?

I force myself out of my room and down to the lobby. The visitation room is already crowded when I enter, but Mom spots me immediately. She barrels into me from the side and wraps me up in her arms.

"Oh my God," she says, tears streaming down her face. "I can't believe it's really you. I thought we'd never see you again." She buries her head against my shoulder, then pulls back and ruffles my hair. A small cluster of lines frames the corners of her eyes. Those weren't there the last time I saw her.

I'm enveloped in a second hug from behind. "We're so glad to see you, Jasper!" Dad's voice warms me like a blanket.

When they withdraw from the hug, they each grip one of my arms and won't let go.

"Let's find a place to talk." I guide us to a corner with an open love seat and armchair. Mom and I sit together, and Dad sits in the chair.

Across the room, Denver catches my eye. He's sandwiched on a small couch between two much older women. I don't know if they're sisters or friends or something else, but it reminds me that my reunions are not nearly as difficult as Denver's. At least I'm not coming back to find my parents fifteen years older.

"We were stunned when we got the news that you were alive," Mom says, wiping away fresh tears. "When we were first notified that you were missing, we held on to hope, even after your funeral, but as the months passed, we started accepting that we'd really lost you."

"It's so wonderful to see you, Jasper," Dad says. "We never thought this day would come." He leans over and places his palm on my knee. Mom clutches Dad's other hand, so we're all connected.

"It's really good to see you guys," I say.

Dad leans even closer. He looks tired. They both do. "Jasper, we have to ask. Do you have any information about your sister? Could she be alive, too?"

I hesitate. I can't bring myself to lie to my parents about Addy. They deserve to know the truth.

"She is, isn't she?" Mom asks, her voice shaking and rising with each word. "She's alive, but you're not allowed to say anything!"

Heads swing around to stare at us.

"Emma, be quiet!" Dad whispers. "You're attracting attention." He squeezes in beside us on the love seat and lowers his voice. "Can you at least tell us whether she's alive?"

I can't lie. Not about this. Not to my parents. They have a right to know.

I stare directly at my dad and tip my chin just a bit. That's all I can risk. There's too much at stake. The last thing I need is to be on the security team's radar. That would make it nearly impossible for me to ditch away at the rally tomorrow morning.

"What does that mean?" Mom asks. She's trying to be quiet but failing miserably. "Richard, what is Jasper saying?" she asks my dad.

"Is everything all right over here?" a guard asks from behind me.

I stand. "Everything's fine. My parents were asking about how I rescued the lost aeronauts. I was just explaining that the details of the mission are classified."

The guard nods. It's understandable that my parents would be curious. "All you need to know, Dr. and Mr. Adams, is that your son is a hero." He extends his hand to my father.

My father stands and shakes his hand. "Thank you, Officer. We couldn't be more proud of Jasper." He returns to his seat in the armchair.

The rest of the visit is strained. Mom wrestles back tears, and it's clear she's struggling not to ask more about Addy. Dad tells me news from our apartment building, and he fills me in on a new research study that Mom is leading at the hospital, but I can tell he's hoping I can slip them more information about my sister.

Every few minutes, we're interrupted by one of the guests asking for an autograph or a picture with me. At first, my parents are impressed, but then they get annoyed having to share my attention. Before we know it, the visitation hour is up.

"Are you going to the rally tomorrow?" I ask my parents. I know they'll be there, even though I wish they'd stay home. Jayne promised the Resistance was only planting smoke bombs, but something could go wrong. If anything happens to my parents, I'll never be able to forgive myself.

"Of course we'll be there," Mom chokes out, pulling me into a hug.

"We wouldn't miss it," Dad says, joining us again on the love seat and waiting his turn for a hug.

I want to warn them to stay away, but I know I can't. It's too risky. If word got out, the Resistance's plans would be foiled. Not to mention, there's nothing I could say that would convince them not to come—certainly nothing I could say under the watch of all these guards. Jayne better be right about the smoke bombs.

MONICA TESLER

One of the guards catches my eye and nods at the door. It's time for my parents to go.

As I escort them to the exit, Jayne appears out of nowhere.

Great, exactly the person I was hoping to avoid.

"Mr. and Mrs. Adams," she says to my parents. "My name is Jayne. I'm part of the Earth Force public relations team."

I can't believe she'd corner my parents just so she could talk to me.

"It's such a privilege to meet you," she continues. "I wanted to let you know that your daughter, Adeline, is one of the most extraordinary people I've ever met."

What? I mean, Addy's great and all, but that's what she came to say? I fix my eyes on Jayne. She seems totally genuine. I look around to see if anyone is listening. Even bringing Addy's name up is a risk, one I'm surprised Jayne would take.

Mom can't even talk through her tears, so instead she pulls Jayne into a hug.

Dad shakes her hand. "Thank you so much, Jayne. That means the world to us."

After saying good-bye to my parents, Jayne gives me a sad smile. Then she walks away.

So I guess that wasn't about me either.

I DIDN'T THINK IT WAS POSSIBLE, BUT the crowds seem even bigger here as the hovers cut through Americana East, transporting me and the old aeronauts to the seaside stage where we'll hold the rally. They bring us in through a rear entrance and hurry us to a backstage lounge, where we'll wait for our cue. The air is thick with the sounds of thousands waiting for us to appear.

As soon as I walk in, Jayne pulls me aside.

She glances around the lounge then narrows her eyes at me. "Are you in?"

I nod.

"You have your gloves?"

I bend down and act like I'm scratching my ankle. Lifting my pant leg, I show Jayne the gauzy fabric peeking out of the top of my sock.

"Good." She turns and heads for the exit.

I grab her arm. "Wait! What's the plan?"

She shakes her head. She still has no intention of telling me. "Just do your part."

She's not even going to confirm where I'm going? What if I get it wrong? What if my attempts at guessing what the Resistance wants me to do fall flat? Things are moving way too fast. "What about you?"

"I can take care of myself."

"Will I see you on Gulaga?"

Jayne's eyes almost bug out of her head. She glances around to make sure no one heard me, then drags me out of the lounge and into the empty hall. "No."

"You're staying on the tour? What if you're caught?"

Jayne shakes her head. "I knew the risks, Jasper. You and I are part of a much larger puzzle. Focus on your piece and nothing more."

"But, what if—"

"It's almost time to take our places." She grabs my arm and steers us back into the lounge, closing out any chance I had at getting answers.

It's not like I trust Jayne after all her lies, but I definitely preferred feeling like we were in this together.

Now I'm on my own, and mostly in the dark.

I hope I know what I'm doing.

We've been lined up backstage for almost fifteen minutes, and there's still no sign of Lucy.

Sheek flicks his hair and lets out an exasperated sigh. "Let's just get on with it. It's not like I've never hosted something on my own. Of course, if *I* were missing, it would be catastrophic."

Jayne checks her tablet. She's stressed. Most people probably think she's stressed because Lucy is missing, but I know what's really wrong. We're minutes away from the biggest attack the Resistance has ever launched on Earth soil. I'm sure they've timed their actions to the rally script. Without Lucy up there saying her lines, the timing will be off.

"Jasper! Coming through! Jasper!" Lucy is gasping for breath when she reaches me. Dev and Nev trail behind her, touching up her hair and makeup.

"Where have you been?" Jayne demands. "We were scheduled to go on ten minutes ago."

Lucy waves her off. "Jasper, my magic worked! With almost zero planning and no preparation, I was able to assemble most of your classmates for a memory walk as you make your entrance! Isn't that amazing?"

"What's a memory walk?" I ask. "Wait a second . . . did you say my old *classmates* are here?" A lump forms in the base of my throat, followed by an even bigger lump in the pit of my stomach.

"We need to move, people!" Jayne says. Her eyes are drilling into me. If we don't stay on schedule the Resistance's plans might be a bust.

"Yes!" Lucy says, answering my question. "They're assembling on the other side right now! Immediately before your entrance, they'll march onstage, and then you can walk the line and greet them while everyone cheers. It will be magical! It's the big extra you were looking for! And it will remind the crowd that a few years ago you were just another schoolkid in Americana East! Jasper Adams, boy next door–turned–Earth Force hero!"

How did I get myself into this? The only reason I asked Lucy for a bigger role was because I was trying to avoid Jayne the day we arrived. The last thing I want is a memory walk with my old classmates. I hated my school in Americana East. The other kids called me Klutz most of the time. I bet half of them didn't even know my name until they heard about the Lost Heroes Homecoming Tour.

"Are we going to do this or stand around talking about it all day?" Sheek asks as he surveys his perfectly manicured fingernails.

"He's right," Jayne says. "We can't delay any longer!" She's looking at me as she talks. Actually, everyone is looking at me. I guess tonight is my night.

I nod. "Let's do this."

Lucy smiles, and her eyes sparkle. For a moment, I see her as she used to be: my dramatic, chatty friend with her hair tied back in colorful ribbons. I've missed Lucy, even the new Lucy. I can tell by how happy she is about what she's planned that she's missed me, too. The memory walk might not be what I wanted, but it's Lucy's way of trying to bridge the gap back to me.

It's too bad I'll never get to cross that bridge. Before the night is over, I'll be long gone, first across the continent to Gedney's labs, then hopefully across the galaxy to Gulaga.

Lucy blows me a kiss and takes Sheek's arm to walk onstage. The roar of the crowd swells, and when it finally calms, they say their opening lines.

I strain to see the opposite wing. A group of kids waits for their cue. The lump in my throat thickens as I try to find some familiar faces.

"Please welcome students from Americana East, District Eight!" Lucy turns to their wing and claps.

My former classmates cross the stage in one long line. They're led by a pretty, petite girl with a huge smile. Dilly Epstein. Even when most of the kids were awful, Dilly was always kind to me.

MONICA TESLER

Jayne gently nudges my shoulder. "It's go time."

I step onstage with my own smile plastered on. I pause a moment to wave to the crowd, then I turn to my former classmates and their starstruck faces.

"Hi, Dilly," I say.

"I always knew you were special, Jasper." She leans in and kisses my cheek.

My feet freeze. I can't believe Dilly Epstein just kissed me. Somehow I get moving again, shaking hands with the next kid in line, snagging hugs and collecting kisses.

Next thing I know, I'm face to face with Will Stevens. His hand is on my shoulder and he's smiling and saying congratulations just like he always expected this would happen.

But he never expected this would happen. The day before I left for the space station he laughed in my face and called me a B-wad.

I smile back and shake his hand even as a slew of unkind words race through my mind. *You always thought you were so great, Will. Now look who's on top of the world.*

Then I'm greeting the last kid in line, and my classmates are clapping, and Denver is joining me onstage. He marches me to the front, and I stand before my city, Americana East, as one of the biggest celebrities in the world.

Down in the VIP section in front of the stage, I spot my parents smiling up at me. In the wings, Jayne gives me a thumbs-up. We're seconds away from the attack. She's counting on me to do what's right.

But how do I know what's right? Last night I felt confident that I was making the right decision, but now that the moment's arrived, I'm not so sure. Dilly said she always knew I was special. Maybe she's right. Maybe I *am* special and I'm meant to use my fame and celebrity status to change things for the better.

If I thwarted the Resistance, I'd be even more of a hero than I am now. I'd be even more popular.

All I'd have to do is warn everyone. Instead of saying my next line, I could announce that an attack was planned and urge the crowd to take cover.

Denver says his lines, describing his time in the rift. Soon it will be my turn to talk.

I scan the crowd, looking for signs of the Resistance. All I see are smiling faces.

Lucy elbows me in the rib cage. It's my line.

If I don't say something, they'll skip over me and improvise. My chance to warn the crowd will be lost.

My parents stare up at me, beaming with pride. Right now, they think I'm a hero. What will they think if I join the Resistance?

"I said, what do you think, Jasper?" Denver asks.

I swallow hard. "I think . . . I think . . ." I steal a glance at

MONICA TESLER

the wing. Jayne's no longer there. In the VIP section, some-one is running through the crowd, shoving past my parents, heading for the exit. Earth Force officers spill out the side doors, weapons raised.

"Watch out!"

Bombs blast in near unison across the sea of faces below. A cloud of smoke billows across the stage as guards storm from the wings, pushing us away from the crowd. I fight through their ranks to the edge of the stage to see what's happening.

Smoke fills the air and the sound of gun fire rings all around. The crowd is in chaos.

This is my chance. All I need to do is run for the exit.

But what about my parents? They're down there. Some-where.

There wasn't supposed to be violence!

I drop down off the stage and jump the rope into the VIP section. I wade through the thick smoke, searching for my parents.

There are people everywhere. I nearly trip over a small girl who must have been separated from her family. Seconds later, a woman cries with relief and scoops the girl into her arms.

I push on, scanning the soot-covered faces. Finally I spot a man on the ground. There's something familiar about his body, his posture. I lunge in that direction.

My dad is kneeling with my mom in his arms. Her clothes are soaked in blood. My dad presses a ripped cloth against her shoulder.

"Mom! Are you okay? I'll go get help!" This is all my fault. How could I let this happen?

"You need to get to safety, Jasper," Dad says. "You might be a target."

"I'm not," I tell him. "Let me get help!"

"She'll make it," he says, pushing me away. "I think it's just a surface wound. Please, take cover!"

"Jasper," Mom whispers. She stretches her hand toward my cheek.

"Quiet, Emma," Dad says. "Don't strain yourself."

I lean close. "I'm here, Mom."

"Find your sister."

My resolve hardens. I lock eyes with my mom and nod.

Then I run for the exit.

Crowds pour out of the stadium onto the streets. I duck into the first alley I pass. I swing my blast pack around and pull out the hat and glasses. Then I strip off my Earth Force shirt and stuff it into my pack.

I can't believe I left my mom! I should go back. She could be dying. Jayne promised there wouldn't be violence. Why did I believe her?

Mom said to find Addy. That needs to be my focus now. I

MONICA TESLER

stay close to the buildings and sprint as fast as I can, but it's a lot of stops and starts as I dodge the crowd. Soon the crowds start to thin, as I manage to outrun most of the spectators. By now, Earth Force is probably realizing that I'm missing. I wonder if one of the lost aeronauts is missing, too, if the Resistance's plan was successful. I wonder who they took.

I keep running. There's only three more blocks to my apartment building. When I finally reach it, I race down the ramp to the parking garage and keep on running to the lower level.

I race to the back where the storage rooms are. I find the one that Addy and I used for our secret meeting before she left with me for the Academy. I try the door. It doesn't budge. Please don't be locked. I shove against it with my shoulder, and it swings open.

A cloud of dust rises to greet me as I close the door and flip the light switch. Dust quickly coats my nose and throat. I try to cough it out, but that only stirs up more dust.

The weird dolls with the red lips look at me. I try not to pay attention to their unblinking stares. Instead, I dig my gloves out of my socks. I slide them onto my blood-covered hands and fit the fingers. They feel exactly like my old gloves. I hope they work the same.

I pull my shirt up over my nose and mouth and take a deep breath. Gedney better be right about the quantum detection scanners not working underground. What if he's wrong?

THE HEROES RETURN

What if there's actually a quantum scrambler in use? Those work underground. They used them in Gulagaven. And they don't block bounds, they just scatter your atoms across the universe if you attempt a bound. That would make a quick end to this whole Jasper-finding-Addy plan.

Here goes nothing.

I drop my hands to my sides and close my eyes. Then I reach out with my mind and feel instantly alive. My skin tingles with excitement. I sense every atom in the room, then in the garage, then in my building, then in all of Americana East. I expand my consciousness until I feel I could fill the whole universe and bend every atom to my will.

But that's not why I'm here. I'm a trained soldier, and now I fight for my own cause.

Flexing my fingers, I raise my hands and draw atoms like metals to a magnet. They crystallize into a great ball of energy, swirling and swelling until my port is complete.

I pull up an image of Waters's and Gedney's labs.

Then I bound.

MY HIP STRIKES THE PAVEMENT OF THE
helipad halfway across the American continent. My land-
ings still need work. No wonder I never healed right after
my fall in the hangar during my first tour of duty. The new
gloves aren't the problem, although they are a bit quick on
the takeoff.

An alarm is sounding—probably a quantum detection
scanner announcing my arrival. I push myself up on my
hands and knees.

A few moments later, Gedney shuffles out the lab door.

"Welcome, Jasper! I'm so glad you made it." He extends
his palm, but I get the rest of the way up on my own. I

brush the dust from the basement closet off my uniform and pull off my gloves, my hands still covered with my mom's blood.

"There wasn't supposed to be violence!" I shout at him. "My mom was shot!"

Gedney's face winces in alarm. "I'm so sorry. Things didn't go exactly as planned."

I bend over and rest my hands on my knees, catching my breath and trying to slow my racing heart. I can't believe I left my mom at the rally. What if she doesn't make it? What if there's more violence? What if they're caught in the cross fire? Sobs build in my chest. I swallow them down. "I think she'll be okay," I say, mostly trying to convince myself. "My dad said it was a surface wound."

Gedney nods. "I'll try to have someone check on her as soon as possible. I'm sorry, son."

I'm furious with the Resistance, and I'm annoyed that Gedney wasn't being honest about his role with them when he visited me on the Lost Heroes Homecoming Tour. But even so, I'm happy to see him. "I guess you were expecting me."

Gedney tips his head. "Let's say I was hoping you'd come."

"I didn't know you were working with the Resistance." We might as well clear the air about that up front.

"It's best to be discreet, don't you think? At any rate, you seem to have found out on your own." He turns and hobbles back where he came from, calling over his shoulder, "Come in. We have much to catch up on."

I follow Gedney into the kitchen of the lab building where one of his assistants is at the stove, stirring a huge silver pot with an old wooden spoon.

"You remember Jasper Adams?" Gedney leans over the pot and inhales the fragrant smell of garlic and onions and spice.

"Of course," the woman says. "Nice to see you, Jasper. The chili is ready. Eat up."

After she leaves the kitchen, Gedney points at a chair. "Sit. I'll dish it out." He pulls two white bowls from the cupboard and ladles chili into both. "You can speak freely in front of my staff. They're loyal to Jon—and to me, I suppose, although it's Jon who brought them on."

"Have you been working with Waters all this time?"

"Not exactly." He places a steaming bowl of chili on the table in front of me alongside a tall glass of water. "Jon and I had a falling-out on Gulaga. I strongly disagreed with his decision to implant the Youli brain patches in you and Mira, as you know. Then so much went wrong on the tour: the disastrous meeting with the Youli, the alliance with the Alks, the unexpected Earth Force offensive at the intragalactic summit. Some of the blame belongs to Jon. He knows it, but it took a while for him to see his part. It took even longer before we were ready to talk it out. But in the end, we want the same things—for you kids, for Earth, for the greater galaxy."

"Why aren't you on Gulaga?"

"It's important to have members of the Resistance everywhere, don't you think? That way we can more effectively do what our name suggests: resist. Here at the labs I'm still doing important research. Yes, it may benefit Earth Force in the short run, but it will benefit Earth in the long run. Waters understands that. Of course, the real value of me staying in place is my ability to pass information and . . . other things, if you will."

"So you're a spy like Jayne?" I cringe as I say her name. What if Jayne was injured at the rally, too? In my mind I see my dad holding my mom, both of them covered in her blood.

"I wouldn't use that word, but if it helps you to frame it that way, so be it."

I press my eyes shut, trying to erase the picture of my parents. I need to focus. Jayne wasn't willing to give me any answers. Hopefully Gedney is. "What do you want from me?"

"You're in a unique position, Jasper. You're one of the few humans alive who has talked with the Youli directly."

I swirl the chili around the bowl with my spoon. I suppose there's no reason to hold back with Gedney. "The Youli gave me a message in the rift. They want peace."

Gedney bows his head and takes a long breath. "That is good news." He sits back in his chair. "You have doubts?"

He must see the confusion written on my face. "Cole doesn't think we should listen to the Youli. He showed me vids of the Battle of the Alkalinian Seat and other clashes with the Youli that happened while I was stuck in the rift. How can the Youli seek peace but still attack our people?"

He folds his hands on the table. "It's complex. We dealt a blow to the Youli when you kids placed the degradation patch on their vessel. It divided them."

"That's what the Youli who helped us escape from the rift told us."

"It's true, and such division is particularly challenging for a species used to acting with a collective mind. Some of their people believed that Earth should be stopped and were willing to do whatever it took to make that happen. But recent reports suggest they've healed their internal differences, and that they're ready to move forward. That's why now is the perfect time to negotiate a peace between our planets and finally join the vast intragalactic community."

Gedney's explanation makes sense and squares with the other facts I've gathered since returning from the rift, but I'm still not clear why the Resistance is so eager for me to join them. They risked blowing Jayne's cover in hopes she'd convert me, and I don't even think they knew about the Youli message. "Where do I fit in?"

He doesn't answer at first. Instead, he studies my face,

then slowly smiles. "We've always said the Bounders are the future, but you kids never understand how important you are, do you?"

When I don't reply, he continues, "The Youli know you can communicate with them, Jasper. They've known since they first encountered you on the Paleo Planet, long before you had the brain patch implanted. Now they've entrusted you with an important message. Don't forget you also have relationships with leaders in both Earth Force and the Resistance. I'd say it's clear how you fit in. And that's not even counting your relationship with Miss Matheson."

My heart jumps. "Do you have news about Mira?"

He shakes his head. "Only whispers, I'm afraid. I've heard she's alive and safe. I believe in my heart that she is critical to the peace process."

I almost wish he hadn't said that. It makes me think—it makes me *hope*—that Mira will come back, that her absence is part of the larger workings of the galaxy that I just don't understand right now. Mira always sensed that kind of stuff. Maybe her leaving with the Youli had all to do with that and nothing to do with me. "I wish she were here. She'd know what to do." And she'd help me calm down. How am I supposed to play an important part in the peace process—how am I even supposed to track down my sister—when I don't know if my mom is okay?

MONICA TESLER

Gedney leans forward and lays his frail hand on my shoulder. "Perhaps Mira will be back someday soon, Jasper. For now, you need to trust in yourself, and something tells me you know what to do, too."

I try not to think any more about Mira or my mom. There's no time for a pity party. Like Gedney said, I need to trust myself and do what needs to be done: get to Gulaga, talk to Waters, and find Addy. "I can't make a difference from here. We both know where I need to go."

Gedney nods. "I was hoping you'd feel that way."

"But first," I say, "I need to know what happened on Gulaga. During our tour of duty, it was clear a lot of Tunnelers weren't fans of Earth Force, and we knew about the Wackies, but all of that was still pretty underground. Literally, underground." I choke out a laugh at my bad joke.

"Good one." Gedney chuckles. He takes my chili bowl and refills it at the stove. When he returns to the table, his tone is serious. "After the space elevator snapped, unrest grew on Gulaga. Waters stayed behind and mobilized the rebels. Earth Force miscalculated. They left repairs in the hands of the Tunnelers, so when the Resistance rose up, there weren't many who were willing to stand and fight for Earth Force. In fact, almost every Tunneler was proud to fight with the Resistance. Soon, the remaining Earth Force loyalists were forced off the planet or . . ."

He doesn't finish the sentence. "Killed," I say.

Gedney nods. "No matter how you look at it, Jasper, this is war."

"That's why we need peace. Too many have died already. I have to carry the Youli message to the Resistance. What's the plan?"

"As soon as the escort arrives with the seized aeronaut, you'll be stowed away on a cargo ship bound for the Nos Redna Space Port. From there, our operative will fly you to Gulaga."

I'd almost forgotten that the smoke bombs at the rally were just a distraction for the Resistance to kidnap an aeronaut. "The plan worked? Things turned ugly and violent pretty quick. I figured the Resistance really botched things up."

Shaking my head free of images from the rally, I ball my hands into fists. When I get to Gulaga, I'm going to have some choice words for Waters about the Resistance and its tactics. It's almost like they're taking lessons from Earth Force, even if their positions are at odds.

"Again, son, I'm so sorry about your mother." Gedney speaks softly, obviously aware of how upset I am. "We believe the Force picked up on our plans at the last minute, but we managed to carry out the operation. If we tuned into the webs, you'd quickly learn that you and Denver Reddy are missing."

MONICA TESLER

My mouth falls open. "It's Denver?"

Gedney nods.

"That's a huge blow to Earth Force!"

"Everything came together, even with the breach in intelligence."

"You're sending us both to Gulaga?"

"That's the plan." He smiles and pats my hand. "Now finish your chili and relax. You probably won't have much good food or rest for a while." He scrapes his bowl and takes it to the sink.

We talk for a few minutes about the logistics of my stay. He promises to check on my mother as soon as he can. Then he leaves the kitchen to return to his laboratory.

I can't believe I'm going back to Gulaga, back to a diet of forage and fungi and BERF bars. It's time to stockpile Earth food. I force down a third bowl of chili, even though I'm way past full. Maybe Gedney will let me bring a duffel filled with snacks to Gulaga.

After I eat, I refill my glass with clean, cold water. I take a long sip and let it trickle down my throat. I try not to think about much—my brain is tired of thinking—but whenever my mind starts to relax, I see my mom on the ground covered in blood.

I have to trust that she's okay, that the wound wasn't serious, that her friends and colleagues at the hospital are giving her good care.

But even if she's not okay, I'm doing exactly as she asked. I'm going to find my sister.

The next morning, I wake to the cutting swish of helicopter blades out the window. Gedney told me last night that the helicopter pilot is an agent for the Resistance, even though he works for Earth Force. Every week he does an authorized supply run for the laboratory, which often includes a lot of unauthorized information and materials for the Resistance. Today, his cargo is a bit different. If Gedney is right, Denver Reddy should be on board.

I pull on the pair of sweatpants one of the lab assistants gave me last night and head for the helipad.

Gedney's already waiting outside. "Your traveling companions have arrived."

The helicopter touches down and the blades start to slow.

I'm not sure what I'll say to Denver. I can't imagine he's in a very good mood after being kidnapped. Plus, I have no idea what they've told him about me, if they told him anything.

The pilot hops out of the cockpit and crouches to avoid the blades. Then he opens the back door and leans inside. Next thing I know, he's pulling Denver out by his bound wrists.

Denver bends low and jogs alongside the pilot to clear the helicopter. When he looks up, his eyes find mine.

His face is a mix of fury and confusion. "I wasn't expecting to see *you* here, kid. You were in on this?"

"Not exactly," I say. "I had no idea you were part of it. I wasn't sure *I* was until a few days ago."

"You're going to have to explain that," Denver says.

Before I can reply, Gedney claps Denver on the shoulder. "Everything will be explained soon, Captain Reddy. We apologize for the manner in which you've been brought here, but it was necessary to—"

Gedney keeps talking, but I can't focus on his words. Someone else is climbing out of the helicopter and running toward the labs.

A dark knot twists in my belly—because even though he's hunched over and wearing a hat, I can tell from the way he moves that it's Regis.

I grab Gedney by the arm and pull him around the side of the lab building. When we're out of view of the others, I turn on him. "You didn't tell me Regis was coming!"

"I wasn't sure he was until this very moment." Gedney keeps calm, even though I'm clearly furious, and even though I just forcefully dragged him across the compound. "The Resistance employs several different escorts, and identities of those on specific missions are divulged on a need-to-know basis."

I clench my fists. "But you knew it was possible."

"I also knew you might not agree to come if I told you Regis would be traveling to Gulaga."

"He's going to Gulaga? With me?" I laugh, if you can call the nasty, stupefied croak that forces its way out of my throat a laugh. "Then you're right, Gedney. If Regis is going, I'm not." I turn away from him, walk the long way around the laboratory buildings, and kick open the gate of the compound. Without a glance back, I jog across the field of wildflowers where I once lay with Mira counting stars and listening to crickets. I shake my head free of the memory and push forward up the mountain.

I'VE BEEN CLIMBING AT A BRISK PACE
for several minutes when I hear footsteps crunching dry
leaves on the path behind me.

"Hey!" Regis yells. "Wait up!"

The dark knot in my gut twists tighter. I can name it now
as the particular mix of anger and wariness that I associate
with Regis. I won't let him see my fear, but I wish I were wearing my gloves.

"Why would I wait for you?" I call over my shoulder.
"What could you possibly have to say to me?"

"Please, Jasper!"

Please, Jasper? Those are words I never thought I'd hear from Regis. I turn around and plant my feet.

Regis stops and bends over his knees, out of breath. It's clear he's been running to catch me. "Give me a sec," he says between gasps.

Smart Jasper would turn his back on Regis and keep heading up the path, but I'm not thinking smart right now. I'm actually curious what on earth he's going to say to try to bridge the chasm that exists between us—a chasm at least as deep and dark as the one he forced Mira and me off in Gulagaven. If it weren't for Mira's quick thinking, he would have killed us both.

Regis takes a huge gulp of air. "Look, I was a jerk, I get it."

"You were a *jerk*? You *get* it? What exactly do you *get*, Regis?"

"I have a lot of regrets, okay?" Regis stands and clasps his hands above his head, still breathing hard. "But it was a long time ago, and I've been working really hard to show I've changed."

I laugh. "You have an odd definition of 'long time.'"

He drops his hands and starts to close the distance between us. "I know it must seem that way to you."

Right. From Regis's perspective, our tour in Gulaga was a year and a half ago. For me, it wasn't half that long.

Regis keeps on talking. "Getting booted from the Academy

was the best and worst thing that happened to me. I blamed you at first, Jasper. I knew it was Gedney who arranged for my dismissal, and I had a hunch you put him up to it. But shortly after I got home, Gedney reached out to me. He explained that some of my behavior has to do with my genetics—I have these impulses that are hard to control. It's not an excuse, but it helps explain things."

"You're right; it's not an excuse."

Regis keeps going like he didn't hear me. "Gedney's been great. He's helped me develop strategies to stay calm and focused."

I curl my fingers tight against my palms. "You've been working with Gedney all this time? You were in touch with him during my mission to Alkalinia?" I talked to Gedney about Regis the day before we left for that slimy, underwater planet. How could he look me straight in the face and talk about Regis's dismissal from the Academy and not mention that he was helping him get all zen or whatever?

"Yes. I'd been leaking information on behalf of the Resistance for months by then."

Wait . . . before Addy and I left for the Academy, there was an anonymous informant who was pumping the webs with Earth Force secrets. The Force was doing everything it could to contain the leak, and promising swift and serious discipline for anyone caught divulging secrets, including

Bounders. Addy and I were interrogated. I was convinced our apartment was bugged. That's why Addy and I had to talk in our building's basement storage room, the dusty old closet with the freaky dolls where I bounded from yesterday. Could Regis have been the leak?

I tip my head and look Regis in the eyes. "Were you the one who tipped off the media about the Bounders and the Youli war?"

Regis nods with a satisfied smile.

"How'd you do it? You managed to keep leaking secrets even when Earth Force swept the planet on a major manhunt for the mole."

"What can I say? I've always been creative in my plans. Remember Florine and the tofu noodles? At least this time I'm fighting for the right side rather than just fighting."

The image of Florine in the trough with the noodles in her hair forces a smile onto my face. "Those noodles were awesome."

"Yeah." Regis laughs and shakes his head. "She was drowning in those things!"

"All you could see were her pink fingernails reaching out for help!"

"Help me! Puh-leeeze!"

Regis's Florine impression is so spot-on, I burst out laughing.

Wait a second! I am *not* sharing a laugh with Regis. No way!

"How about we head back to the labs?" Regis asks, trying to take advantage of our chummy moment.

I backpedal up the path. "Are you kidding? I'm not heading anywhere with you!" The pitch of my voice rises. "It doesn't matter what line of fluff you give me, and I don't care what Gedney says, you can't erase the past! I almost died because of you! Mira almost died! There is no coming back from that!"

Regis takes a deep breath, and this time it's not from running up the mountain. He balls his fists, then flexes his fingers. The seconds pass. I can almost hear him counting to ten in his head.

"I'm trying very hard, Jasper," he says through a clenched jaw. "I want to do what's right."

"Great. Do what's right. If the Resistance wants a civil war, they're going to need soldiers. More bodies can only help."

"That's not what I mean, and you know it!" Regis shouts. "I've spent the last eighteen hours with that has-been aeronaut Denver Reddy and all his arrogant blather. I'm not going to take it from you!"

"You kidnapped Denver. What did you expect? And what on earth did you expect me to do? Hold your hand all the way to Gulaga?"

"I've come to escort you to the headquarters of the Resistance, and you're going to come with me whether you like it or not!"

I stop backpedaling, and instead march right up to Regis. "Are you threatening me?"

He lunges forward, stopping just inches from my face. "What if I am?"

I keep my voice low and level. "I'd say, I'm right. You haven't changed a bit."

Regis deflates. He takes a step back. His face is red, and he won't look at me. "I'm going back to the labs," he whispers. "Please think about this, Jasper. The Resistance needs you. I don't want to be the one who prevents that."

Instead of responding, I turn around and head up the mountain. My muscles are tense, like they're bracing for impact. I'm half convinced Regis is going to plow up the path and tackle me. That's definitely what the old Regis would do.

I can't believe the Resistance is entrusting such an important mission to Regis. First the attack gone wrong at the rally, and now this? I almost died because of Regis and my mom almost died because of the Resistance. Why did I go AWOL to help a bunch of rebels who are just as bad as Earth Force, maybe even worse?

As I climb, the sounds of the forest soon replace the heavy fall of Regis's shoes on the path. Up ahead, a bird whistles—three shrill calls. His mate answers from the left, high in the trees. Every few steps, the brush stirs as a critter scurries to get out of my way.

I want to stay mad, but the calmness of the forest seeps in and relaxes me. I love this place. There aren't many spots left on Earth where you can simply be in harmony with the natural world.

That's why Earth is so obsessed with the Paleo Planet. It reminds us what our planet used to be like. Of course, we're stripping the nature away there as well. They've probably even amped up the occludium mining operations since the Resistance ousted Earth Force from Gulaga.

I can't believe Gedney expects me to travel there with Regis. He knows our history. It's not fair to even ask me to go with him.

Still, what if what Regis said about genetics is true? Could his "behavioral issues," as Jayne called them, be due to his Bounder genes? If so, is it fair to hold him solely accountable? And what if it's possible that he's changed?

I shake the thoughts from my head. I am *not* going to Gulaga with Regis.

For the rest of the climb, I push myself hard. I focus on the burn in my muscles and the strain in my lungs as I climb higher up the mountain. With every step, I get farther away from everything weighing me down and holding me back.

The forest starts to fade and rocks dot the landscape. Soon I emerge on the ridge where my pod mates and I ate lunch when we reunited here before our second tour of duty.

I hunt around until I spot the cairn we built. The tower of rocks still stands, memorializing the strength of our pod. I can almost hear our voices ring out.

It's all about the pod.

So much has changed.

How did things break apart?

Can we ever come back together?

I pound on the laboratory door until Gedney finally hobbles into view.

"Patience, patience, my boy," he says, pulling back the door. "You'll wake the whole compound."

I put my palm against the door and push. It flies open and slams into the wall. "I thought you were all about hurry, hurry, hurry."

Gedney turns around and slowly makes his way to the other side of the laboratory—past the glass aquariums filled with Youli appendages and various other alien body parts used to develop stolen biotechnology. I follow Gedney to the small alcove in the back of the lab, where a metal table is pushed against a side wall. On the opposite wall is Waters's desk. On top of the desk is the glass orb—now empty—that used to store the Youli brain patches Waters implanted in me and Mira.

Gedney drags a rolling desk chair to the metal table and gestures to a nearby stepladder, presumably suggesting I sit.

I don't.

"I can see you're upset," he says.

"To put it mildly."

"Good news, son. We were able to confirm that your mother is doing well. She's already home from the hospital."

Something inside of me unclenches, and I let out a deep breath.

Gedney points again at the stepladder. "Please."

I sit down and immediately regret it. He's already managed to bend me to his will. I'm sure in his mind he's only a few moves away from getting me to agree to go with Regis.

Gedney folds his hands in his lap. "What's on your mind, Jasper?"

"You lied to me."

"I did not."

"You told us you got Regis kicked out of the Academy. Meanwhile, you'd already recruited him for your secret work with the Resistance. How is that not lying?"

"That's exactly what I did," Gedney says calmly, "and I never lied to you about it."

I spring up from the stepladder. "Don't try to trip me up on technicalities! How could you do this? You knew what Regis did to me and Mira!"

Gedney steeples his fingers. "I will always put the interests of the Bounders first. Regis is a Bounder."

"And a psychopathic would-be killer."

"I don't see it that way. Yes, Regis has a history of violence, but isn't that partially Earth Force's fault? We reintroduced the Bounder genes without any support despite knowing that they brought along challenges as well as strengths. If we had intervened with Regis when he young, he may have learned to express his passions in other ways."

"His passions? You sound like he likes to paint or collects vintage comic books! Plotting my death is not a passion!"

Gedney locks his eyes with mine. "I do not excuse Regis's behavior, Jasper, but I do believe in him as a member of the Resistance. People can change. Do you not feel you've changed since entering the Academy?"

Here he goes again, trying to outwit me, and it's working. Lucy's words ring in my mind. *All you wanted, Jasper, was to be popular.* I've tried to convince myself that Lucy was wrong. But what if she wasn't? Maybe that's exactly who I was when I arrived at the Academy. If I've changed for the better, could Regis?

It doesn't matter. "I could never trust him."

"*Never* is an extreme word, but I didn't ask you to trust him. I asked you to go with him to Gulaga. Trust . . . well, that's something for another day. Maybe Regis will prove himself to you and you'll come to trust him."

I laugh. That's the funniest thing I've heard in a long time, ten times funnier than Florine Statton and the tofu strings. Anyone who thinks I might come to trust Regis is out of their mind.

"Will you go with him?" Gedney asks.

I don't answer.

Gedney spins his chair and withdraws a tablet from a file under the table. "That's why you came down here, isn't it? To help make up your mind?" He sets the tablet on the table.

I sit back down on the stepladder. "Can't I go without him?"

"No. Regis has made this trip before, and he knows what to do. You don't. And you certainly don't while smuggling an unwilling hostage."

"Denver."

Gedney nods and turns back to face me. "Jasper, I've said this already. You're critical not only to the Resistance, but to the bigger picture—the movement for peace. For starters, we're going to need Denver's cooperation, and you're the only one who's spent time with him since he escaped the rift. I'm sure your presence will go some distance in ensuring Denver's reunion with Jon isn't a total disaster."

"Denver knows Waters?"

"Of course. The last time they saw each other, they weren't on the best of terms. I'll leave that for you to hear directly from the two of them."

My gaze is drawn back to the glass orb on Waters's desk. I wasn't on the best of terms with Waters when I saw him last either, and now I'm considering joining him in the Resistance. Maybe this whole thing is a bad idea.

"I knew this would be difficult for you, Jasper," Gedney says, "so I enlisted help to convince you." He glides his finger across the tablet. A projection flashes in the air above and then crystallizes around an image of my sister.

"Addy?" I lean forward, trying to get a better view, but the image quality is pretty poor. Even so, I can see that Addy looks different, older. "When was this filmed?"

"Earlier today. We took a great risk with the transmission." He presses the play icon and Addy jumps to life.

"Jasper!" Addy raises her hand to the camera, almost like she can touch me across the stars. "I'm so relieved you're alive! After what happened on Alkalinia, I thought I'd never see you again!" She glances to the side, then bites her lip and nods. Someone outside the camera angle must be giving her directions. She leans closer to the lens. "Jasper, I don't have much time. Just please do as Gedney says and come here right away! We need you. *I* need you. I love you, J! I'll see you real soon!" She lifts her hand again, and the image freezes.

My eyes fill with tears that struggle to escape. Even though I'd been assured that Addy was alive, that she'd survived the Battle of the Alkalinian Seat, I'd never felt 100 percent sure until this very moment. Her message had to have been recorded earlier today, otherwise it wouldn't make any sense. I raise my palm to the projection and hold it against my sister's frozen fingers.

Addy is alive.

She needs me.

And I promised Mom I'd find her.

Okay, Gedney, you win.

"Fine . . . I'll go."

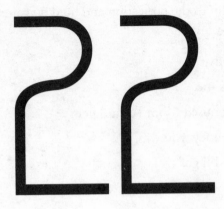

22

REGIS, DENVER, AND I STAND SIDE BY side in the hangar, staring at the small crate.

"You can't be serious," Denver says.

"I'm not excited about it, either," Regis says, "but we have no choice and very little time, so shut your mouth and climb in."

The crate is roughly a meter and a half square on the bottom, and not nearly as high. The three of us won't even be able to sit up straight once we're inside. How on earth will we make it all the way to the space port in that?

This morning at the compound, Gedney laid out the plan as we ate breakfast. The pilot, who doubled as a Resistance operative, would pick us up in the helicopter and transport us to a seldom-used freight hangar at the nearby Earth Force base. From there, he'd smuggle us onto a cargo craft bound for the Nos Redna Space Port and hide us inside a large crate (they consider this crate large?). Once at the space port, we're supposed to meet up with another Resistance agent who will transport us the rest of the way to Gulaga.

"I thought Gedney said there'd be food," I say, not that I'm hungry. In fact, I'm worried my breakfast might make a reappearance the second we're sealed into the crate. I'm just trying to stall.

Regis points at a duffel bag by his feet. "There are the supplies."

"The crate's not even big enough for us and our blast packs!" I say. "Where are we supposed to put that duffel?"

Regis glares at me. "You're worse than Denver. Both of you, get in!"

"Not unless you make me, tough guy," Denver says, "which really means, not unless you make *us*." He lifts his right hand, taking my left along for the ride, and shakes it at Regis.

This morning, when Gedney cuffed Denver to me, I protested. Even if Denver is a flight risk, he's not my problem. He's not my prisoner. Gedney wasn't interested in my opinion. Apparently, Denver couldn't be cuffed to Regis because

Regis needs his hands free in case he needs to use his gun.

That's right. I'm traveling in confined quarters with Regis, who is armed, while I'm handcuffed to an unwilling captive. Nothing could possibly go wrong.

"Yeah, that's what I thought," Denver says to Regis, who's getting angrier by the millisecond. "You just talk tough."

Regis balls his fists as his face turns from pink to pinker to bright, flaming red. Then he closes his eyes and takes a deep breath. His mouth forms words, though no sounds come out. He's counting to ten, one of his calm-down strategies courtesy of Gedney.

Denver laughs. "Keep counting. You're a ticking time bomb."

Regis's eyes fly open, and he jumps forward, shoving Denver in the chest. My arm jerks back as Denver falls to the hangar floor. I land on top of him. Regis knocks me off and sticks the gun in Denver's face. Denver keeps right on laughing.

I glance at my watch. If what Regis said before is true, we only have a few minutes before the pilot comes back with the crew to load the craft. If I'm going to see Addy, I need to get in that crate now.

"Stop letting him provoke you," I say to Regis as I push myself to my knees and yank Denver by the cuff. "Let's go."

Denver doesn't give me too much of a fight, not with Regis's gun now jabbed between his shoulder blades. We haul ourselves up on the loading rack and climb into the crate. I swing my blast pack off my free arm and sink down. There's just enough room for me to sit with my knees bent. Once the lid is on, I'll have to duck my head.

Regis tosses in the duffel then climbs in next to me. There is literally no room between us. We're packed like sardines.

Great. I'm sandwiched between Regis and Denver for the entire trip. This is going to be the longest few hours of my life.

Technically, I guess my hours in the rift were the longest in my life—a whole year long—but something tells me this trip will feel even longer.

A moment later, we hear footsteps, then the pilot's head appears over the crate. "All set?" he whispers. "Nighty-night."

He slides the lid over the crate, leaving us in almost total darkness. The only light comes from four slits carved into the corners, our source of fresh air for the journey. Next, a drill buzzes. He's sealing us in.

My breath comes fast. I'm not good in small places. The tight walls of the crate get even tighter, like they're going to flatten me into a pancake. I close my eyes, but all I can feel is the sensation of being suffocated. I'm back on Alkalinia with a gazillion gallons of water pressing down on me.

I. Can't. Breathe.

"Settle down, kid," Denver whispers. "You've got to stop hyperventilating. It's going to be a long ride. Take a tip from your friend here and try some deep breaths."

"Shut up," Regis says.

"He's not my friend," I say between gasps for air.

"Seriously, shut up, both of you," Regis says. "Don't make a sound until we take off. We can't risk anyone in the crew hearing us."

I focus on slowing my breath and try to send my mind to a different place. Just yesterday I ran through the field of wild flowers where Mira and I lay side by side and counted stars before leaving for Gulaga. I relax my mind and go back to that field. I see the vast sky dotted with tiny pinpricks of light. I hear the insects buzzing between blades of grass. I feel Mira's long fingers weaving with my own.

The crate jerks, and I slide into Regis, even though I didn't know there was any room left to slide. The crate is at an incline; we must be on a loading belt. Once we level out, we're hefted into the air and jostled. When we're set down, I assume it's for good, but then the crate is shoved even deeper into the craft. We must be flush against some other crates, because the small amount of light we have is dimmed in two corners.

"Do you think they blocked the air slits?" I whisper. "If we can't breathe, we're goners."

"Shhh!" Regis says. "You're fine! Keep dreaming about Magic Mira and be quiet."

I clench my fists and bite down on my lip. I want to rail at Regis, but he's right that we need to be quiet. I can't believe he guessed (correctly) that I was thinking about Mira. I can't give him an excuse to say anything more about her. If he does, Denver's bound to ask questions about Mira and how she came to leave the rift with the Youli, a topic I've somehow managed to avoid with him so far.

We're quiet for a long time. At first, I'm convinced we're running out of air, but then I forget to worry about it, and I'm still breathing, so I guess it's not a problem. But what is a problem: the heat. It's getting hotter by the second. And it stinks. I don't know what this crate is typically used for, but it smells like old cheese. I try to breathe out of my mouth, but that's worse. I can still smell cheese, only now I can pretty much taste it, too.

If I could just move around, I might be able to take my mind off the smell and the sweat that's pooling in every crease of my skin. But there's nowhere to go. I shift my legs. Denver shoves my shin. My legs fall the other way. Regis knocks my knees with his own. I keep my eyes closed and try not to think about the absolutely horrible, utterly unfathomable situation I'm in.

Why on earth did I agree to do this?

We haven't even left the ground, and I'm losing it.

A loud noise sounds, and the light in the crate dims even more.

"They've sealed the door," Regis says. "We're probably about to leave."

"Thanks for that nugget of wisdom," Denver says. "We never would have guessed."

"Regis is super smart like that," I say.

Regis elbows me in the rib cage.

"Ow!" I shove him back.

He elbows me again.

Denver slaps my forehead with his cuff-free hand. "Stop it! Both of you! The only thing worse than being locked in this crate for a whole day is being locked in here with you two!"

"You don't need to tell me." My forehead stings, but not enough to distract me from the foul cheese smell.

"Apparently, I do, kid, because you and your pal keep making things even more unbearable."

"I told you, he's not my pal," I say.

"Fine, whatever you say. There's obviously history between you. What's all the bad blood?"

"Regis tried to kill me," I answer matter-of-factly.

Denver exhales in a long whistle. "That would do it."

"I thought we weren't going to bring up the past," Regis grumbles.

"I never agreed to that, nor will I ever. I said I'd try to move on, but that doesn't mean I'm going to forget what happened."

Regis slams his fist against the side of the crate. At least it wasn't the side of my head.

"Why don't you count to ten like they taught you in reform school or wherever they sent you to make you somewhat human?" I ask.

Regis slams his fist again.

"New topic," Denver says. "How long have you been working with the Resistance, kid? Is that why you pulled us out of the rift in the first place?"

"What? No. I'm not working for the Resistance. Or, well, not formally. I didn't even know the plan in Americana East until a few days ago, when Jayne—"

Regis elbows me in the ribs again. This time, I deserved it.

"Jayne is part of the Resistance?" Denver asks. "I never would have guessed. She seems so rah-rah Earth Force."

"Forget I said anything."

"You suck, Jasper," Regis says.

"Since it's already out there," I say, "I have to know: Is Jayne okay? Was her cover blown?"

"Not until right now," Regis says.

Yeah, I suck. "The point is, I have friends on both sides," I tell Denver. "My sister is with the Resistance. I haven't seen her in a long time."

"So all of this is about a family reunion for you?" Denver asks.

"No, there's a lot more to it." There is, but I'm not sure how to explain it to Denver. I rub my head with my free hand. "I agree with the Resistance's principles. And I think they have the best shot at negotiating peace."

"Peace? Are you kidding?" Denver asks. "They attacked us at the rally! They kidnapped me, and now they're shipping us halfway across the galaxy! What does that have to do with peace?"

"Everything," Regis whispers.

Denver leans forward so he can see me and Regis. "No, seriously, both of you, I want to know about the Resistance. I've hardly gotten any answers from Earth Force—not that I'm surprised—and what they have told me has me questioning who the bad guys really are."

That's a pretty bold thing to say—some may even say treasonous. Maybe Gedney was right. Maybe Denver *can* be swayed toward the Resistance.

"And what's more," Denver continues, "there's no way Admiral Eames is going to let that attack go unanswered. So, here's the thing: I'm willing to listen to the Resistance and consider helping you defend against Earth Force's inevitable counterattack, but you'd better start talking."

I take a deep breath of the stale, cheesy air. "A lot has

happened since you got stuck in the rift, Denver, a lot more than they taught you in your recent history classes. You know how they made us lie about our rescue from the rift? That's just the beginning. . . ."

23

OBVIOUSLY, DENVER KNOWS ABOUT THE Incident at Bounding Base 51, but he only knows his part— the part with the failed bound that leaves him and his fellow aeronauts trapped in the rift for more than fifteen years. So I figure that's a pretty good place to start.

I tell him how the Incident changed everything. In its wake, all of Earth's space programs and militaries were formally merged under Earth Force. Space programs make sense—in fact, the space program that oversaw all quantum aeronautics was already called Earth Force—but did anyone question why Earth Force needed to control the military? It's clear now, obviously, but what about then? Didn't it seem suspicious?

My mind is transported back to our pod room during the first tour of duty when we sat on bean bags and listened to Waters talk about the history of the Bounders. Shortly after the Incident, the Bounder Baby Breeding Program was announced. All male-female couples, like my parents, were tested for the Bounder genes. If they carried the genes and planned to procreate, well, let's just say the end results were Bounder babies like me and Addy.

"Yeah, yeah, yeah," Denver interrupts as I go through the history, "because the Bounders are the only humans who can use the alien technology. I thought you were going to tell me something I didn't know."

"They told you all that at the space station?" I'm surprised his clearance level was that high.

"No. It's old news, kid. We knew Earth Force was studying the Youli's biochemistry and comparing it to the human genome back before the Incident. They wanted to expand their research and conduct experiments on an actual alien. That's one of the reasons we engaged in the training exercise the day we got trapped in the rift. We hoped to lure the Youli in and capture one."

"Why did they film it live, then?" Regis asks.

"Who knows? Arrogance? It's not like they planned to stream the alien capture part, just the dashing aeronauts boarding their bounding ships. We filmed all the bounds in those days. Nothing ever went wrong, and the public couldn't get enough of us, which kept the funds rolling in. You think you're a celebrity now, kid? It's nothing compared to back then." Denver shifts, jerking my cuffed arm to the left. "Anyhow, the lure worked too well. The aliens showed up before we expected, and they disrupted our bound. But I understand it wasn't all in vain. Earth Force apparently snagged a little green man, and Waters and Gedney worked their magic. Add fifteen years, and here we are."

"What do Waters and Gedney have to do with any of this?" I ask, tugging my arm back to the right.

"You really don't know? It was their research! Jon Waters was the one who wanted the Youli taken prisoner! Even before they captured one, he and Gedney had hypothesized that alien DNA could be used as a bioweapon, but only certain people would be able to wield it. That's why the Bounder Baby Breeding Program was ultimately started."

Denver's words fall into place in my mind, connecting dots that had dangled far too long. "They reintroduced the Bounder genes because they were similar enough to parts of the Youli genome that we'd be able to use their biotech," I say, thinking out loud.

"Bingo, kid. It's all in the genes."

"And Waters and Gedney were the masterminds from the beginning."

Denver claps his hands, pulling my left hand along for the ride. "You got it! Waters is just a jerk. He thinks he knows everything. But Gedney is the real deal. We used to call him Einstein."

"I used to think Waters knew everything, too," I say. "Now I know he's just another adult with an agenda. For him, the end always justifies the means."

"Think what you want about Waters," Regis says, "just don't lose sight of the real enemy: Earth Force."

Regis asks some more questions about the Incident at Bounding Base 51 and the Bounder Baby Breeding Program, but I tune them out. It's mostly stuff I already know. Plus, I need some time to process what Denver just said about Waters and Gedney. After all this time, neither of them ever confirmed that they were personally involved with the Bounder Baby Breeding Program, let alone that it was their brainchild. I guess I should have known. The signs were all there—Gedney knows more about the gloves than anyone—but I didn't want to believe it. Was the Youli prisoner being held at the space station during our first tour of duty just another one of their science experiments?

The craft lurches forward as it shifts to Faster Than Light Speed, and we end up in a pile at one end of the craft.

"FTL," I mutter.

"I can think of a few different acronyms I'd use to describe that," Denver says, pushing his way off of us and back to his corner.

"It's no treat sharing this crate with you, either," Regis says.

"You're the last person I ever wanted to be in close quarters with," I say to Regis.

"The feeling's mutual."

"Enough," Denver says. "Your bickering is exhausting. Let's get back to the topic. So, you're saying that Earth Force kept the Youli war and the reason for the Bounder Baby Breeding Program a secret all these years?"

Regis must have added those gems while I zoned out.

"That's right," Regis says. "Now here's what I want to know: How did the Youli war start?"

Denver takes a deep breath. "Some things happened before I joined Earth Force, so for the old stuff, I only know what I was told, and we all know how loose the Force is with the truth. But the way it was said to me is like this: Shortly after Earth developed Faster Than Light technology, we were exploring an up-until-then-unknown sector of the galaxy when we were hailed by the Youli. This is known in high-security circles as first contact. As the story goes, it was no accident that we encountered the Youli. The Youli had been watching Earth for a long time and waiting until we achieved space travel technology that took us outside the confines of our solar system. Once we had that, the Youli reached out and basically offered to take us under their wing in the greater goings-on of the galaxy. For a while, we all played nice."

"We started out as friends?" I ask.

"Sort of," Denver says. "It was more like a mentor relationship. The Youli civilization is far older and more advanced than ours, and they never let us forget it. In the greater order of the galaxy, there are rules and ethical standards that have to be followed. Of course, one of the signature features of Earth and its people is our collective arrogance. We don't like other folks' rules and standards, even when those folks are much older and wiser. I guess Earth is like a meta version of your pod leader, Jon Waters. We think we know everything, and that arrogance is always our downfall."

"The Youli war," I say.

"I'm getting there," Denver says. "I was pretty junior when a lot of this was happening, but I'd put it this way: Earth had a *take what we like* approach to Youli mentorship and our introduction on the galactic scene. We took the trade deals and technology transfers, and we ignored some of the other stuff."

"Like what?" Regis asks.

"The Intragalactic Council does not allow interaction with developing planets who haven't reached FTL capacity."

Now we're getting somewhere. "The Tunnelers."

"Exactly," Denver says.

"You were on Gulaga when Earth Force negotiated the terms of the Tunneler alliance, right?" I ask.

"Negotiated? Alliance?" Denver laughs. "Is that what the Force told you?"

I always wondered what really happened on Gulaga. "That's not how it went down? There's so little information."

"No, and I was there," Denver says. "Cora and I were the two youngest pilots deployed."

"Cora?" Regis asks. "You mean Admiral Eames?"

"Um . . . yeah." Denver laughs again, but there's no amusement in it. It's the kind of laugh that masks pain. "Cora has done quite well for herself."

If the rumors circulating at the space station are true, Denver and Admiral Eames had been in love when he disappeared into the rift. Only a few months after the Incident, she stepped up as the admiral of the consolidated Earth Force. How did she have the focus and drive to do that after losing Denver? How was she able to put it all aside and lead her planet in the defense of a secret alien war?

From what I can tell, Denver's homecoming has been strange and strained for both of them.

"You could say that," Regis says. "What actually happened on Gulaga?"

"We wanted to expand our bounding program," Denver continues, seemingly relieved to get back to the facts, "but

MONICA TESLER

we needed more occludium. We tried to trade for it, but the Intragalactic Council blocked us—something about keeping our development at a sustainable pace. Earth Force wasn't having it. So when our sensors located occludium ore on Gulaga, we set out to claim it.

"Frankly, when we arrived, we didn't take much notice of the Tunnelers. They barked and bowed when we landed on their planet, but we thought they were just a primitive species. Pests, really. Only later, when we learned that they'd built an expansive civilization underground and had been mining occludium for hundreds of years, did we realize their utility. We wouldn't even need to set up a mining operation on Gulaga. One already existed, along with a people who could run it."

"Free labor," Regis says.

"That's right," Denver says. "We commandeered them."

"So there *was* bloodshed?" I'd always guessed there was more to the story.

"To put it lightly. When the Tunnelers tried to resist us taking over, we showed them they had no choice. The fighting didn't last long. Our military might and technology far surpassed anything the Tunnelers had ever seen. But they fought admirably. Some of those Tunnelers are the bravest beings I've ever encountered."

The Wackies. I picture grizzly old Barrick with the scar

running across his face. There's no doubt he was leading the charge against Earth. In fact, he's still fighting us.

"The truth is," Denver says quietly, "I've never felt right about it. When I heard you were taking me to Gulaga, I stopped resisting so hard. I'm intrigued to go back. I feel I owe something to its people."

"You're going willingly?" I ask.

"I wouldn't say that," Denver says, "but if I'd really been trying to ditch you guys, I'd be long gone by now."

"What is this? Some tactic to get us to uncuff you?" Regis asks. "Because it's not going to work."

"Why? You don't trust me?"

Regis laughs.

"What about you, kid?" Denver asks.

"I'm not sure."

"Do you trust him?" Denver asks, obviously referring to Regis.

"No," I answer without a second thought.

"Well, then it looks like we all have trust issues."

I don't realize I've fallen asleep until the crate is hefted off the floor of the craft, knocking me into Regis, who kicks me in the shin.

I raise my eyebrows. Where are we?

Nos Redna Space Port, Regis mouths.

I nod. We need to be quiet or risk being discovered.

Voices from outside the box reach us. They're not speaking English. In fact, it doesn't even sound like language. The closest I can relate is the Tunneler bark, but this sounds more like chirping. Seconds later, a translator kicks in. It's hard to hear the specifics, but I think they're asking our pilot for cargo papers.

"Is there a problem?" I whisper.

"Routine," Regis answers and lifts a finger to his lips.

Several seconds pass with nothing happening. Then the chirping starts back up. This time, there's no translation and no sound of our pilot. The crate is hefted up and placed on a transporter that whisks us across the landing bay.

"Still routine?" Denver asks.

Regis nods.

"Where are they taking us?" I ask.

"We usually unload in a private storage bay. I'm guessing that's where we're headed now."

Doors clang shut, and chirping comes from all sides. There must have been a whole bunch of those aliens waiting for us in the private storage bay.

"That's . . . odd," Regis whispers.

"What?" Denver and I say at the same time.

"I don't know why those chirping dudes are still around. Usually we're unloaded by Tunnelers, occasionally by Earthlings, but never by . . . whoever these guys are."

A hush falls in the bay, and then the doors open and close once more. The chirping starts again, but this time it's loud and formal (or at least as formal as chirping can sound). Then the translator kicks in, except that it doesn't translate into English.

The translation is robotic and strange but also familiar.

I look at Regis. He shrugs.

Once I hear the reply, there's no mistaking the language they're speaking.

It's the signature hiss of Alkalinians.

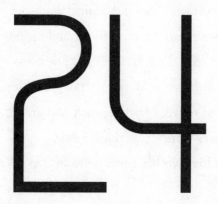

I MUST HAVE GASPED, BECAUSE BOTH
Denver and Regis elbow me hard in the ribs. I bend over and
try not to yelp in pain.

"We're in trouble," I whisper. "Those are Alks."

"That means nothing to me, kid," Denver says.

My heart races, and my breath comes fast. This crate never
felt so suffocating. "The Alks are the aliens who sold us out
to the Youli. I bounded to the rift in the middle of the battle
on their planet."

"Are you sure those are Alkalinians?" Regis asks.

I hush them so I can listen. Outside the box, the chirpers

chirp away. I hold my breath and wait for the translation and reply, hoping I was wrong.

Again, the sinister hiss of Alkalinian fills the bay.

A shiver seizes my body as the terrible reality sets in. The Alks are here, and there can be only one reason why. They're here for us, and they've already got us locked up.

We need to move. I lean forward and grab my blast pack. "Do our gloves work here?" I ask Regis.

He yanks his own blast pack into his lap. "Yes. There's no scrambler."

"Good," I say, already pulling my gloves from my pack, "because they're probably our only chance to get out of this."

Denver yanks my left hand by our shared cuff. Regis hands me the key, and I detach us.

"I don't have any gloves." Denver waves his now free hands in the air. "But I'm an excellent shot." He points at the gun strapped to Regis's waist.

"Don't even think about it," Regis says.

"You'd rather get killed than let me help?"

"He's right, Regis. Give him the gun." I fit my gloves on my fingers. When Regis doesn't move, I add, "Now!"

Regis unholsters the gun and hands it to Denver. Then he pulls on his gloves.

"Plan?" Denver says, disengaging the gun's safety. "What can you guys actually do with those things?"

"You'll find out soon enough," I say. "We need to act fast while we still have the element of surprise. I'll pop off the lid, and you get ready to fire. Regis, you and I will try to immobilize anyone who's armed."

"How?" Regis's voice shakes.

I slap his leg, trying to inject a dose of confidence that I don't feel myself. "However you can. Fling their weapons away. You remember the pillow fight our first tour."

"That didn't go my way," Regis whispers.

I look him in the eyes. "This time it will."

Regis nods.

Denver looks up at the lid of the crate. "Let's do this."

I close my eyes and tap into the energy of my gloves. The familiar current courses through me. Once I've aligned with the source, I point my fingertips at the crate's lid. I take a deep breath, then force all my mental effort into blowing the top of the crate to the roof.

The lid flies off, and fresh air rushes into the crate. The light is so bright after being shut in all day, I have to squint. And I have to move. Denver springs to a squat and starts firing. Regis and I both leap off the sides and take cover behind the crate. My muscles scream from being cramped in a crate all day, but I let the adrenaline surge through me, forcing my limbs to obey.

"How many?" Regis shouts over the sound of weapons

firing. He holds his palms out in front of him. I can almost see the energy radiating from his fingers.

"I'll check." Peeking around the side of the crate, I count five Alks, none of them close enough to see if I know them from Alkalinia. There are also about a dozen other aliens in the bay, who I assume are the chirpers. They're tall and skinny and have three sets of mini wings around their midriff. They don't fly, exactly, but they leap in the air and flutter, making them hard for Denver to target.

Luckily, only about half of the chirpers are armed, and most of them share tandem rifles.

Denver quickly takes out four of them.

The buzz of a laser nearly gives me a haircut. I duck back behind the crate. "Five Alks and about a dozen chirpers."

Regis nods and flutters his gloved fingers. "Now or never."

I steady my breath, and the world shifts into that slow-motion mode like when we placed the degradation patch on the Youli vessel or when I brought the shield down in Alkalinia.

Every minute, every moment of every minute, means life or death right now.

"On my count." I raise a finger . . . one, two, *three*.

I pivot out from behind the box and raise both hands. I whip my right palm at the closest group of chirpers and seize control of their atoms. With my left, I condense the

MONICA TESLER

air around me into a viscous bubble that hopefully will slow down incoming fire. I fling the chirpers against the far wall and fix my sights on the Alks.

Two of them are firing at Denver, and three others hover near the door. I dash behind a stack of empty shipping containers and seize control of the flying throne of the nearest Alk. Focusing my intentions, I flip the seat, and the Alk tumbles to the ground and tries to slither out of range. I seize him by his cyborg arm and send him flying across the bay. On the other side of the hangar, Regis takes out two chirpers and their tandem rifle.

"Behind you!" Denver shouts from the top of the crate.

I swing around just in time to fend off another chirper duo.

Denver trades shots with an Alk wielding a laser staff. "Help me out, kid!" he hollers, nodding at a pair of chirpers targeting him with their rifle.

I grab the atoms of the chirper on the left and toss him to the edge of the bay. Then I fling the other one up in the air. He collides with the ceiling and crashes down. His long, skinny body bends in a bad way on the ground; his paper-thin wings flitter to a stop.

"Yeah, kid!" Denver shouts. He dives into the crate as his Alk adversary lets loose a laser beam from his staff.

Sparks ricochet off the crate and ding across the port,

sending more chirpers for the door. Regis uses the distraction to dash across the bay and take cover behind a stack of empty crates. Now our offensive has the remaining Alks and chirpers pinned in.

Regis freezes the Alk firing at Denver, leaving Denver free to take him out with the gun.

"Nice trick!" I shout.

That leaves a final group of chirpers and a single Alk left to immobilize. As he closes in, his features come into focus. It's Steve, our guide from Alkalinia.

The chirpers break for the door. Regis and I use the same strategy to freeze the chirpers, and Denver picks them off one by one with the gun.

Until Steve is the only one left.

Denver aims the gun.

"Wait!" I raise my gloved hand at Denver. "He's mine."

Steve's back is to me as he races for the exit. I seize his throne and slowly rein it in. Then I spin him like a top until he's facing me.

Anger rises in my chest. My eyes swim with rage at the memory of Addy and Marco racing through the venom tube, Serena sliding in to help them, all of her abandoned babies rushing to greet her and ripping the tube in two.

I pull Steve's throne to the floor then throw it back in the air, launching Steve from his velvet cushion. Before he hits the ground, I grab his scaly Alk body and tear his cyborg arm clean off. He drops to the floor and wriggles for the door.

I don't even bother using my gloves. I run across the bay and step on Steve's tail. Then I bend over my old Alk guide. "Hello, Sss-Steve. Tell Sss-Seelok I say hello."

He hisses at me, but his translator is nowhere in sight. "Grab a voice box from one of those chirpers!" I shout at Regis.

When I have the box, I shove it under Steve's scaly chin. "How did you know we'd be here?"

Steve clicks and hisses. "Sss-silly boy, don't you know what Alksss do? We deal in sss-secretsss. Nothing is off-limitsss at the right price-sss."

"Who sold us out?"

"Molesss are everywhere, Jasss-per, even in the Ressssissstanssse."

Denver walks up behind me. "We need to go, kid."

"Someone squealed. We need answers."

"No time. They'll be on us in seconds if we don't move." Denver grabs my arm.

I shake free. "Not yet." I lift my gloved hand and seize the atoms around Steve's scrawny neck. He struggles to breathe, his hisses leaking from his throat in a weak stutter. All it would take is a bit more pressure. Just a little squeeze. He deserves it. If he'd had his way, I'd be dead. All the Bounders would be dead.

"Let's go!" Regis calls.

Denver gently places his hand on my wrist and lowers my gloved hand to my side.

"He could warn the others," I say to Denver. Why shouldn't we finish what we started? We already took out the chirpers and the other Alks.

Denver stoops over Steve and brings the butt of the gun down hard on his head, knocking him out. "Not anymore."

I scan the bay and take stock. Part of me still wants Steve dead, but I know it's not necessary. If I killed him now, I'd be no better than the Alks.

Regis stands by a rear exit, waving his arms. "This way!"

Denver and I jog across the bay and follow Regis into a dark hallway. We pick our way through the back halls, trying to avoid contact with anyone. Soon, though, the hall fills with chirpers flitting swiftly by, carrying dirty plates and glasses and paying absolutely zero attention to us.

"What's that smell?" I ask. "It's like a mash-up of red licorice and dirty sneakers."

"Where did you come up with that?" Denver asks.

Regis stops us. "We're almost at the kitchens. Beyond them is the bar. That's where we'll meet our ride."

Denver nods and starts back down the hall.

Regis grabs his arm. "Not so fast." He points to the gun. "Hand it over."

Denver dangles the gun in Regis's face. When Regis reaches for it, Denver laughs and shoves it in his waistband. "Not a chance. This gun is mine now."

"No way." Regis balls his hands into fists.

Denver keeps right on laughing. "What are you going to do, fight me for it?"

"Forget it, Regis," I say. "He saved our butts back there. I guess we all need to practice more trust."

Regis shakes his head. "Fine." He flips the hood of his sweatshirt up, then pulls some hats out of the duffel and hands them to me and Denver. "You're two of the most wanted guys in the galaxy. Put these on and keep a low profile. And put your gloves away, Jasper. We don't want to raise any red flags."

As I slip off my gloves and zip them into my blast pack, I think about what Regis said. There are probably a few bounty hunters in that bar who could make a pretty penny bringing Denver and me back to Earth. Maybe Regis was right to ask for the gun back. With our gloves stowed, Denver is the only one of us who's armed. There's not much stopping him from marching us up to the head of the port and turning us in. I'm sure he could catch a ride back to Earth in no time.

Hopefully our heart-to-heart in the crate counts for something.

We follow Regis into the bar. It's shaped in a circle with the bartenders in the center, counter seats surrounding them, and a ring of tables on the rim. The place throbs with a rapid bass beat and whistles with the sound of electronic music blaring a reed setting in a minor key.

It's packed. I'm trying to keep my head down and not attract attention, but I steal a few glances. The chirpers are working the tables. A tall dude who looks kind of like a twig with lots of arms is bartending. And there are dozens of species of aliens I've never seen before. Gedney wasn't kidding when he described the intragalactic scene as vast.

Fortunately, I don't spot any Alks or Youli, but I'm pretty sure I spy a table of Tunnelers in the back. There are lots of humanoid-like aliens with different-colored skins and odd appendages, but there are also aliens I don't even have words to describe and that I never would have imagined existed if I weren't staring at them right now with my own two eyes. Like the giant slug-looking thing that's driving around in a motorized cart, or the table filled with tiny creatures that look more like ants than any alien I've ever seen.

Regis jerks his head toward a table in the corner. We follow him and slide into seats. Seconds later, one of the chirpers flits to our table. She has silver chains wrapped around her body, with coins jangling from hooks. Her wings are dyed purple and pierced with multicolored crystals.

She chirps at us, then presses a button on her translator. A husky woman's voice booms out, "What'll it be, boys?"

Denver laughs. "Who programmed that voice box?"

"Low profile," Regis mutters under his breath. Then he smiles at the chirper. "Three sour ticklers."

"Coming right up, honey." She reaches into her apron and pulls out a handful of small foil packages. "Enjoy your nuts."

I peel back the foil and out roll a bunch of black rocks. I'm about to pick one up when it jumps on the table. I jerk back. "What are those?"

Regis pops all of his in his mouth at once. "Hoppers. They're imported from one of the nearby planets. They taste kind of like soy nuggets."

Denver smells one of the hoppers, then bites it in half. "They're not bad."

"Not bad" is not good enough for me to even try. I push the foil-wrapped nuts over to Regis. "Have mine."

My stomach grumbles. I dig in my bag and pull out a protein bar.

"Not in here!" Regis says. "It's rude!"

"Since when do you care about being rude?"

Denver swipes my bar and shoves it in the duffel. "If you're hungry, eat your hoppers, kid."

I'm about to protest when the chirper arrives with our

drinks—they're blue and frothy and releasing teal steam into the air.

A long, curly straw sticks out of the glass. I take a tiny sip. My lips pucker. It tastes like jelly beans and sour peach candy mixed together. So, in other words, I love it.

Denver tries his drink and makes a face. I guess I'm not the only picky one. "What are we supposed to do? Just sit here and wait for our ride to show up?"

"Don't worry," Regis says, scanning the bar. "She'll show. She's probably just waiting until it's safe. I'm sure security has found our trail of carnage by now."

"Speaking of that," I say, "what if they figure out that we were behind that? We're basically sitting ducks right here."

"Which is why we need to keep a low profile," Regis says.

As soon as the words "low profile" leave his mouth, a fit of barking erupts at my back.

I spin around just as a voice box starts to spit out a long stream of words.

"Oh! Oh! Oh! I was so very worried! Especially when I heard the rumors. And oh! Oh! Oh! They're true! They're true! Jasper Adams! I didn't know if I would ever see you again! But oh! You're here! Give me a hug!"

Neeka throws her furry Tunneler arms around my neck before the voice box finishes translating.

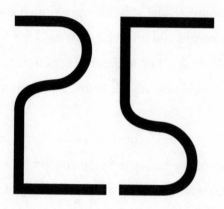

"NEEKA! I HAD NO IDEA YOU WERE GOING
to be here!" I free myself from her furry arms but keep hold
of her paw. My Tunneler friend is wearing an emerald-green
tunic that makes the green of her eyes shine. Gone are the
days of the burlap sack—standard Tunneler attire under
Earth Force control.

"Neither did I," Regis says.

Neeka growls. "Oh! Shut up! You know I didn't come here
for you."

Denver leans back in his seat and folds his arms across his
chest. "Your little reunion is quite possibly the furthest thing

from low profile." Nodding at Neeka, he adds, "Isn't someone going to introduce us?"

"Oh! Captain Reddy!" Neeka says through the voice box. She drops my hand and offers her paw to Denver, who shakes it a little awkwardly. "I do apologize. I am so very sorry! Oh! I was ever so rude! I told myself before I got here that the very first thing I—"

"Hey!" Denver holds up his hands. "Stop talking for a minute! Start off by telling me who you are."

"Oh! Oh! You are oh so right! Where are my manners? Oh!"

Denver looks at me. "On second thought, kid, you tell me who your friend is."

"Denver, meet Neeka." I put my arm across her shoulders. She wraps herself around me and squeezes. "She was our pod's junior ambassador on Gulaga, and she's awesome."

Neeka smiles up at me. "Your sister can't wait to see you."

"You've met Addy?"

She nods.

A swell of emotion rises in my chest, making me feel light-headed and heavy on my feet at the same time. I'm going to see Addy. I'm here with Neeka. Yes, there's a war. And yes, we'll try to push for peace. But it's also about family and friends, the things that matter most in life.

"We should go," Regis says quietly.

"I don't take orders from you," Neeka barks back.

"He's right," I say to her. "We had a run-in with some old friends back in the cargo hold."

"Friends?" Neeka asks.

"Kidding," I say. "They were Alks, and they had a heads-up we were coming."

"Someone's going to want to know who left the mess," Denver says.

"Plus," I say, grinning at Neeka, "I can't wait to see Addy."

We follow Neeka out of the bar and back through the rear hallways until we reach a hangar crowded with small ships. Pilots and crew hang about chatting, cleaning their crafts, loading cargo. Neeka leads us across the hangar, greeting almost everyone we pass. She stops in front of the most banged-up, piece-of-junk ship in the hangar.

"Oh! Here's my baby," she says, patting the ship with her paw.

"This thing flies?" Denver asks.

"Barely," Regis grumbles.

Neeka swats him. "Oh! Excuse me? This beauty is a ruby in the rough. Isn't that how your cliché goes?"

"Diamond, but who's listening to me?" Regis says.

"No one, as usual." She places her paw on the lock sensor, and the loading bridge drops down. "All aboard! Oh! I can't wait to fly you to Gulaga, Jasper! It's where you belong!"

We climb onto Neeka's ship, which looks just as bad inside as out. Once we strap in, she flips a bunch of switches, backs us up, and steers us out of the hangar into open space. While we fly, Denver peppers her with questions about the Resistance. From the way Neeka's talking, it's clear she's a pretty high-ranking rebel. After her dad died during the battle with the Youli, she sought out Barrick and volunteered for the Resistance, and she's taken every chance she can to prove herself and rise in the ranks.

"Commander Krag was your father?" Denver asks. Apparently, he met Krag when he came with Admiral Eames and the other Earth Force officers to hammer out the Earth-Tunneler treaty. "I remember him. He was a fierce and loyal advocate for his people, even when we were much younger. I'm sorry for your loss."

"Thank you," Neeka says. "Even though it's been a year and a half since my dad died, the wound feels fresh. Sometimes I can almost hear him whispering to me." She doesn't ask Denver any questions about his time in Gulaga twenty years ago. She must have already known he was there and accepts that we need to move forward. Plus, the fact that Denver's voice sounded heavy with guilt probably helps.

"I'm sure your dad would be very proud of you, Neeka," I say.

"Definitely," Regis says.

Neeka snaps at him. "Oh! Don't you dare try to ingratiate yourself with me, Regis!"

"You don't want me to kiss your furry butt?"

She hops up barking. "Out! Get out of my sight! Go strap in by the engine and stay there until we land!"

"Gladly," Regis says. He undoes his harness and disappears to the back of the craft.

"What's your deal with him?" I ask once he's gone.

"Oh! What is *my* deal?" Neeka barks, her temper still sizzling. "What is *your* deal? How could you forgive him for all the evils he caused? Do you not remember what happened on Gulaga? He almost killed you and Mira more than once!"

"That explains a lot," Denver says.

"I definitely wouldn't say I've forgiven him. It's complicated."

Neeka doesn't respond. She checks some of the gauges on the ship and prepares for the shift to FTL. Once that's done, she asks in a much calmer voice, "How is Mira?"

Denver perked up as soon as Neeka mentioned Mira's name a moment ago. Now he's practically sitting on the edge of his seat, waiting for my answer. I've intentionally avoided the topic with him. I have no idea what his Earth Force buddies told him about her.

"I haven't seen Mira in a while," I say. "The Youli have her."

"Mira's the girl from the rift, right?" Denver asks. "What

happened? Why did she leave with them? Was that part of the deal—she went with them to save us?"

I ask myself those same questions every day, and I'm still no closer to an answer. I don't know how to respond.

"Kid?"

I decide to stick to the truth. "All I know is she had to leave with them, but also she said it was her choice to go."

We don't talk much for the rest of the ride. Denver dozes off. I'm exhausted, but I can't get Mira off my mind, and I'm too excited to see Addy and Marco to fall asleep. I close my eyes and try to call up happy memories. I'm reliving the epic pillow fight during our first tour when we slam out of FTL.

Out the window, the planet of Gulaga is in our sights, along with the wreckage of the space elevator. A long spire stretches from the surface of the planet out into space. Construction crafts surround the tip of the spire, and repair robots work on a large platform suspended in space. A dozen defense ships dot the perimeter.

"They're rebuilding the space elevator?" I ask.

"Oh! No! It's far too much of a risk. We learned that the hard way, didn't we? We are disassembling what remains of the elevator and bringing the scrap to the surface. We need all the space-worthy building materials we can find."

"Are you building ships with the scrap?" Denver asks.

Neeka's ship isn't the only one that looks like she bought

it at the junkyard. Almost all the Resistance ships look like pieces of junk because, according to Neeka, they mostly are junk. When the Youli snapped the space elevator, much of the Gulagan fleet was lost or destroyed. Later, when the Resistance ousted Earth Force, the Force left with any ship that could fly, hoping to strand the Gulagans on the planet. Fortunately, some of the Tunneler engineers had learned enough from Earth Force during the occupation that they were able to piece together some new ships out of scrap metal and broken-down Force ships that had been abandoned in a repair facility on the surface.

"What's that silvery gauze around Gulaga?" Denver asks.

"That's the occludium shield," I say. "No bounding to the surface."

"Ah!" he says. "I should have guessed. Occludium-based technology has come a long way since I was stranded in the rift."

"Good news, Jasper," Regis says as he returns to the front of the craft. "The Resistance deactivated the scramblers on the surface."

"So we can bound wherever we want?"

When Regis nods, a smile stretches across my face. That is definitely good news. No more getting stuck on the tundra. No more crossing narrow bridges in Gulagaven. No more flying my blast pack without my gloves.

As we cut through the atmosphere and prepare to land at Gulagaven, Neeka calls down to the surface for them to lower the standard force field that now protects the main settlement.

"I can't wait to see Addy," I say. "Will she be there when we touch down?"

"I'm sorry, no," Neeka says. "They keep the exact itinerary of the transports a secret for security purposes, but I'll take you to her as soon as we land. Speaking of landing, we'll be exiting the craft outside. There are parkas stocked in the aft cabin. You'll need to put those on for the short walk into the tunnels."

"I could never forget how frigid your planet is," Denver says. "I almost lost my fingers on my first visit to Gulaga."

"I almost lost my life when I was trapped outside over-night, thanks to Regis," I say.

Regis shakes his head. "Please stop bringing that up."

"I told you before, Regis, I might be able to forgive you eventually, but I'll never forget what you did. And I'm going to make sure you don't forget, either."

"Fine," he says. "Since we're bringing up memories, every time I land in Gulaga, I remember when you put burning foot powder in my boots."

"That was a joke."

"I wasn't laughing."

"And I wasn't laughing when you threw those bugs in my bed. In fact—"

Neeka waves her paws in the air. "Oh! Oh! No! Enough!"

"I'm with her," Denver says. "Shut it until we land. Then the two of you can find an isolated underground burrow and yell at each other all you want."

I'm half-frozen by the time we make it down the entrance ramp. Once we pass through the two containment doors and into the Outfitters, a Tunneler trades our coats for some human-size parkas. I strip the too-small Tunneler coat off and don the parka as fast as I can, but I still feel like I was dipped in an ice pond. Denver, Regis, and I huddle together shivering until Neeka finishes shutting down her ship and joins us.

My excitement grows with each step as we wind our way down into the heart of Gulagaven. I can't believe I'm really about to see my sister. When we reach the central chasm, I place my hand against the mud wall and keep walking. Soon, I have to stoop to stop from bumping my head.

"Were the ceilings always so low in this part of Gulagaven?" I ask. "I don't remember having to bend over until we reached the branch halls."

Neeka laughs. "You're oh-so-much taller than the last time you were here."

"Even I remember these low ceilings," Denver says. "And

how could I forget the bottomless pit? That thing still makes my heart race." He keeps his hand on the wall, too.

After a few turns around the central chasm, we begin to encounter other Tunnelers. Almost all of them have traded their drab brown-and-gray tunics for colorful garb like we saw across the tundra in the Wacky headquarters during my tour of duty. I bet that's how Tunnelers dressed before Earth Force showed up in the first place.

It's not just their clothes that seem different, though. The Tunnelers greet Neeka cheerfully, and many of them smile at Denver, Regis, and me. Some of them give us a far-less-than-friendly stare, which I can understand given their history with Earth. The point is that almost all of them look us in the eye, and that's a huge change from the last time I was here.

We pass through the central market, and it's even louder and rowdier than I remember. Tunnelers bark and wave their paws as they trade for goods and clothes and treats—not that I'd call those creepy crawlies treats. The smell alone is enough to make my stomach turn. I don't bother asking Regis if the Tunneler cuisine has improved since Earth Force left, because I'm 99 percent sure I don't want to know the answer, and I'm going to find out soon enough anyway.

Once we pass the market, Regis cuts off on his own, mumbling something about changing his clothes and taking a nap. We certainly don't try to stop him. All of us are happy to be free of him, at least for now. Maybe Regis has changed, but bad blood runs thick, and he's still annoying, even if he's not actively trying to kill me.

Finally, we find ourselves at the once ornate, carved doors of the Tunneler Parliamentary Chamber. The relief carvings on the doors are filled over with mud, probably because the carvings depict scenes from the Tunnelers' first contact with Earth.

When I stood before these doors during my tour of duty, the Bounders were booed. A disgruntled Tunneler even threw eggs at us. Now, though, there is no sign of protest. I'm hoping these doors and the chamber beyond have regained their status as a place of reverence and pride for the Tunnelers.

Neeka greets the door guards. "Brother, sister, salutations. I bow to your service and fortitude." She tips her head down.

"And we also bow to you, sister," they both respond, inclining their heads.

"Will you grant us access to the chamber?" Neeka asks.

"We will, sister," the one on the right answers.

Both of the guards grip a handle and pull the doors back. As we pass through, they say in unison, "May your days be peaceful and productive, and may your nights provide shelter from the cold."

I step into the large chamber filled with dozens of tiny carrels carved into the high walls where Tunnelers have participated in their government throughout the generations. This is where I first saw an Alkalinian. This is where Admiral Eames rallied the Bounders to fight the Youli. And hopefully, this is where I'll be reunited with my sister.

The chamber floor is packed with humans and Tunnelers, all dressed in brightly colored tunics like Neeka. They're crowded around a projection table. Graphs and charts and pictures rotate in the air above the table.

I scan the room for my sister. She spots me first.

"Jasper!" Addy cuts through the crowd and tackle-hugs me, nearly knocking us both to the ground.

26

I HOLD MY SISTER LIKE SHE'S THE GRAVITY
keeping me on the ground. Now that we're back together, I'm
too afraid to let go. Eventually, Addy untangles herself from
me and cups my cheek with her palm. "I thought I'd never
see you again."

I place my hand on hers. "I thought you were dead. The
Battle of the Alkalinian Seat . . ."

"I know." She hugs me again. "Thank goodness we're both
alive. And thank God you made it here safely."

A hand clamps on my shoulder and gently pulls Addy and
me apart.

"Ace, I thought you'd never show."

I grip Marco's palm and pull him in for a hug. "Good to see you, Marco."

"*So* good, J-Bird. Welcome back from the land of the dead."

"You just can't get rid of me."

Neeka runs over and corrals us all in her furry arms. "Oh! Together again! Happy day!"

When we break apart, another familiar face stands behind Neeka.

"Welcome, Jasper," Jon Waters says. "I'm so glad you chose to join us." He looks the same: tall, wrinkled shirt, tweed blazer.

I expected to feel something more when I saw Waters—anger, I hoped, or intimidation, I feared. Instead, I'm oddly detached, like he doesn't have quite as strong a spell over me as before.

Next to me, Denver clears his throat. "Not all of us had a choice." I was so caught up in my reunion with Addy, I'd forgotten about Denver. His arms are crossed against his chest, and his cold stare makes clear he's not thrilled to see Waters. Two armed Tunnelers stand just behind him.

"Good to see you again, Denver," Water says, extending his palm.

Denver doesn't shake. "I'm not going to say the same. Under the right circumstances, I suppose I might enjoy grabbing a whiskey and talking old times, but those circumstances don't include being kidnapped and shipped across the galaxy in a crate with two kids."

"As I understand it," Waters says, trying to sound friendly while matching Denver's cold stare, "one of those kids—one of *my* students—deserves the credit for you being back in the galaxy in the first place."

Denver clasps my shoulder. "Jasper and I have spent a lot of time together, Jon. I know how he feels about you, and I guarantee you deserve none of the credit for any of his actions."

Okay, so that's out there.

Waters shoots me a glance, then drops his gaze. "Point taken. Now, if you'll excuse me, I need to return to the briefing. They'll see you both to your quarters, where you can rest and change. We'll talk more later." He nods at the two Tunneler guards behind Denver and heads back to the group.

"Mr. Waters," I call after him. I might as well get to the point of why I came halfway across the galaxy, other than seeing my sister, of course: the Youli's message.

He turns around.

"I need to speak with you."

"I'll find you after the briefing, Jasper." He turns to my sister. "Addy, Marco, you're needed over here."

Addy holds tight to my hand. "I haven't seen my brother in almost a year."

Waters stares down my sister. She doesn't budge.

"Fine, you have an hour, but then I need you back."

"Thanks," Addy says, already dragging me to the door. "Oh, and Marco's coming with us."

Marco runs ahead, not waiting for Waters's response.

Soon we're in the hall, beyond earshot of the guards, and it's just me, my sister, and one of my best friends in the whole galaxy. It feels like every millimeter of my body exhales.

"I'm exhausted," I say. "And starving. Is the food any better here?"

Marco laughs. "There's a BERF bar with your name on it just waiting for you in the cantina."

My face falls. "And I'm betting some tasty green forage, too?"

"Don't worry," Addy says. "I have a secret stash of decent snacks. Let's go!"

When we cut down the hall that takes us to the old Earth Force wing, Addy stops. "The fruit balls are in my room. Head to the Nest, and I'll meet you there in a few." She jogs ahead and hangs a left at the next hallway.

Marco and I keep going until we reach a familiar door. He pulls an old-fashioned key from his pocket.

"Since when are the baths locked?" I ask.

"Gotta keep our private hideout private," he says.

"I thought the scrambler was turned off."

"It is. Only Bounders are allowed in. In fact, I rarely use this key. We usually just bound, but I thought I'd treat you to a formal entrance."

"How very kind and un-Marco-like of you."

"I've grown up while you've been gone, Ace. Don't worry, nothing too dramatic, but I can act my age occasionally. Your sister has been a good influence."

I follow him into the baths. The entry looks just like we left it. Puffy stools line the walls, and a desk is on the back wall. That's where the two old Tunnelers sat when they brought us here from the trash tunnel. No wonder they hated us. We stunk!

We cut through the empty shower stalls to the back room—a.k.a. the Nest. The place looks even more homey than I remembered. There are papers scattered around with drawings labeled in my sister's handwriting. There's also a blanket, some pillows, and an overflowing waste bin filled with protein bar and fruit ball wrappers.

I sit down on the bench and kick up my feet. "Speaking of my sister . . ." I leave the words dangling, hoping he'll fill in the blank.

"Yeah, umm, about that . . ." He doesn't finish his sentence, either, but he doesn't need to. He fiddles with a string on his sleeve.

"It's cool." It's not like I didn't assume Marco was Addy's

boyfriend. Their connection was growing back in Alkalinia, and that was close to a year ago.

"Addy and I have been through a lot together, Ace."

I nod, and for a while, we don't say anything more. I lie back and hang my arm off the bench, dragging my fingers through the thick carpet made of mold. The last time I was in the Nest, the whole pod was together.

"You see Lucy and Cole?" Marco asks. He must have been thinking the same thing.

"They've changed."

Marco snorts. "Understatement."

"Cole is this military strategy genius, which I guess was kind of predictable."

"If you say so. He did have mad skills at *Evolution of Combat*."

"Remember that time we synced up and charged Normandy?"

"Epic."

I close my eyes and try to go back to a simpler time when my ranking at *Evolution* was an important focus of my life. It doesn't work. "I spent a lot of time with Lucy."

Marco groans. "It's impossible to watch the webs for more than two minutes without seeing her huge eyes staring back at you."

"She was pretty annoyed with you and Addy the last time we were all together."

Silence filled with things unsaid hangs in the air between us.

"What happened?" I finally ask. I've been wanting to know since I escaped the rift, and for the first time, I might actually get an answer.

Marco shrugs. "It's hard to explain."

"I traveled across the galaxy in a box with Regis to get here, Marco. The least you can do is tell me what I missed while I was trapped in the rift."

Marco laughs. "You make a fair point, Ace." He sits up on one of the mushroom-shaped stools and crosses his legs. He looks eerily like Waters.

"Alkalinia sucked," he says. "After the shield blew, it was a free-for-all. Addy and I were running through the lower levels of the Seat, dodging Alks as they tore about on their scooters. We finally made it up to the siphon bay. It was outright war. Earth Force and Youli were ripping each other apart. We didn't stick around for long because we needed to get to the other Bounders.

"Once we made it to the quarters hall, we were blocked. Steve and a bunch of his throne-riding Alk groupies were holding their position. Steve was hissing orders. Not much of it went through the translators, but one of the Alks had his on, and I'm pretty sure he was telling them to kill all the Bounders.

"We knew we had to do something fast. Addy and I had

our gloves out, but they were useless with the scrambler on. The other Bounders were no help. The ones who were awake were so groggy from the venom they could barely stand. Some of the Alks had those yellow vials. I think they were going to overdose our friends. If it hadn't been for Cole and Lucy, they probably would have."

It's weird to hear what happened to my friends while Mira and I were trapped in the rift. If I hadn't gotten that shield down, they'd be dead. "What did Cole and Lucy do?"

"During the chaos, Cole hacked the system and deactivated the scrambler. They came at the Alks from behind. I'm sure it was Cole's mastermind plan, but Lucy was able to wrangle the other Bounders into our quarters while Cole used his gloves to immobilize the Alks who were fighting off Addy and me from the other side. Once the Bounders were safely in, Cole retreated and sealed the doors."

"How?"

Marco shrugs. "Cole figured out some tech thing. Anyway, they survived the battle, which is a lot more than I can say about a lot of the Earth Force soldiers who fought that day. Eventually the Youli retreated, and a handful of Alks got off the planet on their vessel."

"I know. We ran into Steve at the space port."

"Seriously? What happened?"

"I'll tell you later. Go on with the story."

Marco explained how Cole was hailed as a military hero for saving the Bounders and quickly moved up the ranks. Lucy used her recognition to talk her way into a press position and rose from there.

"What about you and Addy? It sounds like the two of you deserved some credit."

"Yeah, well, Addy—"

As if on cue, my sister bounds into the room. Literally bounds.

"I'm back!" she says, flopping cross-legged to the floor.

"You've been practicing with the gloves," I say.

She winks. "It's been a while since you saw me, J. I'm a bounding expert now. What did I miss?" She tosses me a pack of strawberry fruit balls.

"Actually, I was telling J-Bird what *he* missed when he was trapped in the rift."

"About that . . . ," Addy says, ripping open her own pack of fruit balls. "Time moves differently in the rift, huh?"

I nod. "It was like I was only gone for a couple of hours. The lost aeronauts were only there for two days."

"So, let me get this straight," she says, "you lived for a few hours in the rift while I lived for almost a year in the real world, right?"

I shrug. "I guess."

Addy hops up. "That makes me older than you!"

Umm . . . no. I shake my head and stare down my sister. "It does not."

"Oh yes, it does! And don't forget it!" She twirls around the room chanting, "I'm your big sister! I'm your big sister!"

She eventually sits down beside me on the bench and nudges me with her shoulder. "Seriously, though, what happened in the rift? Where's Mira? All we've heard are rumors."

I tell them about the Youli, their message, and Mira's departure. A thick lump forms in my throat while I talk. Sharing it with my sister makes the wound feel fresh.

"The Youli and their peace talk," Marco says, "that's old news. Isn't that what that guy said to you on top of his spaceship on the Paleo Planet? And then again when we planted the degradation patch on their systems during the intragalactic summit?"

"This was different."

"How?" Addy asks.

"I don't know how to explain it. It *felt* different."

Addy places her hand on my shoulder. "Maybe it just felt different because Mira went with them."

"No, that wasn't it," I say, "and anyway, why are you guys fighting me on this?"

Marco and Addy exchange glances.

"We're not fighting you, Ace. It's just . . . peace can be dangerous. For us."

That makes zero sense. "Peace is the opposite of dangerous."

"Maybe for most," Addy says. "But what about the Bounders? Someone has to look out for our interests."

"We were born to be soldiers," Marco says. "We were bred for war, not peace. If there's peace, there are no more Bounders."

I laugh. "Come on. It's not like they're going to kill us off."

"In a way, I think they will, Jasper," my sister says, "unless the Bounders have a voice at the table." I'm sure she can tell by my face that I don't understand.

"If there's no more need for Bounders," she explains, "no more *military* need, there's no more need for the Bounder Baby Breeding Program, at least how things are currently constructed on Earth."

"I'm still not sure I understand."

"It's like this, J-Bird. Addy and I and the other Bounders in the Resistance, we've had almost a year to reflect on the Battle of the Alkalinian Seat. Yes, we want peace, but we want a say in what that peace looks like. Earth needs to change. We need a planet—a civilization—that has room for all types of people, one where Bounders are welcome and born not because of military need but because it's right." He offers his hand to Addy. They stand together, staring down at me. "If this war has taught us one thing, it's that in our differences lie our strengths."

"And while we're open to talking about our planet's entry into the Intragalactic Council," Addy says, "it can't be on just the Youli's terms. The Resistance needs a voice. The Bounders need a voice."

As I stare at my sister, I'm struck again by how much time I lost in the rift. Addy has always been willful and strong, but the person I'm looking at isn't my kid sister. She's a leader, a warrior.

"Will you fight with us, Jasper?" she asks. "Will you join the Resistance?"

They're both looking at me, waiting for my answer. It would be so easy to say yes, to let Addy and Marco take over, to follow their direction and fight alongside Waters again. The truth is, I do think they stand on the right side of the conflict, even if Waters doesn't always do the right thing. Since my first tour of duty when I learned the depth of Earth Force's deception, I've known in my gut that what the Force is doing is wrong. Plus, there's no one in the galaxy I trust more than Addy and Marco.

The problem is, when I really think about it, I trust Cole and Lucy, too. What Cole showed me about the Youli was really troubling, even with Gedney's explanation about the Youli division. Cole's 100 percent on board with Earth Force, and he has the best strategic instincts of anyone I know. Then there's Lucy. She may be annoying sometimes, but there's no

MONICA TESLER

one who has a bigger heart, who cares more about her friends. I know she thinks she's doing the right thing.

Could there be a middle ground? Is there a road to peace that brings everyone together? That unites Earth Force and the Resistance?

"I have to talk to Waters first," I tell them. I need to speak to him directly about the Youli's message and his intentions.

The air next to Addy shimmers. Half a second later, Regis appears.

I recoil. Maybe I was starting to tolerate Regis, but that definitely doesn't mean I was ready to invite him to the Nest. Unfortunately, it seems someone already issued an invitation.

"What's up?" Marco asks him.

"Waters asked me to get you guys," Regis says. "He needs all the captains in the Parliamentary Chamber, stat."

"*Captains,*" I say. "So the Bounders in the Resistance were promoted just like in Earth Force."

"It's nothing like Earth Force, J. Just wait and see." He turns to Addy. "We should go."

"In a sec," she says. "You go ahead."

Marco shrugs, then bounds away with Regis.

Addy sits on the floor and pats the ground beside her. I slide off the bench and plop down next to my sister.

She wraps me up in a giant hug. "I can't believe you're really here, J. I spent so many nights lying on this rug, trying to imagine you somewhere in the galaxy, alive. Everyone kept saying there was no way you survived, but I wouldn't accept it. I *couldn't* accept it. A world without you just wasn't something I could get my head around."

"When I got to the rift," I say, "all I could think about was watching the venom tube rip open into the deadly waters with you and Marco inside it. I could actually picture your sinking corpse."

"That's gruesome." Addy starts laughing. "Everything about Alkalinia was gruesome. It was so horrible it's actually funny."

I'm laughing, too. "Do you remember how freaked Marco was when he met Serena's babies?"

Addy falls back on the carpet. "So freaked! I mean, who wouldn't be freaked wading across a futbol field filled with tiny, venomous snakes?"

"Welcome to the EarthBound Academy!" I say, lying down beside her. "Was it all you thought it would be?"

"And more!" She giggles. "I nearly died along with all my new Bounder friends, and my brother was lost in a timeless rift! It's awesome!"

Our laughs fade, and the memories recede, and I'm left again with the reality of my post-rift life. "Marco was telling me what happened while I was stuck in the rift. You showed up before he got to the part where you and he joined the Resistance."

"They had a funeral for you, Jasper," Addy says quietly. "It was the worst day of my life. Tons of people spoke, including Admiral Eames. While she talked, a giant screen rose up behind her with a picture of you and the words PROTECTING OUR PLANET COMES AT A PRICE scrawled in cursive letters across your face. That very day, Earth Force posted the picture on the webs and distributed posters across the planet. Your death became their propaganda campaign."

Jasper Adams: poster boy. The way Lucy tells it, everything about the campaign was a huge success. As with most things, though, there's another side.

"I was so appalled," she continues, "I never reported back to duty. Neither did Marco. Neither did a lot of the Bounders."

So that's how so many Bounders ended up with the Resistance. In some weird way, it's because of me. "Is that why things got so bad with my pod? Because Cole and Lucy supported the propaganda campaign?"

"No, that wasn't it. . . ." She props up on one elbow and looks down at me. "Don't you see? Your pod was already growing apart back on Alkalinia. And then you were gone. You were the only thing holding the pod together, Jasper."

"I don't believe that. It can't be that simple."

"Sometimes it is. Bonds break."

Mira's words from the rift come back to me. *You're the glue, Jasper.*

Addy sits up and crosses her legs on the rug. She reaches over and squeezes my hand. "Friends come and go, J. But family is forever."

A sad smile lifts my lips. I'm so relieved to be back with Addy. She's not only family, she's one of my dearest friends. Wait . . . family . . . our parents.

I push myself up. "I saw Mom and Dad."

Addy raises her hands to her face. "Really? How are they?"

"They're worried about you, Addy. They thought you were dead, too, you know."

"Did you tell them I'm alive?"

"I hinted at it."

"Good. I know we're supposed to be all secretive in the Resistance, but I hate keeping them in the dark."

"There's something else, Ads." I scoot my back against the bench. "Mom was injured in the Resistance attack."

Alarm crosses Addy's face. "No! Everything went wrong! It was supposed to be nonviolent. We think someone must have tipped off Earth Force. Tell me she's okay, Jasper!"

"Gedney's sources said she was released from the hospital. But I'm not going to lie, she was badly hurt." I can see Mom's face, staring up at me through blood and tears. "She pushed me to search for you, Addy."

She blinks back tears. "None of that was supposed to happen. It's all our fault."

Silence stretches between us. In many ways, it *is* the Resistance's fault. They may have the ultimate goal of peace, but they're willing to cross a lot of lines to get there. I wish I could tell Addy that everything will be fine, but we'd both know it wasn't the truth.

"It's hard to predict what might happen when you're at war," I finally say, "even when you have the best intentions. I believe in the Youli's message, Addy. Peace is the answer."

She smooths her bounding gloves and rises to her feet. "I don't disagree with you, J, but we need to fight for the kind of peace that protects everyone."

ADDY WALKS ME TO THE BOUNDER BURROW
before heading to the Parliamentary Chamber. She suggested
we bound there, but I insisted on taking the long way around.
I wanted a few more minutes with my sister.

The Burrow—the old Bounders dormitory—is cavernous
and empty. The silver glow of the occludium-powered lights
casts a glare on the glossy walls. I run my fingers along the
shellacked mud. I can almost hear Lucy and Neeka talking
about clear nail polish. I wonder if Neeka misses Lucy. The
old Lucy.

I walk all the way to the last bunk, the one Marco, Cole,
and I shared with Regis and his pod mates during our tour

of duty. It's empty. The beds are stripped, and there's no sign that anyone has stayed here in a long time. It's probably been empty since we left.

There were stacks of bedrolls by the front of the Burrow, but I'm too tired to go all the way back. Plus, everything aches. My body is screaming at me for spending a whole day curled up in a dark box.

I climb up to the top bunk, the one that used to be mine, the one that Regis tossed the creepy crawlies in during our tour. I close my eyes, expecting to fall asleep instantly, but I can't. Instead, I think about what Addy and Marco said about the Bounders, which makes me worry about the talk I need to have with Waters, which reminds me of the Youli's visit to the rift. And Mira.

Why did you leave with the Youli, Mira?

Do you miss me as much as I miss you?

Will I ever see you again?

I must eventually doze off, because the next thing I know, someone is barking in my ear.

I shoot up in bed and almost fall out of the bunk.

"Didn't think I'd see you again," the monotone voice box translates.

I get a look at the source of the bark: an old Tunneler with a scar across his furry face.

"You scared me half to death, Barrick. Don't do that again!"

"It's good for you. Keeps the reflexes sharp. Let's go." He makes some growly noises that don't translate and starts walking toward the exit.

"What do you mean? Go where?" I grab my blast pack and follow him across the Burrow.

"I said, let's go. Waters is waiting," he calls over his shoulder.

"Why didn't he come himself?" I ask once I catch up with Barrick.

"He's very busy."

"Sure."

"I'm sure he's busier than you," he barks. "I just found you asleep."

He has a point. "Why are you still using that old beta-version voice box?"

"Why are you still asking annoying questions?"

Barrick is as grumpy as ever. He saved my life, so he's not all bad, but he's not the best for friendly strolls through Gulagaven. When he had to escort Mira and me back here from the Wacky base, you'd think he was forced to eat an entire plate of those creepy crawlies (although who knows, maybe Barrick likes those things). He couldn't ditch us fast enough.

I follow Barrick through the halls and into another open

chasm. He keeps walking right onto one of the narrow bridges with no guard rails.

I freeze. There's no way I'm crossing that bridge. Mira and I nearly plunged to our deaths off one of those the last time I was here, thanks to Regis. I unzip my blast pack and dig for my gloves.

Barrick stops and turns around on the middle of the bridge. My stomach quakes just looking at him out there.

"What are you doing?" he asks.

"Give me a minute." I shake out my gloves and slip them on my fingers.

"Not in here!" he shouts.

"The scrambler is off."

"Don't care. Don't like those darn things."

I can't bound because he doesn't like my gloves? Tough luck.

I tap in, build a port, and bound, beating Barrick to the other side of the bridge.

He growls at me. I don't need the voice box to tell me he's mad.

"What is wrong with you?" the translation confirms. "I told you not to do that!"

I stand strong. "I don't follow orders from you, Barrick! And let me give you a preview of my meeting with Waters: I don't follow orders from him, either!"

Barrick passes me and heads down the hall. "We'll see about that," he barks over his shoulder.

I follow a few paces behind him. The ceiling gets lower with each step. Soon I'm more hunched over than Gedney on a bad day. I have a horrible sense of direction, but if I had to guess, I'd say we're near the bar where we first met Barrick.

He stops in front of a door guarded by a very large, very well-armed Tunneler. He has at least three guns strapped to his furry body.

Barrick nods at the guard, and he steps aside. I follow Barrick into a wide alcove. At the far end of the room is a long, stone table with a desk chair behind it. A few cushy stools are arranged in front. Maps and diagrams are tacked up all over the walls, and stacks of paper and tech crowd the floor around the table.

Waters is standing in the center of the room, spinning a projection of a galaxy sector. When we enter, he snaps his fingers, and the projection vanishes.

"Ah! Jasper! Come in. Have a seat. The stools look funny, I know, but they're actually quite comfortable. Feel free to take your shoes off. The carpet is incredibly soft. Believe it or not, it's made from—"

"Mold," I interrupt. "I've been here before, remember?"

Waters narrows his eyes and nods. "Yes, of course I do. Please sit." He sinks down on one of the mushroom stools. Barrick leans against the doorframe and crosses his arms.

MONICA TESLER

"I'd like to talk with you alone," I say.

Waters looks at Barrick, who shakes his head.

"Whatever you have to say, you can say in front of Barrick."

"Are you, like, co-leaders or something?"

"We're not co-anything," Barrick says. "You got your meeting. Talk."

I sit on a mushroom and clasp my hands. I don't like this dynamic. I don't like that Barrick isn't sitting. I don't like that I feel like this is two against one, especially since I'd hoped to leave the room feeling like we were on the same page, united.

"Before you start, Jasper," Waters says, "I need to know more about Mira."

At the mention of her name, my heart jumps. "Have you heard something?"

"Only that she's with the Youli."

"Is she okay?"

Waters shakes his head. "I have no idea. I hoped you would shed some light on what happened."

Something inside of me falls, like a piece of glass crashing and shattering into a million tiny pieces. For a moment, I had dared to hope that Waters might have news about Mira. But he doesn't know anything more than I do. In fact, I'm probably his source, indirectly. I told Jayne, who probably told her handler in the Resistance, who probably told Waters.

Or maybe Gedney just called him up and told him the whole story since they're buds again now.

I push aside my emotions and try to hold a neutral expression while I talk to Waters. "I'm sure you heard we were trapped in the rift after the Battle of the Alkalinian Seat."

He nods me on.

I recount how we found the lost aeronauts and learned that time moved differently in the rift. Then I explain how the Youli arrived and offered us a deal. They'd help us escape the rift if we delivered a message. Of course, the "we" was really "me," because Mira didn't come back.

"What's the message?" Barrick asks.

I keep my eyes on Waters.

He taps his foot. "Go ahead, Jasper. Give us the message."

"Peace," I say. "The Youli want us to work toward peace together and discuss Earth's admission to the Intragalactic Council."

Waters steeples his fingers and raises them to his chin. I hold my breath. So much depends on his reaction.

Just when I start to think he's with me, he presses against his thighs and stands. "That message wasn't for me."

I look down at the moldy rug. I need to keep this going in the right direction. I need Waters to agree to work toward peace, and that starts with a peaceful resolution to his conflict with Earth Force. "They didn't specify who it was for."

"Jasper," Waters starts, pacing the alcove as he talks, "we're fighting on the same side as the Youli. I've been fighting on their side for years. We want to stop Earth Force from exploiting early developing planets. We want Earth to be invited to join the Intragalactic Council. As long as we have a meaningful voice on the Council, our interests are aligned with the Youli. We want peace. You are preaching to the converted with your so-called message."

This is not going the way I hoped, but I'm not going to let him run me over with his teacher tone. "You may support the Youli's agenda, Mr. Waters, but you're not practicing peace. The Resistance is openly fighting Earth Force now. You smoke-bombed a rally, and people got hurt, my mom included! And you kidnapped Denver Reddy and shipped him across the galaxy against his will!"

Waters doesn't respond to what I said. Instead he sits back down and leans close. "You talked to Admiral Eames first, didn't you? What did she say?"

Why does he have to be so good at reading the situation?

"She's not interested in peace."

"No, she's not," Barrick says. "She's interested in occludium. We have it, and they want it."

"Don't you think that oversimplifies things?" I ask.

"Usually the obvious answer is the right one," Waters says.

The anger I thought would come when I first saw Waters

starts to simmer beneath my skin. "Who are *you* to talk about what's right?" I say, my voice growing louder with each word. "You can't keep defending your actions that way! The ends do not always justify the means!"

"Let's keep the focus on the topic at hand, Jasper."

"No! I'm done doing what you say. I know the truth now, Mr. Waters. I know what really happened at the Incident at Bounding Base 51. You kidnapped a Youli so that you could conduct experiments on him. That's what caused the Incident. It's *your* fault Denver and the other aeronauts were lost in the rift all those years!"

Waters crosses his legs and tries his best to look unruffled. "I can see Denver has been telling stories. Yes, a Youli was taken prisoner that day, but I didn't order that."

I push to my feet. "But you admit you experimented on him!"

"Gedney and I were scientists instructed by Earth Force to research an alien life-form. Not only did we have no real choice in the matter, it was also a tremendous opportunity for the human race."

"And then you started the Bounder Baby Breeding Program! It was *you* who decided to breed kid soldiers!"

"No!" Waters jumps up. "That is not how it happened! I established a relationship with the Youli. Through him and his collective mind link, I was able to learn that Earth had essentially doomed its development by weeding out certain genes from the population. I argued to reintroduce those genes for the future of our species."

"And you needed a rationale. . . ." Standing up, I see I'm not that much shorter than Waters now.

"Yes, I emphasized the potential military benefit, but it was necessary."

"Again, the end justifies the means."

"What would you have me say, Jasper? That I'd rather the Bounders not be born? That I'd rather *you* not be born?"

I ignore his questions, even though he's baiting me with the same issue Marco and Addy explained in the Nest. Is he the one who planted that seed in their minds? "What about the other Youli prisoner? The one at the space station during our first tour of duty?"

"That wasn't my doing."

"You didn't know about him? Come on!"

"Of course I knew about him, but it wasn't my idea to take him. It ended up being a stroke of luck, though. I was able to communicate with the Youli through him and further our peace talks. You put a real roadblock in those talks with that stunt you pulled at the Wacky outpost."

I throw up my hands. This has gone far enough. "Nice, Mr. Waters! Blame it all on the kid! Way to turn the tables. I'm going to find my sister." I head for the door. Barrick blocks my exit.

"Before you go, Jasper," Waters says calmly, "let's bring things back to the Youli message."

I turn around.

Waters waits until he's sure he has my full attention. "If you're interested in peace, like the Youli, like me, then know that Earth Force is on the wrong side of that line." He snaps his fingers, and the projection reappears in the center of the room showing an image of the space station that housed the EarthBound Academy during my first tour of duty. "Thirty Earth Force gunner ships have just left that space station. Our intelligence indicates they're headed for Gulaga."

"What?"

"See for yourself." Waters flicks his fingers, and the image zooms out, showing a larger galactic snapshot of the space station. He points to a cluster of pinpricks of light moving steadily away from the station. If he's telling the truth, that's the Earth Force fleet. "It seems we've forced the admiral's hand. Eames is launching a full-scale attack. She was embarrassed in front of the whole world when we nabbed you and Denver. She couldn't let that stand."

"You planned this?" A wave of nausea curls from my belly up my throat. Denver said Eames couldn't let his kidnapping go unanswered.

"It's not possible to plan your enemy's behavior," Waters says, "but I'm awfully good at predicting it."

"Why did you provoke her like this?"

"I'm not interested in peace with Earth Force, Jasper, not in the short term. I've tried that route. Now I'm convinced that the only way to achieve long-term peace is to rid the galaxy of the Force once and for all. We need a new government in place to usher in our future as full members of the Intragalactic Council."

"With you at the helm?"

"If necessary, for a time, but that's not my goal. There are plenty of young leaders who share my ideals and who would do incredible things for our planet and the greater galaxy. Your sister, for one, Jasper." He smiles. "Maybe even you."

If what he's saying is true, Gulaga will be under attack in a matter of hours. "So, what exactly are you planning to do?"

"You'll see."

28

THE CHAMBER FLOOR IS PACKED WITH
Tunnelers and Earthlings. Almost every carrel climbing the
walls is filled. The room hums with excitement. It's a totally
different kind of energy from when I stood here as Admiral
Eames rallied Earth Force for Operation *Vermis*. Then, it was
rage, entitlement. We had a common enemy: the Youli. Now
everyone in this room has a common cause. Unity. Indepen-
dence. Ultimately, peace—and they're willing to do whatever
it takes to get there.

Waters stands at the podium. He stands for Gulagan freedom, Bounders' rights, the greater galactic community. He
stands for things I believe in.

Then why is it so hard for me to join him? Especially when joining him means joining Addy and Marco?

"Listen up!" Water says. "Our intelligence indicates that Earth Force will move into position and commence an aerial assault within the next hour. In addition, we must assume they have bounding ships positioned to enter our airspace at a moment's notice. Yes, we have the occludium shield in place, but don't forget that the shield doesn't prevent Earth Force landing on the surface in regular spacecraft."

A smaller group of Tunnelers and Earthlings stands with Waters on the front stage. I'm guessing they're the captains. Many of them I recognize: Addy, Marco, Neeka, Grok (another one of the junior ambassadors during our tour of duty), Minjae (one of the juniors in Addy's pod), even Regis.

Barrick stands next to Waters. "What's the update on fortifications?" he barks. From the way he asks, it's clear he's one of the leaders, outranking probably everyone but Waters.

Grok steps forward. "We reinforced the standard force field around Gulagaven yesterday to prepare for the attack. It should hold."

"For how long?" Marco asks. "Earth Force has far superior artillery. We're outgunned."

"It shouldn't come to that," Waters says. "All we want to do is bait them for a fight."

"Are you sure it's going to work after what happened at

the Lost Heroes Homecoming Tour rally?" Addy asks. "There were injuries, casualties. Admiral Eames has even more at stake." What she doesn't say is that our mother was one of those injured in the Resistance attack.

"She won't risk it," Waters says, "not with the world watching. And after what happened at the rally, you know they'll be watching."

Denver elbows me. "Any idea what the grand plan is, kid?" We're hiding out in one of the carrels on the first level, although we're not really hiding since Denver can't go anywhere without two Tunneler guards on his heels.

I shake my head. "No clue."

"Your friend is right," he whispers. "The Resistance is outgunned. I don't see how your old pod leader can eke out a victory here."

"Still," Waters continues from the podium, "we'll prepare our defensive as a precaution. You all know your roles. Everyone except captains is dismissed to their ready positions. It's a go, friends." Waters pumps his fist, then inclines his head. "Brothers, sisters, I bow to your service and fortitude."

The crowd bows and calls back, "And we also bow to you, brother."

It's the same exchange Neeka had with the chamber guards when we first arrived. I wonder if it's a traditional Tunneler custom.

Waters raises his arms and shouts, "May your days be peaceful and productive, and may your nights provide shelter from the cold."

The crowd cheers and floods out of the carrels, most of them headed for the exit. We join the masses, but before we reach the doors, Denver's guards block our path. They're not wearing voice boxes, but the one on the right raises a paw toward the stage, where Waters, Barrick, and the captains are continuing with the briefing.

"Moment of truth, kid," Denver says. "Something tells me we're about to find out why they shipped me across the galaxy."

"Then why do they need *me*?"

"If you don't think you're part of his grand plan by now, you don't know Jon Waters as well as you think."

Denver marches straight up to Waters. I join Addy and Marco and the other captains. I already know Waters was hoping I'd join the Resistance. He'll take as many Bounders as he can get. After all, another Bounder in the Resistance is one less in Earth Force. But could Denver be right? Could he want me for something more than that? Do I play a part in his grand plan?

Waters and Barrick hear reports from all the captains about armed crafts, artillery, defense, tunnel security—the list goes on and on without any mention of Denver or me. Finally

Waters dismisses the majority of his captains to their posts. All pilots, including Neeka, are instructed to board their crafts and wait for the launch signal.

Soon, the only ones left in the chamber are me, Denver, Addy, Marco, Regis, Barrick, and a handful of other officers, most of whom are strapped with guns. I'm guessing they're here to enforce whatever Waters is about to say.

Once the doors close behind the departing captains, Waters clasps his hands. "I'm sure all of you have had a chance to meet our guests, Denver Reddy and Jasper Adams. I trust your—"

"Get on with it, Jon," Denver interrupts. "I'm not your guest. I'm your prisoner. What I want to know is why."

Waters purses his lips. "Very well. Earth Force relies heavily on its media campaign to control public opinion and support. Right now, the population of our home planet is carefully waiting to see how Admiral Eames will respond to your . . . disappearance, if you will. As of now, rumors run rampant, but the Force hasn't confirmed that the Resistance is behind what occurred. In fact, we strongly believe that, once again, Earth Force will blame this on the Youli. As you know, the Force hasn't confirmed the existence of the Resistance at all, although reports are all over the webs." Waters pauses, letting his words sink in.

"And?" Denver asks impatiently.

"And that's about to change."

He walks to the center of the stage and activates a projection. This time, we're seeing Gulaga. He flicks his fingers, and the image zooms out until we can see the Earth Force fleet closing in. For several moments, he doesn't speak. He lets us watch the fleet as it gets closer and closer. He lets the gravity of the situation sink in.

"I need you to stop this," he finally says.

"How exactly do you propose we do that?" Denver asks.

"You are two of the most recognizable, popular people on the planet. I need you to tell Earth that you stand with the Resistance, and that the Resistance stands for peace. I need you to convince them that it's time to move beyond Earth Force and usher in a new era as members of the Intragalactic Council. I need you to tell Earth Force to stand down."

He needs *me* to do that? Why did he factor me into this? How did he know for sure I would come? The Resistance kidnapped Denver, but I came by choice.

"How on earth is that even possible?" Denver asks.

"It's all set up. We have a high-level contact in Earth Force public relations. She's arranged for the broadcast to stream globally. Once it's out, the webs will run with it. Earth Force won't be able to shut it down."

"Jayne," I say.

"That's right," Waters says. "Jayne is an extremely valuable asset of the Resistance, as I believe you already know, Jasper."

Waters must have been the one who told Jayne to bring me into the fold. He sent Gedney to see me on the tour. He made the recording of Addy begging me to join them. He knew I would come, and he knew I would be a far more willing participant in his plan if I thought I came by choice. And he knew I could help get Denver on board.

"As for timing," Waters continues, "we'll wait until the Earth Force fleet is within range, perhaps even draw combat. That way, we'll have excellent footage of the Force's savagery to include with the broadcast."

Wait a second. This is moving too fast. I may agree with the Resistance's objectives, but I don't approve of all their methods, including this one. There's way too much that could go wrong.

"You're risking everyone on Gulaga for this?" Denver asks.

"It's a calculated risk. I'm confident Admiral Eames will cave. Once she knows that you're on Gulaga, Denver, she'll call it off. We both know she wouldn't do anything that might result in your death."

Denver throws up his hands. "That's ridiculous. You've never understood how the military works, Jon. Cora is a soldier. She'll prioritize the mission, not her personal feelings. And trust me, her personal feelings are no longer a factor."

"You've been gone a long time, Denver. I understand the military. And I know Cora. Trust *me*."

Denver clenches his jaw and starts to shake. Every muscle in his body is coiled tight, like he's about to spring on Waters. His Tunneler guards take a step closer.

I'm no expert on Admiral Eames, but no matter how she reacts there's a lot that could go wrong. I have a very bad feeling about this. I glance at Addy. She bites her lip and looks away.

Barrick's com link buzzes. He relays the report to Waters. The first Earth Force vessels have been detected on standard satellite. They should be in Gulagan airspace within minutes.

"Excellent," Waters says. "We'll watch the initial engagement. Then we'll broadcast live. Regis, please oversee the setup for filming, load the script into the teleprompter, and confirm Jayne is ready to go."

Regis nods and exits the chamber.

We crowd around the projection, watching as the Earth Force fleet closes in. When they're within striking distance, Waters gives the order to send the Resistance ships out to meet them. Sweat beads on my forehead. I clasp and unclasp my palms, watching for the first sighting of the Gulagan vessels.

"You're sending those heaps of junk out there?" Denver asks. "That's a suicide mission."

"They're trained in evasive tactics," Waters says. "We won't keep it up for long."

"Neeka is piloting one of those?" I ask my sister, remembering the ride in Neeka's craft and how the inside looked like it was held together with duct tape and wire.

"Yes," she says gravely, still not meeting my gaze.

How did it come to this? We're out of options. Earth Force is retaliating for the Resistance's attack at the rally. Their counterattack was predictable. All of this is part of Waters's plan. And our only shot at calling off the fleet is Waters's broadcast.

If it's the only way, we might as well minimize the risk. "Can't we just broadcast now instead of—" I start.

Waters raises his hand. "Timing is everything."

Regis comes back into the chamber with a group of Tunnelers. At the far end of the stage, they set up two chairs and a small recording device on a tripod in front. Now that I see the setup, I realize it must be the same place they filmed Addy's message to me.

Marco elbows me in the ribs and points to the projection. A dozen Tunneler crafts zoom out of the atmosphere in a V formation, preparing to engage the Earth Force fleet. I'm pretty sure Neeka's craft is the leader.

The Tunnelers shoot, then roll out on the sides, circling back to form a perimeter. Earth Force returns fire, but the Tunnelers shuffle position, evading the brunt of the assault. All the while, they rain fire on the Force ships.

"Earth Force isn't taking damage from those hits," I say.

"They're shielded," Marco says. "Our shots are all deflected."

"Well, how do we expect—" My words are cut short when a burst of orange light showers across the projection. One of the Resistance ships was hit. It spirals away from the others. A second round of fire finds its target, and the Tunneler craft explodes.

"No!" I shout.

"Is everything prepared for the broadcast?" Waters asks Regis, his voice low and urgent.

Once Regis confirms, he looks at me and Denver. "Okay. It's time." He crosses the stage in long, swift strides, headed to the area set up for the broadcast.

Denver folds his arms against his chest. "No."

Waters stops. "What did you say?"

"I said no. It doesn't matter what you do, Jon. Torture me, if you want. I'm not doing your broadcast. I am not your pawn. I'm not going to read your words to the people of Earth. I may not agree with Earth Force, but that doesn't mean I agree with you."

Waters waves his arm at the projection. "You see what's happening out there, and I know you're sympathetic to our cause!" He marches over to Denver. "You're not going to stand here and do nothing while countless Tunnelers die. *Again*. You don't have a choice!"

"There's always a choice, Jon. You miscalculated. Threats may work on Eames, but they won't work on me. I have nothing to live for. Life passed me by while I was stuck in the rift."

"You couldn't save the Tunnelers before, Denver, but you can save them today!" Waters shouts. "If you don't, their blood is on your hands!"

"Do you still not get it, Jon?" Denver shouts back. "Their blood is on *your* hands!"

"THEY'RE NOT GOING TO MAKE IT!" I
plead with Denver. "We have to stop this!"

"It's not our job, kid. We didn't start this, and crowning
Jon Waters the winner is not going to end it."

"My friends are going to die!" For all I know, Neeka is
already dead.

"This is war, kid. That's what happens. If you want it to
stop, convince your pod leader to raise a white flag and admit
defeat."

"And . . . what? Keep fighting a war with the Youli that will
ultimately destroy us?" I ask. "Allow Earth Force to decide
the future of our planet? Even *you* know that's a horrible idea!

Please!" When Denver shakes his head, I turn back to Waters. "Mr. Waters, you've got to do something!"

Waters doesn't hear me. He's fixed on the projection. Three more Resistance ships have taken hits. Two have disengaged with engine failure. Meanwhile, the Earth Force ships continue to press without any sign of damage.

A second ship explodes in a crater of light. My breath catches in my throat. When the image clears, half of the Earth Force ships are no longer visible on the projection.

"They've entered the atmosphere," Addy says. "We need to get out there!"

"The Bounders need to stop them on the ground," Marco says. "If they make it through the force field, we're done for!"

My sister and Marco stare at Waters, waiting for their orders.

Waters nods at Barrick.

"Romero, Adams," Barrick barks, "gather the other Bounders, get in position, and await further orders."

Adams . . . not me, my sister. He's sending her into battle. "Let me do the broadcast on my own!" I beg.

"No," Waters says, he takes a deep breath, then softens his voice, probably to sound less threatening, more like a friend explaining a plan, but his expression oozes with desperation as he turns to face me and Denver. "It needs to be both of you on the broadcast, or it won't work. The people of Earth know you both were taken. If you don't appear together, Earth Force will be able to spin the story their way. They'll likely claim you're responsible for the kidnapping, Jasper, that you're working with the Youli."

Denver grabs my arm. "Don't let him manipulate you like this, kid. There has to be another way."

"There is no other way!" Waters shouts at Denver.

"Surrender!" Denver shouts back.

"You know we can't do that!"

Barrick refocuses the projection. At least ten Earth Force vessels are nearly on the ground. He barks into his com link. "The Bounders are ready to engage," he relays to Waters.

"Give the order," Waters says, then turns back to me and Denver. "Are you really going to send Jasper's sister into the line of fire?"

I look at Denver, hands clenched to my chest.

"The Bounders have departed," Barrick reports.

Denver shakes his head. "I'm not doing it, kid. I'm sorry."

"Convince him," Waters says to the armed guards.

The Tunnelers drag Denver across the stage.

"Stop it!" The Tunnelers ignore me. I run after them. "I said stop!"

Denver takes the first two punches standing up, then hits the chamber floor. The Tunnelers kick him in the ribs, flip him, and kick him in the back. I wrap my arms around my waist and rock back and forth. All I can do is watch in horror as they beat him to a pulp.

But it doesn't really matter what they do. They need Denver to cooperate or this won't work. They can't put Denver on a live broadcast with a gun to his head. That would make the Resistance look like the bad guys. It would justify Earth Force's actions.

Another one of Waters's plans backfires, and we're left paying the price.

Barrick's bark calls me back to the moment. "The Bounders are taking fire."

I spin back to the projection, expecting to see bounding ships engaging the Earth Force gunners on the ground. Instead, my jaw drops as I process what I'm witnessing on the projection. Addy, Marco, and the other Bounders don't have ships. They're out there on foot, engaging Earth Force on the frozen Gulagan tundra, fighting with their gloved hands.

"Are you insane?" I scream at Waters. "They're going to get killed!"

"Bounders are a priceless commodity," he replies. "I doubt Earth Force will fire on them."

"You *doubt* it?" I shout. "I'm done gambling on your guesses, Mr. Waters!"

I pace back and forth in front of the projection. Every second wasted is a second closer to Addy's inevitable death. I can't believe I came all the way to Gulaga only to watch my sister be slaughtered.

"Do something!" I scream.

No one responds. Waters and Barrick urge on their guards trying to beat sense into Denver.

Regis grabs my arm and bends close. "Let's go."

"Where?"

"Where do you think?" He nods at the projection. "They need us out there."

He wants to fight with Addy, Marco, and the other Bounders? I glance back at Waters and Denver—that's hopeless. Regis is right. My best bet is to join the fight. I nod.

Regis takes off running. Once we pass through the doors of the chamber, he loosens the control straps on his blast pack and lifts off. I'm right behind him.

We weave through the narrow tunnels of Gulagaven, slowly making our way to the surface. Regis is flying because of me. He could just as easily bound to the force field—after all, the scramblers are off—but I don't know the way.

I push myself faster and suddenly my brain seizes on a memory. I'm racing Regis in the hangar during our first tour of duty. More than anything I wanted to humiliate him. My hatred fueled me.

Now, as I race to help my sister and friends, I'm fueled by determination. If anything, Regis and I have a common enemy. And maybe, as much as I don't want to admit it, maybe Regis isn't the enemy anymore.

He touches down and darts forward. He hurries us through a door into a small outfitter and tosses me a bundle of outerwear. I shove my arms and legs into the suit, don the helmet, and force my feet into boots. Regis is ready by the time I'm dressed.

"Right through these doors!" He activates the sliders, and we pour into the first exit chamber. The door slides closed behind us. One more door and we're in the battle.

"Hey," I say to Regis. "Thanks."

He looks at me and nods. "The Bounders will be the ones who end this."

He lowers his visor and seals his helmet. The door slides back, the frigid air rushes in, and Regis and I take off across the Gulagan tundra.

Up ahead, the Earth Force gunner ships close in. The Bounders hold them back with their gloves. Regis breaks left, but I bolt straight ahead toward the point where I spotted Addy on the screen.

My mind is a jumble. I'm clenched in fury over Waters's failed threats and riddled with fear that my sister and friends are going to get killed. Plus, I probably know some of the soldiers in the Earth Force vessels. They might be Bounders. For all I know, Ryan or Meggi or even Cole might be right here on the tundra. I don't want them to die either. There must be another way to force Admiral Eames to call off the attack. If I could only clear my head enough to think.

The thing is . . . Waters isn't wrong. Threats *will* work on Admiral Eames—the threat of exposing her propaganda campaign and the threat that Denver's life is at stake.

What if all we needed to do was lay down the threats?

We don't actually need to broadcast, we just need to *threaten* to broadcast.

What comes after the threats is what's important. And if I can get Waters and Denver to buy into the next steps, we might be able to stop this.

Voices swirl in my head.

Regis's words from moments ago: *The Bounders will be the ones who end this.*

Addy's words from the Nest: *The Bounders need a voice.*

Mira's words from the rift: *You're the glue, Jasper. It has to be you. It's always been you.*

I skid to a halt.

This needs to stop.

And *I* need to be the one to end it. I *want* to be the one to end it.

I'm one of the most popular people on Earth right now. I thought that no longer meant much to me, but the truth is, it does. It does because it might help me end this and finally achieve peace for our planet.

I spot Addy up ahead. I lock in visual contact and bound to her side.

"What are you doing out here?" she screams. Her arms are raised. She's trying to block the fighter guns of the nearest Earth Force ship. I raise my gloved hands and help. Slowly we're able to turn the metal so that the gun is pointed in upon the ship.

"Listen, I have a plan. I think I can convince Waters, but it will take a few minutes. Bound back with me."

Addy targets the second gun on the ship. "No way. We're outnumbered, J. Without my help, we're doomed, if we're not already."

I scan the line of Bounders. There are far too few. No matter how powerful we are with the gloves, they stand no chance against this artillery, especially when the other Earth Force ships land. The best they can do is buy us time.

Which means I need to hurry.

I nod at Addy. "I'll be as quick as I can."

Pulling up a mental image of the Parliamentary Chamber, I build my port and bound, landing half a meter away from Denver.

"Where were you, kid?" he asks with a strained voice. The guards have kept his face free of bruises, but his insides are a different story.

I unseal my helmet and throw it on the chamber floor. "I have an idea. Please listen."

356   MONICA TESLER

Denver locks eyes with me. At first, I don't think he'll agree. Then he dips his chin in a small nod.

I jump to my feet and run to the projection, where Waters stands with Barrick. "There's another way!"

Waters spins. "Where were you?"

"There's no time to explain. My idea will save us."

"Unless you can talk sense into Reddy, don't waste my time."

"Hear him out, Jon." Denver pushes to standing, wincing from the beating.

Waters narrows his eyes at me. "Ten seconds."

"You don't have to broadcast live. You just have to threaten to do it. Get Admiral Eames on the line. Tell her what you plan to do. Make her call off the invasion."

Waters's face crinkles and his gaze drops as he processes what I said.

"The most that gets us is a cease-fire," he says.

"For now, that's enough! They're dying out there!"

Denver nods, catching on to my idea. "The kid's right. Start with a cease-fire and move on to diplomacy. Someone needs to negotiate, Jon, and by 'someone,' I do *not* mean you."

"Well, if you think I'm sending you—"

"Send me!" I shout. They all turn to me, one face more incredulous than the next. "Send the Bounders!"

Suddenly the Youli's message resonates in stunning tone.

Their message wasn't for Earth Force. It wasn't for the Resistance, either. It was for me, and I know exactly what needs to be done. "I've spoken to you, Mr. Waters, and I've talked to Admiral Eames. Neither of you is capable of reaching terms. You need fresh voices. Like you said, there are plenty of young leaders who share your ideals, who would do incredible things for the galaxy, who can move Earth toward peace." Regis knew exactly what he was talking about. "The Bounders will be the ones to end this."

"What exactly are you suggesting?" Waters asks.

"Both sides send representatives to a neutral location to negotiate—Cole Thompson and Lucy Dugan for Earth Force, Marco Romero and Adeline Adams for the Resistance." I swallow hard before continuing. ". . . as long as all of them are still alive. I'll facilitate the discussion."

Waters laughs. "Don't be ridiculous. You're just kids."

Denver places his hand on my shoulder. "Maybe so, Jon. But this kid rescued me from the rift, helped lead a publicity campaign across his planet, and talked sense to me in a cramped crate. Not to mention that much of what you're fighting over is technology that only the Bounders are capable of wielding. I'd say our futures lie with these kids."

Waters closes his eyes and rubs his chin.

"They're closing in on the force field!" Barrick barks.

We're out of time.

"Your plan has a major flaw, Jasper," Waters says. "Earth Force will never agree to it."

"That's where you're wrong, Jon," Denver says. "Get me a secure line to Cora. I'll get her on board."

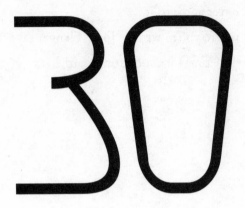

THE SECONDS TICK BY AS WATERS TRIES
to secure a channel to Admiral Eames. On the projection, the
battle intensifies.

Addy and Marco work together. They manage to stop one
of the ships from progressing, but it's clearly draining them.
Minjae and another Bounder arrest a second ship, but the rest
of the gunners continue their advance.

"We need to hurry!" I shout. "What's taking so long?"

"They've nearly breached the force field," Barrick says.

As soon as the words squeak from Barrick's voice box, the closest gunner ship fires at the invisible wall, the only thing separat-
ing Earth Force from Gulagaven and the heart of the Resistance.

One of the Bounders runs to the front to defend the force field, trying to knock away the laser fire with the power of his gloves.

He's too close. He can't hold back that kind of firepower.

I see the moment when his energy gives out. One second, he has control of the laser with his gloves; the next, his arms collapse inward. Then he's lying in a heap on the cold ground, his protective gear burned through and steaming in the cold Gulagan air.

Only now can I clearly see his face.

Regis.

"No!" I slam my fists into the projection and stumble forward, nearly falling to the ground.

"Denver!" Waters shouts. "Get over here now! I've got Cora on the line!"

No matter how quickly Denver manages to convince Admiral Eames, it might not be fast enough to save the Bounders. Every second counts.

I grab my helmet. "I'm bounding out there."

Barrick grumbles and dodges for me. I duck out of the way. "Don't you dare—" his voice box is translating, but I build my port and bound before it finishes.

I land half a meter from Addy. My skin burns. I didn't have time to seal the coat sleeves tight against my gloves. And I don't have time to worry about that now. I aim my gloves at the advancing gunner ship and help my sister hold it off.

"What's happening?" Addy asks with a strained voice. She's tired. The Bounders can't keep this up for long.

"Denver is negotiating with Admiral Eames. We're hoping for a cease-fire."

Please let it work. Please. Everything I've done, all the choices I've made, have led me to this moment. If I'm wrong, I might as well go lie down next to Regis.

Addy turns back to the ship. I feel her command of the atoms slipping. This isn't going to work.

"We need to make them defend from both sides," I say. "That will buy us time."

"But the force field . . ."

"All we need is a few minutes, Ads. If it takes longer than that, we're goners no matter what."

She nods and refocuses her energy at the ship. "Go!"

I bound to the flank, where Marco and Minjae are holding back another gunner.

"Come with me—attack from the rear!" I shout.

Marco gives a thumbs-up and nods at Minjae. The three of us open ports.

I hit the frozen ground behind the middle gunner, the same ship my sister fights from the front. I flash my gloves at its thrusters. The ship jerks back. I grab the straps of my blast pack and shoot up in the air, barely avoiding getting run over. Addy darts to the side to target another ship.

"Good one!" Marco calls, copying my move on the thrusters of another ship. We're disrupting their attack plan and causing confusion. Some of the ships try to turn around; others stop firing. If we can keep up the disruption for a few more minutes, hopefully Eames will stop the advance.

I shift my focus to the ship advancing on Addy. She disarms one of the guns, but the ship still edges forward. Her arms bend inward. She collapses to her knees.

"No!" I grab the ship by its right wing and fling it with all my might. It spins in a circle and comes to rest facing me.

Lasers blast from its remaining gun. I bank right in my blast pack then zoom low to the ground out of firing range. I touch down and turn, raising my palms.

This is it. Give me all you've got.

I brace for the impact of the lasers, hoping my new gloves and my wavering strength are enough to shield myself. Otherwise, I'll end up fried on the ground like Regis.

But the shots don't come.

The ship drops its rocket vents and lifts off. It slowly rises above the frozen ground until it's high enough to shift its engine and blast through the Gulagan atmosphere.

The other Earth Force vessels follow, departing the surface.

Oh my God. It must have worked. Eames must have agreed to a cease-fire.

Soon, all of the Earth Force ships are gone, and only the slim line of Bounders remain.

I run across the tundra and sweep up Addy in a huge hug. Marco collides with us from behind, and we fall to the ground in a giant pig pile.

I'm freezing and crying and so tired I might never get back up.

But we're alive.

We're wonderfully, blissfully, gratefully alive.

For now.

What comes next is up to the Bounders.

It's all set. Denver talked Admiral Eames into a cease-fire, and she agreed to send Lucy and Cole to negotiate, as long as they're allowed to talk with her before reaching an agreement. Waters isn't too happy with the plan, but he's going along with it. After all, what choice does he have (other than to be soundly beaten by Earth Force in a costly battle)?

Funny how it turns out that Waters is the one with no choice, although nothing about today is really funny.

Was it only this morning that I climbed into a crate with Regis? That we battled Alks and chirpers side by side? And now his body lies on the tarmac, frozen, covered in a tarp and awaiting a final trip home to Earth. He'll be traveling in a different kind of box this time.

I won't ever forget the way Regis treated me at the Academy, the way he treated Mira. But I do forgive him. He acknowledged his wrongs, and he did right in the end.

Twenty Tunnelers lost their lives in the space fight. Only two Resistance ships made it home. I feel guilty being happy that Neeka was spared, but I am. She piloted her hunk-of-junk craft to the surface on the other side of Gulaga once her first engine was hit, saving her from the brunt of the battle. A ground crew is crossing the tundra now to bring her home.

Other than Regis, the Bounders all survived, but a lot of them sustained injuries. I'm one of the lucky ones. My only battle scars are the patches of skin on both of my forearms that were exposed to the Gulagan air. They're covered in salve and wrapped in gauze. The painkillers they gave me in the infirmary seem to be working.

I can't afford to dwell on the day's losses. I need to focus on the negotiation. The meet is set to convene at Bounding Base 32, the place our pod went on our first bounding trip. The base is evacuating right now. Addy's never been there, but the Resistance has a BPS, so she can scan the coordinates pre-bound.

Since I'm going to serve as an impartial facilitator, I left Addy and Marco to talk strategy with Waters and Barrick. Denver and I are sitting in the cantina. I didn't even bother getting food. He filled a plate with forage and fungi, and has spent most of the time pushing it around his tray with a spork.

Shortly before I'm supposed to join Addy and Marco in the Parliamentary Chamber, Waters walks into the cantina.

"I need to speak with you privately, Jasper."

Denver raises his eyebrows. He'll stay if I want him to. I shake my head, letting him know I'm okay. He leaves the table and heads to the other side of the cantina, clutching his side as he walks. He's pretty banged up from the Tunneler beating.

Waters pulls back a chair and sits. He waits until Denver is out of earshot, then leans his arms on the table. "We've been contacted by the Youli. We know they monitor most of our communications, and apparently today was no exception."

I nod for him to go on.

"They intercepted the call between Denver and Admiral Eames. The Youli know about the meet, Jasper, and they want to send a representative."

Include the Youli in our negotiations? Eames would never agree to that. Plus, it doesn't fit the spirit of the meet: young leaders taking their planet in a new direction.

"No way," I tell Waters. "My pod knows one another, and they know Addy. They may not all trust one another now, but the seeds of trust are still there. Injecting a Youli into this would erode all that."

Waters pushes Denver's tray away. He sits up straight and looks me in the eye. The silence is heavy, because I know he has more to say.

"It's Mira."

My breath catches in my throat so badly I almost gag. "Mira? How?"

"Easy. She'll bound there, just like you."

"Yes, but how did this come about?" I swallow hard. "And how is she?"

Waters leans back in the chair. "I haven't spoken to her, but I have no reason to suspect she's been harmed. The Youli likely suggested they send Mira because they know it's the only way we'd agree."

"So it wasn't her idea?" This probably has nothing to do with Mira wanting to see me. The Youli are probably making her do this.

"I really don't know any more than what I've already told you, Jasper."

What if she doesn't even want to go? She may not care if she ever sees me again.

I know I should tell Waters that Mira can't come. She'll make me jittery, and it's not like she's going to persuade the others of anything—at least, not with words. On the other hand, Mira's a keen judge of a situation. Maybe having her there will be helpful.

Who am I kidding? Would I ever turn down a chance to see Mira again? Of course not.

"Tell the Youli she can come."

I expect Waters to leave, but he sits there staring at me.

"Can I ask you a question?" he finally asks.

I shrug. The last thing I want is to keep talking to Waters, but I know he's going to ask no matter what I say.

"Do the brain patches actually work?"

After everything that happened today, that's what he wants to know? I can't think of a good reason to lie anymore. "Yeah, they work, although they have a range. It's not like I can talk to her right now."

"Hmmm." Waters runs his hand through his hair. "You know, Jasper, I never wanted things to go the way they did. I messed up. I guess I keep messing up. But I'm trying to do the right thing. People are counting on me."

I shake my head. What is he expecting me to say? "Is that an apology?"

"Not a good one. How's this: I'm sorry."

Too little, too late. His words don't even touch me. I sit back in my chair and cross my arms. "How's this: There's nothing you could say that would make me fully trust you again. You used me. You used my friends."

Waters nods. "That's fair."

Fair? Who cares about fair? I grab the table and lean

forward. "What part of this war is fair, particularly to the Bounders?"

"Look, Jasper," Waters says, pushing away, "I said I was sorry, and I meant it. But let's get one thing straight between us: I don't regret what I'm fighting for."

I lower my voice and narrow my eyes. "Neither do I."

We lock eyes, and I know he's expecting me to turn away first. The Jasper who showed up at the EarthBound Academy for his first tour of duty would have. Not anymore.

Eventually Waters drops his gaze. A tiny part of me feels victorious, but there's too much at stake today to care for long.

"I need to respond to the Youli," he says.

I nod.

He stands and places a hand on my shoulder before leaving the cantina. That used to be comforting. Now it just feels like another weight on my back.

31

"YOU READY?" I ASK ADDY.

"I've used the BPS before," she says. "Stop big-brothering me. I'm the older sibling now, remember?"

"Very funny," I say.

"We need to go," Marco says.

"Remember, we'll be available via com link the whole time," Waters says, "and you need to return and confer before reaching a deal. Jasper, per the terms Captain Reddy negotiated, you need to bound in first."

I give Addy a quick hug then tap in and build my port. I pull up a clear image of Bounding Base 32 and *bam!*

My knees buckle as I hit the flight deck. Another botched landing.

As we agreed, the bounding base is deserted. It's downright creepy to be standing alone on an empty building in space. Beyond the flight deck, the endless blackness is dotted by stars light-years away.

A shimmer next to me announces the next arrival.

Bam! Lucy bounds in.

As soon as she gets her bearings, she charges at me, fists raised. "I can't believe you, Jasper Adams! After all I did for you! I made you a star! You were breaking hearts across the planet. And then you betray me? I'll tell you what, Jasper, you broke *my* heart! You—"

"Lucy! Stop!" I grab her wrists to stop her pounding on my chest. "I didn't know what the Resistance had planned until right before it happened." That's not entirely true, but it's not wildly far off, either. "Please understand, Lucy. I had to see my sister."

Addy bounds in.

Lucy takes a step back. She adjusts her uniform and wipes a makeup-filled tear from her cheek.

"Hello, Lucy," Addy says.

Lucy smiles the fakest smile I've ever seen. "Adeline." She looks Addy up and down, taking in her bright,

Tunneler-inspired clothes. Her lip turns up in disgust. "What are you wearing?"

Addy glares at Lucy. "Why? Does my outfit offend the new face of Earth Force?"

Geez. Things aren't going well. Maybe this was a bad idea. Maybe I was wrong to assume we could move past everything that happened while I was in the rift. I don't even know all that went down. I should have made Addy give me the gritty details before this meet.

Cole bounds in next. He stands rod straight in his perfectly pressed Earth Force uniform. He commands an authority I never could have imagined when I first met Cole. He nods at me and Addy.

When Marco arrives, Lucy raises her clenched fists again. Fortunately, this time she doesn't charge.

"Hey, Wiki, DQ!" Marco says.

"Don't you dare." Lucy's voice is a grumbled whisper filled with menace.

I have to keep things under control. I kick Marco's foot. "No nicknames."

"Whatever you say, Ace."

"I see you haven't changed, Marco," Lucy says.

Before Marco can respond, I step forward. "See, that's one of the reasons I pushed for this meet. We know one another really well. If there's anyone capable of hashing out a truce, it's us." I take a deep breath, hoping one of them will jump in and at least agree with the idea that this meet could work. Silence.

Eventually Cole nods. "Let's get started, then."

"In a second," I say. "We're waiting on one more person."

"What do you mean?" Lucy says. "We agreed to a specific attendance list! If you're already breaking the negotiated rules, we're going to leave. In fact—"

The air between us shimmers, and a second later, Mira is standing on the deck.

Her blond hair hangs loose around her shoulders and glistens like real gold. She's wearing a long white dress that catches the light with a faint iridescence. Her bare hands glow.

I try to keep my expression blank. Inside, my heart hops against my ribs.

"Oh my God!" Lucy shouts. She runs across the flight deck and throws her arms around Mira. "How is this possible? We all thought you were dead!"

I almost remind Lucy that she made up the story about Mira being dead, but I decide it probably won't advance our talks. "The Youli intercepted the communication between Captain Reddy and Admiral Eames," I explain. "They insisted that Mira come to the meet."

"We should have been informed," Cole says.

"Actually, you were." I try to keep my voice from shaking.

"We said we wanted the pod here. Mira's been staying with the Youli, but she's every bit a member of this pod." I swallow hard. I can't believe Mira is standing a few meters away.

I steal a glance at her. She turns. As soon as our eyes meet, a whole world opens in my mind. Love, joy, and comfort pour in, but a layer of sadness and longing hangs at the edges.

Mira smiles. *Hello, Jasper.*

I take a deep breath. "Hi, Mira."

"I'm okay with Mira being present," Cole says, "but I must insist that there be no brain-talk. That's not fair to the rest of us."

"And it's not fair to Mira to disallow it," I say. "We both know Mira doesn't speak in the customary Earth way."

"Then *you* can't brain-talk, Jasper," Marco says to me, "and if Mira does, you have to translate everything she says." He turns to Cole. "Does that work for you?"

Cole nods.

"Everyone else?" I ask.

Addy and Lucy nod.

"Mira?"

Yes. I've missed you so much.

I take another deep breath. Everything in me wants to reach out and touch her, make sure that she's real. For now, though, I'll have to settle with letting our minds touch. I take a moment to feel her familiar presence inside my brain. Now I need to stay on track.

"She says she agrees," I say. "Should we go inside? I asked the officers at the bounding base to leave some food for us in the cantina."

Marco laughs. "Why is it always about food with you?"

The joke doesn't reach Cole. "We'll stay out here."

"Fine," I say. So much for keeping things casual.

I stand up straight and launch into the remarks I prepared on Gulaga. "So to start, I'll remind everyone that Cole and Lucy are here on behalf of Earth Force, Marco and Addy are here for the Resistance, Mira is here for the Youli who consider themselves an interested party, and I'm here to act as a neutral facilitator. I'm hoping we can keep our discussions as informal as possible. Who would like to speak first?"

Glances flicker around our circle. Is no one going to talk? I shoot a glance at my sister. I traveled halfway across the galaxy for her. The least she could do is help me out now.

Addy steps forward. "I know I'm kind of the outsider, here, so why don't I start?" She side-eyes Marco, who nods her on. "I've always admired your pod. You're all so different, but you achieved so much together. I know things were difficult after the Battle of the Alkalinian Seat. I know I certainly wasn't on my best behavior. I said things I regret, things I didn't mean. I'm sorry for that. But here's the thing: you guys, your pod, you're the best thing about Earth. It doesn't get better than you. I hope you know that, and I hope we can talk together and get on the same page about moving forward."

Lucy puts her hands on her hips. "I don't know where that speech came from, little sister, but don't think for a minute that you can excuse your behavior by writing it off as emotional distress. I'm emotionally distressed every day, and it doesn't stop me from showing up and doing my job for Earth Force. Do you think you were the only ones reeling from Jasper's death? I was devastated and charged with rolling out Earth Force's biggest PR campaign since the launch of the Bounder Baby Breeding Program. The two of you went AWOL when I needed you most!"

"Lucy," Marco starts—I think it may be the first time I've ever heard him use her actual name—"we were all devastated, and we all had different ways of dealing with it. But that's not where the divisions in the pod began, and it's not when our views split with the Force. Even in Alkalinia, we didn't see eye to eye on the Force's tactics. I don't expect us to agree on everything today, either, but I do think we can reach a reasonable solution to our immediate problem."

"I'd prefer if we kept emotions out of this," Cole starts.

Like that has any chance of success.

"Let me summarize why we're here," he continues. "Our

fleet is positioned to destroy Gulaga. You have Denver Reddy, and he's prepared to publicly declare support for the Resistance with Jasper by his side. We're at a standoff, and we're here to see if we can stand down."

Lucy is dramatic but reasonable, Mira says. *She understands the media dynamics. Tell her that the Resistance has no desire to air the broadcast if Earth Force agrees to terms.*

"Mira thinks we can reach a deal," I say. "The Resistance won't air the broadcast as long as we can reach an agreement, which obviously includes Earth Force's immediate exit from Gulagan space."

"Any deal must include Denver's return," Lucy says. "And you, Jasper."

I anticipated this. "Neither Denver nor I are Earth Force prisoners."

"No," Lucy says, "you're hostages of the Resistance."

"Actually, they're not," Addy says. "They've both decided to stay on Gulaga of their own free will."

"Remind me why you're here again?" Lucy says to Addy. "You were not in our pod. And frankly, you add nothing to this discussion!"

"She's right, Lucy," I say. "Denver and I don't want to go back. That's our choice."

"Let's leave," Cole says to Lucy and begins building a port. I'm almost sure he's bluffing, but I can't risk it. "Wait!

Maybe there's a middle ground. I'd be willing to return to Earth to finish out the Lost Heroes Homecoming Tour if it meant we could reach an agreement today."

"And Denver?" Lucy asks.

"We will discuss it during our caucus," Addy replies.

"Even if Captain Reddy agrees," Cole says, "it's not good enough. The Resistance must answer for its attack at the rally."

Addy balls her fists and puffs her chest, the same stance she'd always take before pummeling me over taking the last chocolate chip cookie Mom baked. "And Earth Force must answer for shooting down more than half our ships today!"

Lucy takes an angry step toward my sister.

"Hey!" I say. "We're here to find a way forward, not dwell in the past. Let's cool things down."

"How can I cool things down when you destroyed my narrative?!" Lucy shouts at me. "Any solution we reach has to address the publicity nightmare you left us!"

"We'll get to that, Lucy, if we can agree to some preliminaries. For starters, no more violence. Both sides stand down. Earth Force leaves Gulagan airspace. The Resistance ceases all attacks on Earth. We'll discuss whether Denver and I are willing to return."

"No way, J—" Marco starts.

"It's reasonable, Marco," I say. "If we're going to reach a compromise, both sides have to give something up."

"That's what *compromise* means, in case you didn't know," Lucy says to Marco.

"Don't start with me, Lucy," Marco says.

"What are *they* giving up?" Addy says through gritted teeth.

"Our ships are poised to destroy you," Cole says. "We're willing to discuss letting you live."

They would never destroy Gulaga. They value the occludium ore too much.

"Mira rightly points out that you'd never risk the destruction of the occludium or the mining operations on Gulaga, Cole, so please stop bluffing. It's getting us nowhere."

"Then what do you want?" Cole asks.

"Publicly acknowledge the Resistance and formally listen to our demands," Addy says.

Lucy laughs. "If you think Admiral Eames will agree to that, you're dumber than I thought."

"Agree to return Captain Reddy permanently, and I'll present that to her," Cole says.

"We already said no," Marco says. "Denver doesn't want to go. The best we *might* be able to do is convince him to finish out the tour."

"Then I don't see how we move forward," Cole says. He lifts his gloves.

"Wait," Addy says. "We'll ask him."

"Okay, then," I say. "I know Admiral Eames and Captain

Reddy discussed this already, but any deal reached today must include an agreement for both sides to meet within the next month with their leaders and the delegates here today— meaning us—to hammer out a formal deal and next steps. Understood?" They nod in acknowledgment. "Great. We'll break and reconvene here in twenty minutes." That didn't go the best, but I suppose it could have gone a lot worse.

"We'll be back," Cole says to Addy and Marco. "Make sure you are, too." He builds a port and bounds away.

Seconds later, Lucy vanishes.

"You coming?" Marco asks me.

Stay.

"No," I say. "I'm supposed to be neutral in all of this. I'll wait here."

Addy and Marco bound back to Gulaga, leaving Mira and me alone on the flight deck.

32

MIRA LOOKS SO BEAUTIFUL THAT I HAVE to shade my eyes. I don't want her to know my thoughts—although it's not as if covering my face and twisting my neck will make a difference in her ability to read my mind.

Even though I'm not watching, I feel her take a step closer, then another.

I can't help it. I turn back to her.

Words don't flow from Mira, but feelings do, a full spectrum of feelings. She encapsulates us in a bubble of contradictions: joy and sorrow, hope and despair, love and resentment.

"You left me." I blink, spilling tears onto the flight deck. "You said you didn't want to come back with me."

I'm sorry.

"Why?"

I can't explain.

"You can't say that! You can't just disappear with the Youli and then refuse to tell me why. That's not how friendship works, Mira!"

What I don't say—what I know she hears anyway—is that I thought we were more than friends.

Mira takes a step closer. She raises her palm, her long fingers spread wide like a sea star. Then she places her hand on my heart.

A sizzling current seizes my body. My head falls back as my chest juts forward against Mira's palm. The current intensifies. Our connection strengthens. For a moment it isn't me and Mira, two separate people. It's *us*, together, merged in a place beyond time and space.

She curls her fingers and lowers her hand, severing the connection.

I fall to my knees. My hips strike the flight deck. I'm empty. It feels like Mira grabbed my heart and ripped it right out of my rib cage.

Mira kneels beside me. *Okay?*

No, I'm not okay! I want her hand on my chest. I want her arms wrapped around me. I want to bury my head in her neck and cry.

I want her to stay.

I shouldn't ask. I shouldn't dare hope, but I can't help it. I watch her face until her eyes meet mine. *Will you stay?*

She drops her gaze to the flight deck. *No.*

No? It feels like my heart is ripped out all over again. *Why not?* I slam my hands against the flight deck. "Why not, Mira?!" My words spill out through tears and clenched teeth. "Oh, wait, that's right . . . you can't explain. You're not going to explain, you're just going to abandon your friends again, is that it? You're going to abandon *me* again, Mira!"

It's not about what I want. This is just what has to be.

Maybe she thinks she can't come back. Maybe she thinks Admiral Eames would lock her up or even execute her for joining the Youli. She might be right.

I stand and gather her hands, pulling her to her feet. *It's okay, Mira, you can come back. You can come to Gulaga with me. Waters would love for you to join the Resistance. There's a place for you, Mira. There will always be a place for you.*

Mira jerks her hands away and walks to the edge of the flight deck. In the light of the stars, her golden hair seems to glow.

I don't need her words to know her answer. It doesn't matter what I say, she's not staying.

Please, Mira.

She turns back to me. *I will try to explain, but not here, not now.*

"When, then?"

When you come.

An image forms in my mind of a huge crystal city glisten-ing under the light of a trio of suns, its buildings stretching like thin fingers to the sky.

Is that the Youli home world? I ask.

I can't wait to show it to you. We can be together there, Jasper, at least for a little while.

What on earth does that mean? Why is she talking in riddles?

A flicker of light flashes in my peripheral vision, followed by a second. By the time I turn around, Cole and Lucy are standing on the flight deck. Addy and Marco arrive seconds later.

I straighten and try to calm my insides. There's no time to decipher what Mira is saying, not when so much depends on this meet. It's time to finish what we came here to do.

"Have both sides had a chance to talk with their leaders?" My voice trembles as I ask my pod mates. They confirm that they have. "What do you think of the terms?"

"We have a question for you, Jasper," Addy says. "Are you sure you're willing to finish out the Lost Heroes Homecoming Tour?"

I look from Addy and Marco to Cole and Lucy. "If it means we leave here today with an agreement, then yes."

"Captain Reddy agrees to return for the tour as long as Jasper does," Marco says.

"And after?" Lucy asks.

"That's up to him," Addy says. "Captain Reddy hasn't made a decision about what to do after the tour. As you all know, he just rejoined society after being stranded in the rift for fifteen years. He would like time to weigh his options, and he wants free passage back to Gulaga after the tour ends if that's what he decides."

"We can live with that," Lucy says and nods at Cole.

"Earth Force will withdraw its troops from Gulagan space," Cole says, "as long as the Resistance stops all attacks."

Marco nods. "Agreed."

"Then it looks like we have a deal," I say, relieved that something productive is actually going to come from this meet.

Wait.

Mira walks into the middle of our group—Addy and Marco to her right, Cole and Lucy to her left, me directly in front. She raises her arms, and her palms shine with a golden light.

Then she's in my brain. But more than that, I can tell from the expressions on Addy's and my pod mates' faces that Mira is in their brains, too.

The Youli also have a demand.

"Are you hearing this?" Cole asks.

Marco taps his head. "Loud and clear, Wiki."

"I don't think it's Mira," I tell them, remembering what Waters said about the collective Youli mind. "I think it's the Youli talking."

Mira's face is blank, but the words continue to flow from her into our minds. *Earth must present itself before the Intragalactic Council. We have selected the five of you as representatives of your planet.*

"We can't just agree to that," I say.

"How are you speaking to us?" Lucy asks Mira. "Did you learn this from the Youli?"

"Is this what brain-talk always feels like?" Addy asks me.

You have one Earth month. Then we will meet here again and travel together to the Youli home world to meet with the Council.

"What if we don't?" I ask.

As soon as the words leave my mouth, the space around the bounding base illuminates and three silver spheres appear. They spin faster than light, and as they do, they unfurl into giant saucers, just like the Youli ship we saw on the Paleo Planet.

Earth Force may be poised to destroy Gulaga, but the Youli are positioned to destroy Earth and all its peoples. You have not yet witnessed the extent of our power. We have tolerated Earth's unethical acts long enough. You must appear and negotiate your planet's admission to the Intragalactic Council. It is time Earth understands its role as a planetary citizen of the galaxy.

Mira's words fade. The Youli ships begin to spin. They circle back into spheres. In a flash of light, they're gone. For the briefest moment, Mira's eyes meet mine.

And then she is gone, too.

The five of us are left behind on the flight deck.

Marco and Addy exchange glances. So do Cole and Lucy. Then Cole looks at Marco, who shrugs. Addy and Lucy both look like they're about to laugh. And then we're all communicating silently, without words, almost like Mira. Even though something unexpected and dangerous just happened, it kind of feels like old times. Because . . . really . . . the threat of the Youli annihilating us is nothing new.

I push aside the well of emotions bubbling inside me and break the silence. "So I guess we have a deal. Or, at least, Earth Force and the Resistance do. As for the Youli, you should talk to your leaders, but I suspect I'll be seeing you back here in a month." Even though that sounds totally bizarre, it also sounds somehow right.

Is that the only reason Mira came? To threaten us into appearing before the Intragalactic Council? Was she happy to see me? If it was up to her, would she have stayed?

All I know is she's gone, like before, and I'm left with more questions than answers.

"Thank you, Jasper," Cole says, nodding formally.

"Yes, thank you." Lucy gives me a hug. "I love you even though I'm still mad."

I squeeze Lucy tight. Love is a strange thing. I think I love Mira. But I also love Addy—in a different way, of course. In fact, I love everyone standing on this flight deck.

Marco slaps his hand on my back. "Thanks, Ace. Now, didn't you say something about food?"

Addy smiles. "Why not? Anything is better than BERF."

"Blah!" Lucy says, pretending to puke. "You couldn't force me to eat that stuff again!"

Despite the drama, Lucy heads for the base and the rest of us follow like it's the most normal thing in the world.

With each step, the stiffness seems to seep out of Cole. "I can't believe you went back to Gulaga, Jasper, not with all the forage and fungi."

Marco swings his arm over Cole's shoulder. "He just wanted to pay a visit to the trash worm, Wiki. If I remember right, you had a close-up view of his insides."

Lucy pretends to vomit again. "Leave it to you guys to gross me out twice."

"Nothing's as gross as your signature scent," I say. "I left your office smelling like a rose garden."

"I love roses," Addy says, glancing cautiously at Lucy.

Lucy looks surprised for a moment, and then her expression

softens. "Thanks for coming to my defense, sweetie," she says to Addy. "Us girls need to stick together."

Once we're in the mess hall, we pull up seats around an old metal table. Marco fills a tray with tater tots and slides it into the center.

Soon we'll have to get back. Waters will wonder where we are, and I'm sure Admiral Eames is just as antsy about Cole and Lucy. But for now, even if it's strained, even if it's fleeting, even if it requires a whole tray of tater tots to keep it going, we're a pod again.

And I don't think any of us want to let that go.

Not yet.

Acknowledgments

The last few years have been a whirlwind of writing, marketing, and interacting with incredible booksellers, teachers, librarians, publishing professionals, authors, and, of course, readers. I have so much gratitude for those who have supported me, worked alongside me, and taught me by example since I first sent the Bounders series out into the world.

With the publication of *The Heroes Return*, special thanks are owed to my fabulous editor, Sarah McCabe, and the entire team at Simon & Schuster/Aladdin. Also, I will be forever grateful to my agent, David Dunton, and my first editor, Michael Strother, who both saw the potential in the Bounders series from the beginning.

I draw my inspiration from many places, but no place greater than my own family. My husband, Jamey, and our children, Nathan and Gabriel, will forever have my heart and gratitude. Thank you so much for your continued support and love on this journey.

Creativity needs to be nurtured. Fortunately, I come from a family that celebrates and supports my creativity. My parents,

Lynne and Richard Swanson, have always been my biggest fans, whether it be at a piano recital, a theater performance, or a book launch party. Thank you, Mom and Dad, for helping me fill the creative well from which I continue to draw. This book is for you.